ABOUT TH

Melissa Hemmings was b
Having put a pin in a map
up in the Bristol Channe
prospect of living on a san
and moved the pin down a   , ...ppcu
sticks to live by the sea in Somerset, whereupon she awoke one day and decided to open an organic delicatessen. This sort of behaviour has blighted Melissa's life and, whilst it has, undoubtedly, afforded her a very rich and eventful time of things, she now finds herself in need of a sit down.

Hence the advent of her love of writing. She has always written. All manner of things; from stern letters of complaint to poetry, as well as having the pleasure of ghost-writing others' literary works.

She is also an artist and when she's not writing, she's creating pictures. All artwork promoting her books are hers and more can be found hung on people's walls, in books and magazines.

This is Melissa's second novel.

OTHER BOOKS BY MELISSA HEMMINGS:

Observations From The Precipice

Fortitude Amongst The Flip-Flops

MEANDERINGS OF A CUCKOO

By

Melissa Hemmings

MEANDERINGS OF A CUCKOO

Published by Happy Mayhem Media Ltd

20 – 22 Wenlock Road, London N1 7GU

This is a work of fiction. Names, characters, businesses, places, events and incidents are either the products of the author's imagination or used in a fictitious manner. Any resemblance to actual persons, living or dead, or actual events is purely coincidental.

The rights of the author of this work has been asserted to her in accordance with the Copyright, Designs and Patents Act 1988. No part of this book may be reproduced in any form, by photocopying or by any electronic or mechanical means, including information storage or retrieval systems, without permission in writing from both the copyright owner and the publisher of this book.

ISBN: 978-0-9927277-9-6 (Paperback)

First published 2015 by Shameless Miming Ltd
Published 2022 by Happy Mayhem Media Ltd

Text Copyright © Melissa Hemmings 2015

All Rights Reserved

Cover Illustration Copyright © Melissa Hemmings 2022

A CIP catalogue record for this book is available from the British Library

This book is dedicated to my family

I have spread my dreams beneath your feet. Tread softly because you tread on my dreams.

W.B. Yeats

Prologue

Quote: *It is never too late to be what you might have been.* George Eliot

The man sat down, nervously, in the Merrythought Café and looked around at its newly painted interior; everything was pristine.

Stood behind the counter was a greasy-haired man. He was wearing chequered chef's trousers and a white shirt with bulging buttons which was struggling to contain a pronounced paunch. Upon seeing the customer, one of his blue gloved hands nudged a rather irritated young girl who was struggling to contain her long hair in a wispy hairnet.

She wandered over to where the newly arrived customer was seated.

Wispy hairnet girl: "Hello, what can I get you?"

Man: "A cup of coffee please and a pot of tea for my friend."

Wispy hairnet girl, looking around: "Your pretend friend?"

Man, patiently: "My friend. She will be here in a minute."

He shuffled uncomfortably on his plastic chair, looked at his watch and sighed.

Wispy hairnet girl: "Right you are; back in a tick."

Wispy hairnet girl, hollering towards the counter: "Dave! One coffee – normal and a pot of tea for an invisible woman!"

Dave huffed, irritably.

Dave: "Belinda! How many times have I told you? You take the order and you deal with it now. I can't be messing up my clothes. This refit has cost a fortune; I can't afford any more!"

Belinda scrunched her nose up at him and sloped off towards the kitchen to prepare the drinks.

Another customer entered the café and skidded on the highly polished new tiles. They hastily grabbed the back of a passing chair and threw themselves into it.

After checking they weren't injured, Dave walked over to the man who was awaiting his drinks order.

Dave: "Hello. You haven't been here before, have you?"

The man looked up at Dave.

Man: "Oh, hello. No, I thought it was time I frequented it."

Dave: "I'm most grateful. I've just had a shockingly high renovation bill so all custom is most welcome."

The man looked towards the door.

Man: "I'm waiting for my friend."

Dave: "Yes, you said. Bit late, is she?"

The man nodded, sadly.

Man: "Yes, but I'm sure she'll be here in a minute."

Dave nodded in agreement.

Dave: "Of course she will."

Belinda came out, plonked the drinks on the table and the man thanked her. Dave made his excuses and went back to stand behind the counter.

A few minutes later the man finished his coffee and looked dispiritedly at his watch.

Belinda seeing that he had glugged his last mouthful pounced on his cup and whisked it away.

Belinda: "What do you want me to do about the tea?"

Man: "I'll have another cup of coffee please and a new pot of tea for my friend as that one went cold."

Belinda: "Okaaaay."

Belinda picked up the untouched pot of tea and shouted towards the counter

Belinda: "Dave! Another coffee – normal and another pot of tea for the woman who's stood him up!"

Dave looked at her with daggers and signalled for her to go into the kitchen that instant.

Belinda poked her tongue out and did as he motioned.

Dave scuttled over to the man.

Dave: "I'm sorry about that. She has insolence issues. I blame rap musi... Oh, your friend has arrived by the looks of it."

Dave moved out the chair opposite the man, and guided the newly arrived customer into it.

She sat down gratefully and Dave slid back quickly behind his counter.

Man, smiling gently: "Hello. I was starting to think you'd stood me up."

The woman sitting opposite him shook her head.

Woman: "I'd never do that again."

The man took her hand across the table, leant down and kissed it, lightly.

Man: "Sometimes life does offer a second chance. It's up to us if we choose to take it."

They looked at each other over the gleaming Formica table; lost in each other.

Just then Belinda thundered out of the kitchen armed with the drinks.

Dave sensing the emotion stepped sideways away from the counter and pulled Belinda back in her tracks.

Belinda: "Oi! I've got bleedin' hot stainless steel here, you moron!"

Dave motioned her urgently to shut up, took them off her and placed them on the counter.

Dave and Belinda looked on silently and Dave signalled to another customer to wait a minute.

The man looked intensely into the woman's eyes.

Man, barely audible: "Do you choose to take it?"

The woman sitting opposite him nodded and added quietly: "I do."

The man exhaled loudly and kissed the woman's hand again; she lifted it and gently stroked his face.

Belinda pulled an "aww" face to Dave and he gulped back a tear.

Belinda: "Are you crying?"

Dave, wiping a tear from his eye: "No, now go and see to that customer."

Belinda, smiling: "Yeah, you were."

She went off and took the other customer's order whilst Dave picked up the drinks from the counter and gently placed them on the couple's table and melted back behind the counter.

Belinda joined him a few minutes later and they looked at the couple across from them chatting quietly.

Belinda, whispering to Dave: "I want that."

Dave: "It's lovely, isn't it? True and natural. Everyone wants that, Belinda; it's what we live for."

Belinda: "You probably won't get it though."

Dave: "Must you be so blunt, young lady?"

Belinda: "You go for women way out of your league. Just like Will Evans is out of mine."

She tutted, loudly.

Belinda: "That whore Leanne's got him instead. She's huge; got tits around her knees and thighs like an elephant. He must have to use GPS to find out where to put it."

Dave: "Yes, well, you certainly know how to kill a moment. Go and do the dishes."

Belinda: "Eh? Oh, alright."

Belinda went into the kitchens and Dave watched the man get to his feet and help his companion with her coat.

The man nodded goodbye to Dave and motioned that he'd left the money for the drinks on the table.

Dave stood and watched as the man went one way and his companion went the other. He rubbed his forehead for a moment in contemplation then fetched the money from the table.

Belinda shot out from the kitchen with the antibacterial spray and started cleaning it. She tutted at Dave.

Belinda: "You're not meant to wear the blue gloves all day, especially after handling money."

Dave shook his head in dismay.

Dave, muttering: "It's too stressful; a few germs never killed anyone."

Belinda shook her head and continued to wipe the table over.

Belinda, muttering under her breath: "Knob."

***

Second Chance

If I could get a second chance
To see your face again
To get lost in your smiling eyes
And in your arms remain.
If I could turn back the clock
And see you one more time
I'd tell you what you mean to me
And how you should be mine.

If I could have one wish
Answered for me today
It would be that you were with me
Forever and a day.

Eliza Wakeley

The Main Characters

Now then, this is the second book of a trilogy and, as such, it's quite important you've read the first one. If you haven't you've missed out on four hundred pages and eighty thousand words of back story. That's quite a lot by anyone's standards. It also took quite a lot of effort on my part to think it all up, so by the mere virtue I'm now a recluse from society is enough to warrant its purchase.

In the meantime, however, I shall assist and give you a quick rundown of the relevant characters so you can get cracking...

Eliza Wakeley:

This is Eliza's journey. The first book is her mental ramblings and view on the world as she adapts to her new life. This book continues her journey. In the first book I suggested you should like her as she's quite funny and you'll want her to do well. From the lovely feedback you've provided, that does indeed appear to be the case... Bravo! You wanted to read what happens next. This book tells you just that.

Lewis Wakeley (Lewy):

He is Eliza's ex-husband and, as you'll recall, remarkably boring. As it transpired, he did her a favour when he left as it freed her from a life of meal planners and instruction book reading. Of course, Eliza didn't realise that at the time. When he announced he was jumping ship, it was as if her world had imploded. That's what life does though, isn't it? It makes you realise that the path you were on wasn't the right one for you but you never thought to change it.

Anyway, he gave Eliza his sports car, which was decent of him, but he also gave Geraldine (husband taker) a bun in the oven which is quite unfortunate as he isn't up to much on the father stakes.

Geraldine Copeland (Gerry):

As I just mentioned, she's now pregnant and has a swollen everything (which makes Eliza very happy). She's dispensed with the black bras and hair straighteners for elasticated waistbands, oversized 'slouch' jumpers and once a week hair washing. (All of which upsets Lydia to distraction.) You'll also recall Tom mistook her for Jabba the Hutt. This made everyone very happy, except Geraldine and Lewis.

Tom Wakeley:

Eliza's beautiful, funny and endearing little boy. He's now started school but is still a lover of Cheddar Chicken and chocolate buttons. He now speaks fluent child and cockney.

Lydia Perkins:

Lydia is Eliza's best friend. I filled you in previously on her back story. In a nutshell – she has a bully of an ex-husband, Roy. No one liked him and with just reason. He's unpleasant but still managed to get another girlfriend – this one is called Charmaine. On principle, Lydia doesn't like her.

As I warned you before, Lydia comes with a disclaimer as she's a bit near the knuckle on occasions and, not to put too fine a point on it, a bit hectic on the seduction front. If your life mirrors hers, you might want to think about visiting a clinic of some description.

Brian and Clive:

Owners of the restaurant Manners. They still have Carlos, though he's proving a pricey, emotional handful. For the uninitiated, he's the chef not a dog, though I fancy they'd quite like to tie him up and put him in a kennel. He's haemorrhaging pork loins in his attempt at menu domination.

Dave:

Owner and general dogsbody of the Merrythought Café; Eliza and Lydia's usual greasy spoon. Dave is still smitten with Eliza even though she inadvertently got him closed down by Health and Safety due to the unfortunate wasabi incident. You'll feel a bit sorry for him as you know he's never going to get the girl, but hey-ho that's life, it can't be helped.

Philip Hargreaves:

Divorcee and Eliza's eccentric neighbour. Barmy as a badger. You read a lot about him during book one and he has a blast in this book.

Ellington and Norris:

Ellington is Tom and Eliza's Border collie and Norris is their grey Persian cat. I told you previously how they came to be part of the family. I could cut and paste but I'll let you read from book one instead.

Mr Hicks:

He's the ex-baker freeholder of Eliza and Lydia's shop – Illusions of Grandeur Crafts. He had quite a time of it in Observations From The Precipice. I don't know about you, but I'm still recovering from the mental images. He's featured a lot in this book but you'll be pleased to note macaroons don't make another appearance. I saw some in Asda the other day and had to look away; I've scarred myself.

Bunty Hestington-Charles:

Who'd have thought it, eh? I'm shocked at her deviousness and general thievery. It's hard to believe someone who wears pop socks and pearls could stoop so low but now you know, trust no one – not even people who wear fur lined gilets and have double barrelled surnames.

Jude (The Mighty Sword):

Ah Jude... It was love at first sight for Eliza when she saw him. So much so she thought she was having a stroke. You'll like him. How can you not? He's got sparkling eyes, dark shiny hair and a wonderful disposition. I've made him sound a bit like a race horse which wasn't quite my intention. However, you'll also recall how he got his nickname The Mighty Sword, which, quite frankly on that strength alone, makes him quite the catch.

Others:

There's plenty more of them. You will be introduced as the book proceeds. Keep your eyes peeled for Dorothy. She'll make your heart twang; make no mistake.

You're now fully armed with the characters.

Plump up a cushion/adjust the sun-lounger and grab yourself a drink.

I hope you enjoy.

Chapter One

Quote for the day: *In three words I can sum up everything I've learned about life: it goes on. Robert Frost*

Eliza turned her attention back to the auction in hand and opened her brochure to see when Mrs Hestington-Charles' lots were up.

Make them soon, so I can get out of here and have a cuppa with Jude.

Tea and Jude. The perfect combination.

Flippin' flip-flops, I'm excited. Things might really be starting to work out for me.

Thank you, karma fairy, I shall make a celebratory cake later.

She flicked through the catalogue and felt a tap on her shoulder.

Oooh, you're back quick.

She turned her head round with a massive beam to be faced with a very red-faced Lydia who, unusually, had jogging bottoms and an over-sized jumper slung on. Eliza's face fell with dismay.

What?!

Eliza: "Oh! You?! What do you want?"

Lydia: "Yes and a good morning to you too, darling. I'll choose to ignore your transparent disappointment at seeing me. I'm here as an emergency, obvious by the fact I am wearing clothes fit for recycling. You have to come! There's a problem at the shop; Mr Hicks just called me."

Eliza sighed heavily.

Eliza: "Oh god! What now?"

Lydia: "He sounded very agitated... Here, I caught sight of Henry on the way in. Ooh, he sets my bits all of a quiver!"

Henry! Oh my god, I'd forgotten about him with Jude turning up.

Just then, Jude strode back into the room and stopped dead in his tracks when he saw the back outline of Lydia.

Eliza stared at him, helpless, over the top of Lydia's head and watched as a look of horror crept across his face.

Her eyes widened, as did his.

He swiped his hand across his throat urgently and shaking his head, panic stricken, he rapidly backed out of the room.

Brilliant, just bloody brilliant!

Lydia, seeing the crestfallen look on Eliza's face: "Are you alright, darling?"

Lydia searched around the room, trying to follow Eliza's gaze, but he'd gone; as quickly as he'd materialised.

Eliza: "I've been better."

Eliza tutted with irritation and Lydia turned her attention back to her.

Lydia: "Hasn't Bunty's stuff gone for much? It doesn't matter; we can go round there and clear her house out. I'd really enjoy that!"

Eliza, sadly: "They've not come up yet. I've just missed out on a very special lot."

Lydia: "Ah well darling, no use crying over what you weren't destined to have. There'll be other lots."

Eliza: "Not like this one. This one should have been mine."

Lydia looked at her perplexed.

Lydia: "Anyway, we need to go and quick. Mr Hicks sounded most urgent on the phone."

Eliza sighed very deeply.

Eliza: "Yeah, ok. I'll tell Henry we're off."

Eliza dragged herself off the chair and searched out Henry. He was stood near the exit and she waved at him. He smiled in acknowledgement and made his way over to them.

When he got to them, he nodded at Lydia, cautiously.

Henry: "Er, hi Lydia."

Lydia: "Hello, Henry. You look as gorgeous as ever."

Henry: "Oh right, erm, thanks."

He looked enquiringly at Eliza.

Eliza, flatly: "We've got to go."

Henry: "Oh ok. Do you still want that ottoman?"

Eliza, huffing: "Not really."

I want its new owner.

Henry: "Ah, fair enough. You must have just got caught up in the moment; happens a lot."

He ripped up a piece of paper he was holding and lobbed it in a nearby bin. Eliza stood rigid as she watched it flutter in amongst empty paper tea and coffee cups.

Huh? What was that?

Eliza grabbed his arm, urgently.

Eliza: "What are you doing? What was that?"

Henry: "Eh? Oh, the bloke who bought it left his number and said he'd meet you somewhere, just in case. He said he would have given it to you direct but had to rush off as something unexpected turned up."

Didn't it just?

Eliza, shrilly: "Well I do want it! You silly man! How could you rip that piece of paper up without explaining?! Oh, that's just marvellous. Absolutely flip-flopping marvellous!"

Henry, shrugging: "But...? You just said..."

Eliza, screeching: "I was not fully furnished with the facts, was I?!"

Eliza scrabbled into the bin to try and retrieve the pieces of paper. Both Lydia and Henry looked on with bemusement. Henry nudged Lydia and tilted his head towards Eliza, elbow deep in the bin.

Lydia, shaking her head: "Don't ask me, I haven't the faintest idea what she's doing."

The rotund man she was bidding against previously, broke through the threesome and threw a half-finished cup of tea into the bin. Eliza looked up at him from bent over the bin.

Eliza, baring her teeth at him: "You?! I've had quite enough of you for one day. Drink your tea if you're going to buy it. Do not throw it into a bin, half finished! Not only is it wasteful, it's ruined my chances of ever seeing my box again!"

The rotund man stared at Henry with confusion at the outburst. Henry patted him with assurance and gestured for him to go back and sit down. The man hastily did so, whilst muttering 'nutty people, they're everywhere these days.'

Henry tried to placate Eliza.

Henry: "Calm down Eli, it was just a swanky box."

Eliza, slightly hysterically: "It was NOT just a swanky box! It was the best, most perfect box I have ever seen. It was meant to be my box and now I'll never see it again."

Henry and Lydia exchanged flummoxed glances.

Lydia: "And you thought I was the mental one."

Henry, shaking his head: "Indeed, you make quite the pair. Anyway, I have work to do, if you'll excuse me. I'll call you later Eli with the result of Mrs Doubled-Barrelled's pieces."

Eliza forlornly stopped scrabbling through the bin and stared sadly at its contents whilst Henry backed away.

Well, that is very much that then.

I feel sick.

Lydia: "Cheers Henry. Come on Loopy Lou; let's see what's so urgent that I've had to leave the house in tramps' clothes."

Eliza: "It had better be a death or I'm going to be very pissed off."

Lydia grabbed Eliza by the arm and led her forcibly out of the auction house.

Lydia: "Get in the car, you crazy mare. We'll go in mine and collect yours later. I'm a bit concerned you've gone over the brink. I'm not letting you go to an auction again; it messes with your brain."

Eliza: "It does. I think it might take me a long time to recover."

Amount of silent swear words uttered on the way to the car: *Three hundred and twelve (with the distinct absence of flip-flops).*

Chapter Two

Sub quote for the day: *Get your facts first, then you can distort them as you please. Mark Twain*

Eliza sat slumped in the passenger seat of Lydia's car and stared forlornly out of the window as they drove to their shop.

Well, thank you very much, karma fairy.

How am I going to get in touch with him now?

I don't know where he works.

Maybe he's on multitudeofmates.com – Lydia never said how she met him.

I wonder if he subscribes to all things social media. No, he strikes me that he has a life.

He doesn't seem to be the sort who uploads pictures of a Bolognese he's made.

Is it deemed stalkeresque to try and Google him?

Lydia looked over at Eliza and threw her a packet of wipes out of her door panel.

Lydia: "You might want to clean the beverage stains off you. How are things going with Henry?"

Eliza took a few and half-heartedly mopped herself down.

I have a very strong dislike for him at this moment in time.

Eliza: "Alright. I'm not sure I should be going out with him."

Lydia: "Why? He's delicious. I'd have him like a shot."

Eliza tugged at Lydia's arm as they were sat at some traffic lights which were on red.

Eliza, seriously: "Lydia, can I ask you something?"

Lydia turned and stared at Eliza.

Lydia: "This sounds big. Go on then."

Eliza: "Would you go out with someone your best friend had gone out with or is there a law against it?"

Lydia looked quickly across at Eliza.

Lydia: "Laws, shmaws. They're made up by men with no morals. They're all busy dictating to us how we should act whilst they're happy swindling their expenses and knocking off their best mate's wife. If you weren't with Henry, I'd go out with him if you let me and that's no lie. Love is a butterfly – it goes wherever it pleases and pleases wherever it goes."

Oh. That does put quite a different inflection upon things.

Lydia parked up and they both walked towards the shop where they were greeted by the closed sign across the door.

Eliza and Lydia exchanged glances and both pushed their way in.

They were greeted by the sight a very red-faced Sebastian Hestington-Charles brandishing an arts and crafts chair at Mr Hicks, who was pinned up against a dresser.

Eliza, in a state of alarm: "Mr Hicks! Are you alright?!"

Sebastian turned to face them slightly but still kept the chair within whacking distance of Mr Hicks.

Sebastian: "Keep out of this ladies; this doesn't concern you."

Lydia: "I bloody think it does. It's a Friday morning, in our shop and it's closed!"

Mr Hicks, slightly panic stricken: "I'm sorry I called you Lydia, only I was hoping to take the morning off as I had a slight personal matter to attend to but whilst I was on the phone to you, the matter arrived. I'm afraid he's already damaged your heart."

Eh?

Lydia and Eliza looked around to find a smashed heart sculpture by Mr Hicks's feet.

Oh, the ceramic ornament.

Sebastian: "Come on then, you interloper. Stop shilly-shallying. Let's take this outside!"

Eliza: "Now hang on just a minute!"

Lydia: "Yeah, hang on! You probably want to have a word with your strumpet of a wife before you start having a street brawl with Mr Hicks. It takes two to tango."

Mr Hicks's eyes widened with horror and he started coughing loudly to try and drown out Lydia.

Sebastian: "Eh? What are you saying? I can't quite hear over the coughing. What's my Bunty got to do with this?"

Mr Hicks, urgently: "Lydia, be quiet! Sebastian is here over a furniture matter!"

Eliza pulled Lydia back, widened her eyes in a 'shut up this instant' look and stepped in.

Eliza: "What's all this about, please Sebastian. You either explain to me here and now or I call the police."

Sebastian looked at her determinedly.

Lydia: "Yeah and you can put down that chair whilst you're at it. Eli spent a long time tarting that up. We can do without you smashing it around Mr Hicks's head."

Sebastian put down the chair and flumped into it.

Mr Hicks visibly relaxed and scuttled to relative safety, behind the counter.

Eliza: "Would you like a cup of tea?"

Sebastian nodded.

Sebastian: "Milk, no sugar please."

Eliza: "I was asking Mr Hicks actually, but fair enough. Lydia, go and put the kettle on please, would you?"

Lydia: "Why me? I want to know what's going on."

Eliza glared at her.

Lydia: "Ohhh alright then, moody pants."

She stropped off into the kitchen.

Eliza turned her attention back to Sebastian.

Eliza: "Well?"

Sebastian: "Colin, from number fifty-two, saw Mr Hicks helping some chap put my grandfather's Spanish marquetry table in the back of a van. I can scarcely believe it! Blatant! At lunchtime too!"

Eliza looked at Mr Hicks, carefully, wondering how much he'd divulged. Mr Hicks taking his cue, stepped in.

Mr Hicks: "Yes, Mrs Hestington-Charles was out at the time and, apparently, she has no knowledge as to why this and an armoire were removed from their house. It transpires; she believes they were a victim of daylight robbery. I was going to explain to Sebastian the real reason why they were taken."

She said she'd think of a reason why they'd gone.

I didn't think burglary was going to be it.

She needs to be slightly more imaginative with her alibis.

Eliza, slightly incredulously: "You were?!"

Mr Hicks: "Yes. I was going to explain that they were exchange items as Mrs Hestington-Charles had bought a dresser some weeks prior but had not been able to meet the purchase price and had offered the items in return."

Mr Hicks stared at Eliza, square in the eyes and Sebastian looked enquiringly at Eliza.

Sebastian: "Is that right, Eliza?"

Absolutely not.

Eliza: "Absolutely, yes. All those words he just said."

Phew.

Sebastian covered his eyes with horror.

Sebastian: "Oh, my goodness gracious! We do indeed have a new dresser. Mr Hicks, I am so desperately apologetic. To think I thought you were a pilferer and was about to punch your lights out."

He put his head in his hands, dejectedly.

Lydia wandered back in with a cup of tea for Sebastian and handed it to him.

Sebastian, shaking his head in his hands: "What on earth was Bunty thinking?"

Lydia: "Now hang on! Mr Hicks's not all that bad. He makes a lovely farmhouse cob."

Eliza, slightly hysterically: "Lydia, you've missed quite a lot of conversation whilst you've been boiling the kettle, you might want to just shush!"

Lydia looked most put out.

Sebastian, sighing loudly: "I have been under a lot of stress lately. Bunty says I have anger issues."

Lydia: "She's got plenty of her own, I shouldn't worry."

Eliza shot Lydia a warning glance.

Sebastian: "You may have a point young lady. To sell inherited antiques in exchange for a repro dresser, she must have taken leave of her senses."

Eliza: "Ah well, at least that's all sorted out."

Sebastian looked up, suddenly.

Sebastian: "What have you done with the pieces?"

Eliza: "They're in auction today at Billington."

Sebastian: "Really? You mean they haven't been sold yet?"

Eliza: "Well, I think the armoire's probably being sold about now but should imagine the Spanish table is up in about fifteen minutes."

Sebastian: "Do you have the auction house number to hand? I shall call them and bid to get it back. I'm not fussed about the armoire; I never liked the bloody thing. It always reminded me of Bunty's loony great aunt, Mary."

Eliza: "Of course, it's here."

Eliza fumbled about with her phone pulling up her contacts list.

Lydia: "Can you afford to? Bunty said about your buyout thing going tits up."

Sebastian tutted and shook his head with annoyance.

Sebastian: "I really must have a word with her about discussing our personal matters with virtual strangers."

Oh, my dear Sebastian, if only that were the case.

Eliza: "If it makes you feel better, we've seen quite a lot of her recently, so we're not strangers."

Lydia: "Yeah, I can assure you, we've seen more of her than most."

Ain't that the truth?

Lydia pulled a disapproving face.

Sebastian: "Ah ok, that makes me feel somewhat comforted. Well, we have a new backer. It's all systems go. Give me the number, my dear. I have no time to lose."

Sebastian clapped his hands, excitedly.

Mr Hicks: "Sebastian, would you care to use my phone upstairs? The girls can then open the shop up again."

Sebastian: "Of course, I'm so sorry ladies and of course you, Mr Hicks, for the misunderstanding. I shall pay towards the lost revenue for this morning's closure and for the broken sculpture. Send me the bill and my secretary will sort it."

Lydia: "I'm going home; I have to change. I can't have the public seeing me like this. They'll think I'm destitute. You can watch it can't you Eli?"

Eliza: "Yes, I have nothing else to do."

Now.

I did have a wonderful afternoon planned but that was quickly obliterated by a broken heart.

Just when I thought things were going so well...

Track playing on Billington FM: *Things Can Only Get Better. D.Ream*

Chapter Three

Quote for the day: *It is better to remain silent at the risk of being thought a fool, than to talk and remove all doubt of it. Maurice Switzer*

It was Monday morning and Mr Hicks had resumed his duties staffing the shop after taking the weekend off due to Sebastian related stress.

Eliza and Lydia were trawling the aisles at their usual supermarket doing the weekly shop.

Eliza: "Poor Mr Hicks, he could sue us you know."

Lydia: "If he had a work contract, probably. Remember though, it's thanks to his shenanigans with old Bunty which got us in the pickle in the first place. If he hadn't been having it off with her, she'd never have had access to the till."

Eliza walked past her and went towards the tinned section.

Eliza: "I suppose."

Lydia called after her.

Lydia: "We could sue him. Extra-maritals in a craft shop!"

Just then Dorothy, occasional visitor to the shop, wife of the Managing Director of Pilkington on the Moors' prime employer, Cuthbert Promotions Ltd and resident of the poshest, most hanging basket festooned road in Pilkington, tapped Lydia on the shoulder.

Lydia: "Oh!"

Eliza turned to see Lydia frozen with horror. She watched on helpless.

Dorothy: "Hello Lydia, I thought it was you. Sorry to interrupt your conversation but I wanted to tell you, I found a very similar cake to the one you won Pilkington's show with in M and S the day. Yours was obviously better, but I think I might be cheeky and pass it off as my own at my next dinner party. I can pretend to Joyce, I made it. Apparently, it cost a fortune in eggs when she tried to replicate yours, the other week."

Lydia, shrilly: "Yes, ha! You could, but it's classed as cheating, I think."

Dorothy, in shushed tones: "Well, it can be yours and my little secret, can't it?"

Lydia, nervously: "Ha ha. Of course."

How much of that last exchange did she hear?

Dorothy: "I'm very good at secrets, which is good to know. Isn't it dears?"

That'll be all of it then.

She directed a knowing gaze to Eliza. Eliza smiled, uncertainly, and grasping her tin of beans, made her way to them both.

Dorothy: "I must be off; I have a coffee morning to arrange. You must both come sometime, now you're so much part of the village. As you're such a good cook Lydia, perhaps you'll provide the cakes?"

Eliza, cutting in: "That would be lovely, we'd like that wouldn't we, Lydia?"

Lydia: "Would we?"

Eliza widened her eyes.

Lydia: "Er, yeah. It'd make our week."

Dorothy: "Wonderful! I'll pencil you in for next Tuesday. Shall we say, half ten? Cheerio for now."

Dorothy whisked off towards the checkouts.

Lydia and Eliza both exhaled audibly.

Lydia: "Fuck."

Eliza: "Quite."

Lydia: "She's going to hold us to ransom for the rest of our lives now. I'll be eighty-two and still making her bloody fairy cakes."

Eliza: "Better that, than the whole village knowing about Bunty. Come on, let's get this done and out of here."

Lydia: "Agreed. I can't be coping with the stress of ear-wigging villagers."

They finished their shopping and after checking out the till operators, plumped for a middle-aged woman with cherry red hair. They unloaded their shopping onto the conveyor but when it came to their turn, cherry haired woman got up to change with another member of staff... The member of staff Eliza and Lydia dread and the one they deliberately avoid.

Lydia, urgently: "No! Stay on! Just until we're done!"

Cherry hair till operator, derisively: "It's me break, I've been on since six. Here you go Derek."

Deliberately avoided Derek: "Thanks Barbara. Ba – ba – ba. Ba – ba - ba ram. My Ba - ba..."

Cherry haired Ba – ba – ba - bara walked off, ignoring him.

Derek plonked himself down and started scanning their purchases.

Derek: "Ooh apples. Healthy, are we? Spanish, though. They've travelled a long way to be with you, make sure you eat them. We waste far too much food in this country. Were you aware that ninety two percent of our five a day ends up in landfill?"

Eliza and Lydia sighed and studiously ignored him.

Don't engage in any form of dialogue.

Derek continued scanning the conveyor of shopping.

Derek scanned a tin of tuna and picked it up to inspect it.

Derek: "Is this pole line caught?"

Eliza and Lydia exchanged glances, neither replied.

Stay strong, do not answer.

Derek: "They kill whales, you know? Do you have any idea how cruel they are? They call it a sport. Cycling is a sport, not harpooning whales. Cycling allows you to look at the countryside and breathe in the air. You can't look at trees when you're harpooning a whale, can you?"

Lydia: "Depends how far you are from the shore, I would presume. Plus, it'd bugger up your aim. Now give me the tin."

Oh, she's cracked.

We've had it.

Derek held on to the tin and Lydia attempted to wrestle it off him.

Lydia: "Release your grip! Anyway, it's about dolphins not whales, the pole line thing."

Derek reluctantly let go of the tin and Lydia flung it into the shopping bag.

Derek: "All created by God."

Lydia: "Indeed, but so are you, so there's always room for debate."

Derek: "Don't you love the whales?"

Lydia: "I have no wish to have a discussion regarding my love of all things nautical with you. Scan our purchases, please."

Derek, in a childish voice: "Whoooh! Who's a wittle gwumpy pants?"

Lydia straightened up and put her hands on her hips.

Lydia, huffing: "I'm sorry, do we actually know each other?"

Derek looked her up and down.

Derek: "Er, no. I don't think so."

Lydia: "Oh fair enough. It's just the way you threw an over familiar insult at me, led me to believe we did."

Cease wordage with the mad man.

Eliza cut in.

Eliza: "We're in a hurry. Please can you just do your job and not talk to us?"

Lydia: "Yeah, it upsets her aura."

Derek: "What does it do to yours?"

Lydia: "Nothing, mine was shot years ago. You just piss me off."

Derek: "Creating a customer dialogue is to be encouraged. It said so in the new starters' pack."

Derek carried on scanning their purchases and they flung them haphazardly into their bags.

Eliza, whispering to Lydia: "We'll sort them out properly when we get out by the car."

Lydia nodded and lobbed frozen peas in with a top she'd just bought for Freya.

Lydia: "What page in the new starters' pack does it say about entering a discussion about the harpooning of whales?"

Derek: "Oh, that wasn't in there. I am an expert about all manner of affairs. I can look at food and tell you so much about its origins."

Knowledgeable Derek held aloft a bag of carrots.

Derek, aka The Food Oracle: "Did you know these carrots have as much radiation as Chernobyl?"

Eliza looked at the pack of carrots, dubiously.

Really?

Hmmm.

Eliza leant forward and whispered to Derek.

Eliza: "You're a bit mad, aren't you?"

Derek, quietly: "Yes."

Eliza: "Ok, just checking before I eat the carrots."

Derek finished scanning and Eliza paid for their shopping.

Lydia: "Hang on; I'll pay for my bit."

Eliza: "We'll sort it out at home; let's just get out of here, shall we?"

Derek looked on, expressionless.

Derek: "I've never seen real lesbians before. You don't look like how I thought they'd be."

Lydia: "We're not lesbians, you stupid man! I love willies. Not yours, I hasten to add, before you offer to thwack it out on the self-scan. They have to be attached to people who aren't demented."

Derek looked down at his crotch as Lydia wrestled the trolley away from his lane.

Lydia shouted over her shoulder to him as they left.

Lydia: "We'll try and not spear any whales on the way out!"

Derek, calling after her: "You only get them in the ocean, you silly woman! I told you I was an expert on affairs. Anyway, we don't sell harpoons!"

Derek turned, conspiratorially, to the next woman in line on the conveyor.

Derek, tapping his nose: "She'd never get a harpoon past Trevor on security. Someone tried to nick a baguette last week and he was right on it."

Time spent Googling radioactivity of root vegetables: *Entire journey home.*

Chapter Four

Sub quote for the day: *Sometimes good things fall apart so better things can fall together. Marilyn Monroe*

They got back to Eliza's and proceeded to let Norris and Ellington out and sort out the shopping.

Lydia: "I've got to scoot; I've got to unpack before I relinquish Mr Hicks from his duties."

With that, Lydia swept out of the house leaving Eliza to unpack her shopping.

As Eliza pottered around her kitchen she mulled over the past week's events and chatted to Ellington who was hovering, hopefully, by his food bowl.

Eliza: "What am I going to do Ellington?"

Ellington looked at his bowl, by way of suggestion.

Eliza, continuing: "Not with regard to you, I mean about Jude. I'm gutted, I really am."

Ellington looked nonplussed; as well he might, considering his limited understanding of the English language. Accustomed to Eliza's rambling, however, he went over and wiped his nose on her leg by way of comfort.

Eliza, tutting: "Thanks."

She looked out of the window to see Philip stepping over the ridiculous fence, spade in hand, up her garden path.

I once found this alarming but now it's normal.

I've become desensitised to madness.

This does not bode well for my future.

Ah well, I'll see if he wants a cup of tea.

Eliza threw a couple of dog treats into Ellington's bowl, opened her back door and hollered down the garden to where Philip was heading.

Eliza: "Philip! Want a cuppa?"

Philip raised his spade by way of acceptance as he carried on up her path and she put the kettle on.

Once she'd made the tea she wandered down to where he'd resumed digging and plonked his tea on the top of an upturned pot.

Eliza: "Have you found any more treasures?"

Philip: "Well, my dear girl, I think I might be onto something really rather special. Do you want to see?"

Not really.

Eliza: "Go on then."

Philip pointed to the soil at something metal.

Eliza: "Is that it? Looks like a lump of rust."

Philip, patting her arm: "Don't you worry your pretty little tousled head about it."

Condescending, how nice.

That's my cue to leave.

Eliza: "I must go, I have work to do. Important work."

Philip looked up with raised eyebrows.

Philip: "Really? Well done you, dear. Not more leg sanding then?"

Shut up.

Eliza strode off down the garden back to the house, stopping on the way to pick up a sanding block from the shed, which she surreptitiously wedged into her jeans pocket.

Meh.

She went inside and as she did so her mobile rang. It was Henry.

Henry, cautiously: "Hi Eli, how are you feeling?"

Ah, the up-to-my-elbows-in-rubbish incident is still firmly entrenched in his mind.

What he's actually enquiring is "Are you safe to approach yet?"

Eliza: "Hi, I'm ok thanks, Henry. How did Bunty's bits sell?"

Henry: "The armoire not so good, I'm afraid, but the Spanish table had a phone bidder who bid right over the odds. You got a fair old penny for it."

Blimey, Sebastian really did want it back.

Eliza: "That's a relief. Thank you."

Eliza paused and started to speak, as did Henry.

Eliza and Henry, in unison: "Erm, I've been thinking…"

They both stopped.

Eliza: "You first."

Henry, awkwardly: "No, no, I insist."

Do it. It's easier over the phone.

You cannot continue to go out with him. It's not fair on either of you.

He might be perfect on paper but he's not Jude.

Eliza, gabbling: "Ok, I've been thinking, you know, about us, me and you, together – you know – as an item and thought we might be good as friends, if that's ok? I don't think I'm the best girlfriend material for you. You're lovely and deserve someone who is perfect. I don't think I'm quite right."

And breathe.

Henry, audibly relieved: "Oh Eli, thank goodness, I've been thinking the same. I agree you're not quite right. I think, mentally, you have a few issues."

Oh charming.

I meant as in the right fit, actually, you and me.

It wasn't an admission of insanity.

Ah well, what does it matter? It all amounts to the same conclusion.

Let it go.

Eliza, slightly piqued: "Yes, quite. Anyway, I'm glad we're agreed."

Henry, happily (a bit too happily for Eliza's liking): "Yes indeed. I'll pop by the shop later if you're around to sort out the auction paperwork. Let me know when your friend isn't there."

It would never have worked. He is scared of Lydia.

Eliza: "Will do. I'll text you."

They said their goodbyes and Eliza sighed at a passing Norris who wrapped himself around her legs. She picked him up and nuzzled his head with her nose and Norris purred loudly in appreciation.

I can quite see the appeal of becoming a mad cat lady.

Eliza: "You wouldn't care if I was caught with my head in the bin, would you Norris?"

Norris rubbed his face against hers and started dribbling.

Eliza: "Of course not, you do it all the time."

She put him down and wiped the cat drool off her chin.

Eliza: "I can't cuddle you all day. I've got to sand my legs."

She shot a look up the garden towards where Philip was still elbow deep in mud and scrunched her nose up at him.

It is important work.

People will always need beautifully sanded legs.

She wandered off into the lounge and started on the awaiting table.

Amount of concentration expended sanding table legs: *Eight percent.*

Chapter Five

Quote for the day: *One thing you can't hide - is when you're crippled inside. John Lennon*

Eliza and Lydia were sat in the car psyching themselves up for their coffee morning with Dorothy.

Lydia: "Just for the record, I'm not happy about us having to do this. I'm not a coffee morning sort of woman; I still buy my clothes at H&M."

Eliza: "It's our own fault, we have to or she'll blab."

Lydia huffed in the passenger seat, beside her.

Lydia: "Can't we just cancel? Let's drive off now, she'll never know."

Just then her mobile went off.

Lydia: "Ooh message alert! Stop the world, I need to read."

Lydia scrabbled about in her cavernous handbag, pulled her phone out, scrolled to the message and after reading it, tutted disapprovingly.

Eliza: "What? Who is it?"

Lydia: "Some guy I met off multitudeofmates.com. He's sent me a photo."

Eliza: "From the look on your face, it must be a bit dubious."

Lydia waved her phone in front of Eliza's face and she was greeted with the sight a rather buff looking man, reclining on a sun lounger; naked, save for a book covering his nether regions.

Eliza peered closer at the photo.

Eliza: "What's the book covering his willy?"

Lydia: "War and Peace, I think."

Eliza: "Gosh, I thought it looked big."

Lydia: "He's showing off, I can assure you. 'The Little Book of Calm' would have sufficed from my knowledge of 'down there'."

Lydia rolled her eyes and shook her head.

Eliza: "Who is he?"

Lydia: "He's called Toby and he's currently on holiday in Marbella, hence his apparent need to send me naked selfies. I'm going to get rid. I had a rabbit called Toby when I was a child and it was a right bastard; bloody thing kept biting me. I still have the scars, look."

Lydia held out her hand and pointed to a faint white mark between her thumb and forefinger.

I bet you were hopping mad.

Eliza: "Ooh, nasty."

Lydia: "I can do without the memory every time I see him. Plus, he's too self-indulgent, he's very preoccupied with himself; it's a very unattractive trait. I can't be doing with that, it's all about me, not him."

Quite.

Eliza's attention was taken from Lydia to Dorothy's downstairs curtains which were swishing madly. Having realised she'd caught someone's attention; Dorothy held aloft a tea pot and did a thumbs up sign.

Eliza prodded Lydia and she followed Eliza's gaze to the gesticulating tea pot holding woman.

Eliza, solemnly: "It is time."

Lydia: "Shall we just kill her?"

Eliza: "Let's see what her cakes are like first."

They both sighed and got out of the car. Lydia shoved Eliza up the garden path in front of her.

Eliza: "Why me, first?"

Lydia: "You're better at this sort of thing, than me."

Better at what? Walking? Ringing a door bell?

Eliza went to tap on the door but it was flung open wide before she got her knuckles to make contact.

Dorothy was still holding the tea pot and had garish lipstick smeared over her cheek. She beamed at them both.

Ohhh, she's got luminous, fuchsia lipstick stuck to her teeth.

I'm going to stare at that, I just know I am.

Dorothy, excitedly: "Hello! Hello! Oh, it's so wonderful to see you! I couldn't sleep last night with excitement. Kenneth went absolutely barmy as I was tossing and turning all night."

She looks a bit wide eyed and dishevelled.

Eliza and Lydia exchanged confused glances.

Eliza: "Er, it is just a cup of tea we've come round for, isn't it? We haven't missed something?"

Dorothy: "No, no! It's just marvellous to have you here."

Lydia: "Is it?"

Dorothy: "Fabulous!"

My, we are using lots of excited words today.

Wonderful, marvellous, fabulous.

Eliza looked carefully at Dorothy.

Hmmm, I think you might be a bit tipsy.

Eliza and Lydia stood, awkwardly, waiting to be invited over Dorothy's threshold and a silence descended upon them.

Eliza and Lydia exchanged glances and raised their eyebrows at each other in silent communication.

Lydia: "Erm, we've brought some cake by way of hush money, but if you're a bit busy we can always do this some other time?"

Nice try, Lydia.

Dorothy looked horrified.

Dorothy: "NO! Oh, my goodness me, how rude of me! I'm mortified by my bad manners. Come in, come in! Excuse the mess."

Dorothy stood back and flamboyantly waved them into the hall. A pristine hall, as it transpired.

Lydia handed her cake tin to Dorothy on the way in which she plonked, along with the tea pot, on a mahogany writing bureau.

Mess? Are you kidding me?

It's like a show home.

What must people think when they see the state of my place?

It's full of child toys, half painted furniture and a neighbour knee deep in a hole in my garden.

Lydia: "Blimey! Nice gaff, Mrs Cuthbert."

Dorothy: "Oh Lydia, how kind of you to say so. I'm sure it's not a patch on your home. I bet that's absolutely stunning, just like you."

Lydia coughed slightly at the effusive compliment.

Lydia: "Oh, erm, thank you."

Dorothy, wistfully: "I truly think you are one of the most beautiful women I have ever seen, Lydia."

Lydia gulped loudly and flushed with colour.

Lydia: "Oh, erm..."

She's sinking. Throw her a life buoy.

Eliza: "She is indeed a vision of beauty. Shall we put our coats over here?"

Lydia, fanning her face: "Yeah, I'm getting a bit warm."

Dorothy put her hands to her mouth and shook her head.

Dorothy: "My manners! I am appalled. Good job Kenneth isn't here."

Dorothy took their coats, turned heel and tottered off to the cloakroom, leaving Eliza and Lydia standing alone in the hall.

Lydia grabbed Eliza's arm.

Lydia, whispering loudly: "She's pissed!"

Perceptive.

Eliza: "It does rather appear she has partaken in a couple of morning tipples, yes."

Lydia grabbed Eliza's other arm and swung her to face her.

Lydia, whispering hysterically: "She's pissed and she loves me!"

Eliza: "It does rather appear to be the case, yes."

Lydia: "What are we going to do?"

Release your vice like grip for a start.

Eliza flapped her arms like wings to shake Lydia off.

Eliza: "Keep calm and eat cake."

Dorothy blustered back into the hall with freshly applied lipstick which had missed most of her mouth.

Oh, that really is quite annoying.

Dorothy: "Now then ladies, shall we put the kettle on?"

With that she shambled off to the kitchen, still leaving them standing in the hall.

Eliza and Lydia looked at each other and Lydia drew around her mouth with her finger.

Lydia, whispering: "I don't know if I can cope with that, she looks like Janice from The Muppets. Am I allowed to mention it?"

Eliza, also whispering: "I think you might have to."

Lydia nodded and they strode off into the kitchen to join Dorothy.

They found her, spoon in hand, delving into the middle of a trifle which was on the work surface beside the kettle.

Hmmm.

Eliza went over and sniffed it.

Just as I suspected.

Eliza: "It's a bit early for sherry trifle isn't it, Mrs Cuthbert? How about you have a fondant fancy instead?"

Lydia: "Yes, Mrs Cuthbert, and I think you may have missed a bit with the old lipstick."

Lydia waved her finger wildly around her face by way of demonstration.

Dorothy wiped the back of her hand over her mouth, smearing the lipstick still further.

Lydia tutted loudly.

Dorothy: "Oh call me Dorothy, please. We are best friends now, after all."

Lydia: "Are we?"

I can tell you for nothing, Lydia wouldn't befriend anyone who couldn't apply make- up.

Dorothy looked at her imploringly.

Oh no, she looks like she'd going to cry.

If in doubt - lie.

Eliza: "Oh yes, we're all one big, happy friend family. Aren't we Lydia?"

Lydia took in the shambolic state of Dorothy.

Lydia: "Oh god yeah. Eliza and I just love everyone. We're very giving like that. Eliza learnt all about it in her self-help books."

Eliza: "I can lend you one if you like?"

Lydia: "Good plan. Give her the one about self-loving."

Dorothy's eyes widened in horror.

Dorothy, stuttering: "I'm not sure Kenneth would approve."

Lydia: "Not that sort of loving, though it probably wouldn't go a miss. Beats troughing trifle from the bowl in the morning. No, I meant mentally."

Dorothy pondered the suggestion for a moment.

Dorothy, nodding: "Perhaps I'd like that, thank you."

Dorothy started to quietly sob.

Oh, marvellous.

Dorothy, continuing: "You're right; of course, there was a time when I'd not even look at sherry trifle at any time other than Christmas. Now it's before ten in the morning. I'm falling apart."

Don't we know it?

Eliza: "How about you sit down in the lounge and we'll make the tea."

Lydia: "Oh yeah, great plan. Off you go Mrs Cuth... I mean, Dorothy, we'll sort the brews out."

Dorothy nodded gratefully and picked up the trifle to take in with her.

Eliza, grabbing it off her: "We'll have that, thank you very much."

Dorothy wandered off towards the lounge, still holding the spoon and Lydia followed after her.

Lydia yanked the spoon out of Dorothy's hand.

Lydia: "Spoon! We can't be having custard on your swanky upholstery, now can we?"

Dorothy: "You're so thoughtful, Lydia. You are a goddess both inside and out."

Oh dear!

Lydia, awkwardly: "Ohhh, erm... Ok. You sit down and look out the window or something, we'll be in shortly."

Eliza was laying out a tray of cakes and teas as Lydia came back into the kitchen.

Lydia: "I never thought I'd say this but I feel rather ill at ease with the level of flattery being directed at me."

Eliza: "I don't know what you mean; you image of perfection, you walking wonderment, you glittering spectacle of womanhood."

Lydia: "Shut your cake hole."

Eliza: "That's exactly what I intend to shove in it."

Lydia: "I might have to imbibe in a bit of trifle, I'm feeling decidedly peculiar."

Eliza: "You carry the tray and I'll take the plates... Are you ready?"

Lydia: "As I'll ever be. Let's get this over with."

Mental reminder for the morning: *Look up amount of sherry required in trifle to get pissed in case life gets too much and need a stress relieving pudding.*

Second mental reminder of the morning: *Must only have stress relieving pudding after dusk.*

Chapter Six

Sub quote for the day: *Every human walks around with a certain kind of sadness. They may not wear it on their sleeves, but it's there if you look deep. Taraji P. Henson*

Eliza and Lydia carefully carried the tray into Dorothy's immaculate lounge. The whole soft furnishings ensemble was fresh out of the pages of Ideal Home magazine.

Cream carpets? Oh my, that's very brave.

Ellington and Norris would never be allowed entry into here.

They'd be confiscated at the front door - contraband.

I base my home accessories on whether they won't show the dirt or if they're wipe clean.

And those cushions, they're stacked to perfection.

Granted there's so many you can't sit on the seat but fair play to her, they are balanced impeccably.

I feel really rather inferior.

It's the jealousy fairy... Ignore.

What would be the point of stacked cushions in my house? Tom would only climb up them, fall off, hit his head and we'd end up in Accident and Emergency with a towering cushion related injury.

Eliza looked at the pitiful state of Dorothy slumped in a winged armchair; tear stained, with lipstick smeared over her face.

I might have more functional adornments but at least I'm not indulging in sherry trifle before noon.

How could I have felt a pang of jealousy at material possessions?

Have I learnt nothing from the endless stream of hippiness I've been feeding myself for the last few years?

Stop mentally rambling, something is very wrong here.

Eliza poured Dorothy a strong, black tea and handed it over to her. Dorothy downed it in one and wiped away a bead of sweat from her top lip.

Jeez, that was scalding hot! She must have asbestos innards!

Eliza, cautiously: "Are you alright, Dorothy?"

Dorothy was rubbing her chest and puffing.

Dorothy, over brightly: "Yes! Yes! Absolutely! Now, let's have a proper girlie gossip."

Lydia: "You're looking a bit flushed, Dorothy, why don't you take your cardigan off?"

Dorothy, pulling at her sleeves: "No, no, I'll be fine. I like to be covered."

Lydia: "Fair enough. I can't think of anything worse, ha ha!"

Dorothy looked Lydia up and down, adoringly.

Dorothy: "You have the body to carry it off."

Lydia, awkwardly: "Ooooh...!"

Rescue the situation from becoming a Lydia love-fest.

Right, small talk.

We have nothing in common. Seize something and quick!

Eliza: "You've got a lovely house, Dorothy; you must spend a lot of time cleaning it and stacking cushions. How long every day does it take to get it looking like this? I'm most interested in knowing how long the cushion stacking takes."

Lydia shot Eliza a bemused look due to the random line of questioning she'd veered off into.

What?

Dorothy: "Ah, Kenneth likes order. It's his influence. He doesn't like me to work so I spend most of the day ensuring it's up to standard. I used to be much more relaxed."

Dorothy leant forward and whispered conspiratorially.

Dorothy: "Do you know, before I met him, I used to only vacuum twice a week. Can you believe?!"

Shocking. You slob, Dorothy!

I'd best not tell her I only do it twice a week if I know someone's coming over.

I bet she moves her furniture too.

Eliza: "Do you move your settee every time and vacuum under it?"

Lydia shook her head slowly at Eliza.

Well, you come up with something better!

Dorothy: "Of course! It's not done properly, otherwise."

I knew it.

I must move the settee and see what's under there when I get home.

I don't think it's seen the light of day for over a year.

Lydia shoved the plate of cakes under Eliza's chin.

Lydia: "Cake?!"

Eliza nodded gratefully, selected a lump of Millionaire's shortbread and shoved it in her mouth, whole.

Ooh, that's a bit rich.

Lydia, proffering the plate to Dorothy: "Do you want one?"

Dorothy: "I shouldn't really; Kenneth doesn't like me to eat cake."

I'm getting a bit sick of Kenneth.

He sounds a right killjoy.

Not allowing your wife to eat cake and making her tidy up every day. Isn't that illegal?

Lydia shot a look at Eliza who was still slowly chewing her shortbread.

Lydia: "You're your own woman, Dorothy. If you want cake then you eat cake!"

Ah, I'm not the only one sick of hearing about him.

Dorothy: "Oh Lydia, you are so stupendously strident. Go on then, just a little one."

Dorothy dithered about deciding which cake to have and chose the smallest one.

Dorothy, giggling: "Ooh I feel so naughty!! Rebellious, almost!"

Lydia, dryly: "Yeah, you're really pushing the boundaries now; cake at elevenses."

Eliza finally swallowed the shortbread and downed her tea with it.

Eliza: "Do you have many coffee mornings?"

Dorothy fidgeted in her seat and looked down at her lap.

Dorothy, sadly: "I've tried to encourage the other ladies in the village to come round but they seem to cancel, mostly last minute, which is disheartening as I spend a lot of time making the cakes, especially."

Oh, that's a bit tragic.

Eliza: "That's awful!"

Dorothy: "It is a bit demoralising, yes, especially as Kenneth doesn't like me to eat the cakes that are left."

Kenneth the killjoy - Cake denier.

Dorothy: "Can I be perfectly honest with you, dears?"

Lydia: "If you must."

Dorothy: "You're the only friends I've had who have actually turned up. I was fully expecting you to cancel. I was so excited when I saw you sitting in the car outside."

Ok, now I feel awful.

Eliza: "We were looking forward to it, weren't we Lydia?"

Lydia, nodding feverishly: "Beside ourselves. Now we're friends we can keep everything we ever know about each other and any silly little thing we happen to have inadvertently overheard to ourselves, can't we?"

Specifically, the bit about villagers conducting extramarital affairs in our shop, that bit would be good to keep to yourself please, Dorothy.

Dorothy mopped her brow with the corner of her cardigan.

Dorothy, nervously: "Have you heard things?"

Lydia and Eliza exchanged confused glances.

Lydia, carefully: "Noooo, have you?"

Dorothy, relieved: "No, I know nothing about anything and certainly nothing about Bunty Hestington-Charles and her willingness to conduct infidelity with Mr Hicks."

She gazed wistfully, looking into the middle distance.

Dorothy: "He truly is a delightful man, of whom I have much affection for. The loss of his wife to that Portuguese waiter must have discombobulated him. It's the only reason I can think of why he would copulate with Bunty; she's got shocking taste in curtains."

Dorothy went ever pinker as her fury rose.

Dorothy, in full flow: "I'll never forgive Patricia for what she did to him, the harlot. She never even liked paella when she lived in Pilkington but I bet she eats scallops now. She was getting on the train at Billington once when a gust of wind caught the hem of her skirt and I saw the state of her thighs; no Portuguese man will put up with them for long, not with the amount of thread veins she has. It's worse than a map of the London Underground."

Eliza and Lydia in unison: "Okaaay."

I've had enough, this is exhausting.

Eliza: "We ought to be off in a minute, Dorothy; we've got a lot of work on at the shop."

Lydia nodded, feverishly.

Lydia: "Oh god yeah, overrun with it. Tables everywhere you look."

Calm down, we're leaving.

Dorothy looked disappointed and wrung her hands, nervously. She looked resignedly at them both.

Dorothy: "Of course you do."

She pulled herself out of the chair and continued as she guided them towards the hall.

Dorothy: "You're both very gifted, dears. I admire you and your independence so much. Sometimes, you sort of women are frowned upon but I think it's wonderful and liberated of you to have the confidence to undertake parenthood and your business to the exclusion of men. It is to be applauded."

I got stuck on the 'you sort of women are frowned upon' bit of the monologue but I think it was generally flattering.

Eliza: "Thank you."

Lydia: "Yes, thank you, I think. I do love men though, don't misunderstand. I'm not into women so you can forget about that sort of caper. I love men probably more than is good for me, to be honest. I could have loads of them; I just adore them that much. Women don't float my boa...."

Lydia trailed off as Dorothy had already wandered off to collect their coats.

Eliza whispering to Lydia: "Yes alright, we've got the message."

Lydia, whispering back: "Soz, just needed to clear that up. She was a bit keen with the old womanly praise for my liking."

Eliza: "Adoration is slightly different to fornication, dear. Though, how I keep my hands off you, I'll never know."

Lydia: "Ha de ha. You know what they say about sarcasm."

Dorothy lurched back into view holding their coats and held them out in turn for them to step into.

Dorothy: "It's been so tremendous; I can't thank you enough for taking the trouble to visit me."

She really does use a lot of enthusiastic synonyms.

Eliza: "No problem. We've enjoyed it, haven't we Lydia?"

Lydia: "It was like nothing I've ever experienced before."

Ain't that the truth.

Dorothy, imploringly: "Can we do it again, now we're so close?"

I don't know how much Millionaire's shortbread my hips can stand.

Eliza: "Yes of course. We'll arrange it sometime."

Vague but not a no.

Dorothy, beaming: "Wonderful, you've made my year!"

I do rather feel that to be the case.

That's really rather sad.

Dorothy waved them off as they almost ran down the path to the car. They flumped into the seats, gratefully and slammed the doors shut.

Lydia: "Oh shit, I left me tin."

Eliza: "Never mind you can fetch it next time."

Lydia: "Oh you are soooo funny today, aren't you? You and your peculiar fixation with cushions."

Eliza started the car and they made the short journey to the shop.

Eliza: "What's the matter with her, do you think?"

Lydia: "Apart from the overbearing husband, the drink habit, haphazard make-up application and anally tidy home?"

Eliza: "Yeah."

Lydia: "Nothing, darling. She's got excellent taste in women. Ha ha!!"

Eliza: "Ha ha, I'll drop you off at the shop and you can relieve Mr Hicks."

Lydia screwed up her nose.

Eliza: "You know what I mean... I'm off to collect that coffee table from number eighty-six."

Eliza dropped Lydia off to mind the shop and they went about the rest of their day, whilst Dorothy

Cuthbert sat forlornly looking out of her lounge window at the birds pecking at the crumbled remains of the Millionaires' shortbread she'd put on the bird table.

Important research carried out during afternoon: *Calorific content of Millionaires shortbread.*

Chapter Seven

Quote for the day: *Make yourself at home... clean my kitchen. Anonymous*

The next day, Eliza wandered into the kitchen to be greeted by a whimpering Ellington who was scraping at the door to go out.

Eliza: "Blimey, Ellington, you must be desperate."

She let him out and looked out of the kitchen window to be greeted by, what can only be described as, a forensic tent in her vegetable patch.

What the...?

He wasn't desperate for a wee; he'd obviously heard activity in the garden.

Ellington bounded down the path to investigate and Eliza followed him.

Ellington reached the tent before her and started barking excitedly at it.

That's unlike Ellington; he's not generally a woofer.

Out of a flap at the end, Philip poked his head out.

Philip: "Hold your noise canine, it's only me."

Eliza, upon joining them: "Philip, what on earth is going on now?! Ellington, stand easy!"

Ellington stopped barking but continued to bounce, frantically.

Philip put his finger to his lips.

Philip: "Shhh, my dear girl. Subterfuge."

He scrambled out from the tent, stood and brushed down his cords.

Philip, expanding his arms: "It's a greenhouse."

Eliza pointed at the white canopy which covered the rickety frame.

Eliza: "Are you sure? It looks a bit opaque to be a greenhouse."

Philip: "We can't have prying eyes looking in, can we?"

Eliza: "Why? In case they steal your tomatoes?"

Philip: "It's not tomatoes, dear girl. It's a helmet."

Eliza: "You're growing a helmet?"

Philip, slightly exasperated: "No, my dearest Eliza, you cannot grow such things. I do wonder about your education, sometimes. You'll be thinking spaghetti grows on trees next. No, I think I have struck gold."

Eliza: "You've struck a gold helmet?"

Ooh, that's got to be worth a bit.

Philip, sighing: "Something like that. Anyway, I need to investigate further so to prevent any unwanted attention and to preserve its integrity; I decided to erect a tent."

You think shoving a white tent up in my garden will prevent attention?

The other neighbours will think there's been a murder.

Eliza: "It's a bit of an eyesore Philip and you should have asked me first, really."

Philip: "Of course I should have. Please forgive me. However, I think you will be thanking me, if this turns out to be treasure. We can split the proceeds."

Eliza, tutting: "Okay, how long will it take to find out if it's worth anything?"

Philip: "I've telephoned Mr Regis; he's trustworthy and very knowledgeable, if a bit deaf courtesy of the mortar bombs. He's off to Margate for a few days so the earliest opportunity for him to peruse is next week. Put the kettle on, there's a dear. Thirsty work this treasure hunting."

Now hang on.

Eliza: "I was just making one actually, so you're in luck, otherwise I might have been too busy."

Philip: "Uh huh, now run along there's a poppet. I'll have a biscuit with mine."

Grrrrr.

Philip bent down, crawled back into the tent and closed the flap behind him.

Eliza called to Ellington to follow her and he trotted alongside her back into the house.

She made Philip his tea and plonked it outside the tent on an upturned flower pot and went back into the house and absentmindedly drank her tea.

I so wish I could see Jude again.

Just to look at his perfect face and crinkly little smile.

She smiled at the recollection of his face, then she tutted.

It's all a bit rotten.

I'm not very happy about the whole state of affairs, quite frankly.

He's going to think I don't want to see him and I don't want him to think that he's not wanted.

I used a lot of wants there.

It was just circumstances and me not knowing where he was waiting for me.

She gulped her drink and tried to think of surreptitious ways of finding more about Jude.

Time spent Googling Jude: *Seven minutes.*

Time spent Googling gold helmets: *Ten minutes. (Most of those spent with mouth open).*

Time spent deleting browser history: *Fifteen minutes.*

Chapter Eight

Quote for the day: *There is no greater agony than bearing an untold story inside you. Maya Angelou*

A few days later Eliza, Lydia and Mr Hicks were stood leaning on the counter in the shop, mulling over where to place a newly painted console table. Mr Hicks was handing out freshly made ginger nuts as they sipped their teas.

The shop door opened and Dorothy bustled in.

Oh no. Not another coffee morning invite so soon.

Dorothy, brightly: "Hello! Hello! How are we all?"

Eliza clocked Dorothy's make-up choice for the day.

Whoah! That's a lot of orange foundation and you really ought to blend it in to your neck more.

And that's an awful lot of blusher.

Who do you get your application advice from? Aunt Sally?

Lydia's mouth fell open in horror and dropped her ginger nut into her cup.

Lydia: "Oh my dear Lord! I'm sorry, I can't allow that. Mr Hicks, get me a wet wipe."

Mr Hicks remained motionless and was looking carefully at Dorothy.

Lydia: "Don't you possess a mirror, Dorothy?"

Lydia tutted at Mr Hicks for his lack of obedience and fished about under the counter for the pack of wipes.

Dorothy held her hands up to protect her face as Lydia went towards her with one.

Dorothy, screeching: "Move away!! Do not touch me!"

Mr Hicks walked in front of Lydia and pushed her back slightly.

Lydia: "'Ere, steady on Mr Hi..."

Mr Hicks shot her a sharp look and she shut up.

Mr Hicks, gently: "Good day to you Dorothy, are you alright?"

He touched her elbow slightly and she flinched at the physical contact.

Eliza and Lydia looked at each other and Lydia threw the unused wet wipe into the bin.

I think the answer to that, is 'no.'

Eliza: "Would you like a cup of tea and a ginger nut?"

Dorothy, flatly: "I don't know if I'm allowed biscuits."

Lydia, shoving a biscuit in her hand: "We'll not tell anyone."

Mr Hicks pulled a nearby seat over and guided Dorothy to sit down, which she did, gratefully.

Eliza looked at Dorothy and noticed her face looked a bit puffy.

Don't stare.

I need to. Something's not right.

Be subtle.

Lydia, peering closely: "Have you got something wrong with your face, Dorothy? It looks a bit swollen."

Ok, no subtlety then.

Dorothy, laughing awkwardly: "No, no! I'm just very clumsy; I'm forever wandering into things."

Okaaay. Walking into things with your face?

You might want to consider giving up the trifle.

Mr Hicks: "Dorothy, how can we help you today?"

Dorothy, quickly: "Sorry? I don't need any help. It's all perfectly fine."

Mr Hicks, patiently: "I mean, you came to the shop. What can we do for you?"

Dorothy: "Ohhh, silly me. Kenneth always says I'm silly. He's right, of course."

Dorothy looked at her hands.

Mr Hicks, softly: "You're not silly, Dorothy; you're very creative. I remember the time you made that beautiful flower arrangement when Princess Whatsername came to visit the hospital at Billington."

Dorothy looked up at Mr Hicks, wide-eyed.

Dorothy: "You remember that?!"

Mr Hicks, nodding: "Of course! It was greatly admired."

Dorothy, smiling: "Was it? Well, I never. Thank you."

Mr Hicks crouched down so he was level with Dorothy and looked her in the eyes.

Mr Hicks, quietly: "Never underestimate yourself, Dorothy. You are capable of so much, if you allow yourself the chance."

Dorothy stared straight back at Mr Hicks and there was silence as they looked solemnly at each other.

Eliza looked at Lydia over the top of their heads and they shrugged, unsure of what they were witnessing.

Dorothy nodded, imperceptibly, at Mr Hicks and he groaned slightly with exertion, as he stood.

Mr Hicks: "Right, I've got some muffins to attend to. I'll be in the kitchen if anyone needs me."

With that, he walked off out the back, leaving a seated Dorothy in the middle of the shop with a baffled Eliza and Lydia.

Eliza: "Er, right then. It's lovely to see you, what can we do for you today?"

Dorothy gathered herself.

Dorothy: "Huh? Oh, sorry, of course. I dropped by to give you back the tin. You left it the other day."

Dorothy handed the uneaten ginger nut back to Lydia and reached into her canvas shopping bag for the tin.

Lydia: "Oh right! Thanks. That's very thoughtful."

Dorothy: "It was no trouble, it's lovely to see you, dears."

Eliza: "Would you like that cup of tea?"

Dorothy pulled herself up out of the chair.

Dorothy, shaking her head: "No, I won't stay; I need to get back. There's housework to do. If I don't leave now, I'll not get it done."

Dorothy headed towards the door and Lydia shouted after her.

Lydia: "We'll come by yours again, if you'd like? Next week or something."

Eh? Will we?

Dorothy's face lit up and she put her hand to her mouth with surprise.

Dorothy: "Really?! Oh, my goodness, that would be just wonderful! Do you mean it?"

Lydia: "Yes. Count us in for Tuesday again, same time as before."

Dorothy: "Marvellous! I'm so pleased! You really are a generous soul making time for me considering you're so busy. Lydia, you are a true beacon of joy. I'll mark you on the calendar as soon as I get in!"

Dorothy left the shop with a visible spring in her step and as the door shut behind her Mr Hicks emerged from the kitchen.

Mr Hicks: "Do you mean it, Lydia?"

Lydia: "Eh?"

Mr Hicks: "About going next Tuesday?"

Eliza: "Yes, did you mean it?"

Lydia shrugged her shoulders.

Lydia: "Well, we can always cancel. She just looked so sad and pathetic; I thought it'd cheer her up."

Mr Hicks's face clouded over.

Mr Hicks, seriously: "Under no circumstances will you cancel. Do you understand me?"

Lydia: "Whoooh, Mr Hicks, we are masterful today!"

Mr Hicks, soberly: "I mean it Lydia. Do not make offers like that and not adhere to them. They might be an off the cuff remark to you but to others they mean something."

Lydia: "Okay, okay. Why don't you come with us? You seem very keen on her and her flower arrangements."

Mr Hicks, tersely: "Be quiet, Lydia. I'm going out for a while. I'll move that console table this afternoon, when I return."

Lydia: "I thought you had muffins to attend to?"

Mr Hicks shook his head at Lydia.

Mr Hicks: "Sometimes, Lydia, you are very obtuse."

He walked out of the shop without another word.

Lydia put her hands on her hips and looked mystified.

Lydia: "I think I missed about ninety eight percent of that. The only bit I got was the tin being given back to me."

Eliza: "I'm not sure what went on either."

Lydia: "Ah well, who cares. Ginger nut?"

Eliza: "Don't mind if I do."

Later that afternoon, Mr Hicks stood at the end of Dorothy Cuthbert's road, wondering whether to proceed further. He bid good day to a passing dog walker and decided to bite the bullet.

He walked purposefully towards her house and reaching into his coat pocket, pulled out a leaflet. He glanced at it and nodded to himself. He strode up her path, hastily poked the leaflet through Dorothy's letterbox and promptly left; relieved he'd acted upon his instinct and not let the moment pass.

Poem: *A Place to Reflect*

Is what we all need
As essential as the sun
For our souls to breathe
Quietude and contemplation
Allows serenity to flow
Stop awhile
And ask which direction
You wish your life to go.

Eliza Wakeley

Chapter Nine

Quote for the day: *Insanity is hereditary. You get it from your children. Sam Levenson*

Tom was in his first year at primary school and, a few days later, Eliza picked him up on her way home from the shop.

Eliza: "Hello darling, good day at school?"

Tom: "Yes fanks, mummy."

Eliza: "What did you learn?"

Tom: "Nuffink, we did sticking and I fell off the slide at playtime."

Eliza: "Nuffink? You learned nothing, dear, nothing."

Tom: "That's what I said, nuffink."

Eliza shook her head.

I blame mum and her cockney accent.

She says it is part of his heritage.

They got back home to be greeted by an over excited Ellington. She absentmindedly let him out of the back door and looked out of the window as she went to put the kettle on.

What the...?!

Ellington had started barking manically at the sight before him.

Eliza shot out the back door with Tom following her to be greeted by a group of people crowded around near the 'greenhouse' at the end of her back garden. They were bent over looking at the soil.

Eliza, spluttering: "Who the flipping flip-flops are you lot?!!"

Random person in wellies, above Ellington's woofing: "Ah! Good day to you!"

Eliza: "Shut up Ellington!! I can't hear myself think."

Ellington ignored her and continued to bark, madly.

Tom: "Ewwington, stand easy, me old chum."

Ellington stopped barking immediately but continued to bounce, madly.

Random person in wellies: "Are you the occupier of this dwelling?"

Eliza: "I might be, not the tent, I don't live in there; there's no room for a kitchen. I might be the dweller of the dwelling that dwells behind me... Depends."

I'm gabbling. It's the sight of unknown people in my garden.

They have spades.

I'm not reacting well to people with spades.

Eliza, asking again: "Who are you?"

Random person in wellies: "I'm Raymond. I'm the founding member of PHARTS."

Eliza: "What in god's name does PHARTS mean?"

Tom: "It is a naughty word, mummy. It means trump."

Eliza, slightly exasperatedly: "Yes, Tom, that I know. I mean his PHARTS. What are his PHARTS all about?"

Tom, pondering: "Baked beans? They always make me trump."

Raymond the founding PHART, self-importantly: "It stands for the Pilkington Heritage and Relic Treasury Society. I've come with a few colleagues."

He waved expansively at the accompanying group of dishevelled people. The other PHARTS looked momentarily up from the ground they were peering at, waved amiably and turned their attention back to the soil.

Oooh, they must be after Philip's helmet!

There's no sign of him.

I'm sure he said he wanted to keep it a secret.

Eliza: "Does Philip know you're here?"

Raymond, the founding member of the ridiculous acronym: "No, I do believe he may be otherwise detained today. He was on the old sauce last night and was last seen wandering southwards through Farmer Glynn's wheat field."

A bespectacled woman looked up and leant on her spade.

Female from PHARTS: "That's how I – we - found out. Philip was down The Anchor last night and got absolutely plastered. I feel for his liver, I really do. Anyway, he said he'd found a Roman helmet from the Second Century! Can you believe?! He told me in confidence by the fruit machine; you know the one with the iffy button... Well, anything else, I would have kept mum about; I'm very reliable on all manner of confidences. I shall take the rather alarming information I was imparted about Sharon from number eleven being a swinger, to the grave; but this is far too important. I felt I had to divulge the information."

Raymond, nodding: "You did the right thing, Penelope. This could put Pilkington on the map... We are of course on the map; otherwise, we'd never have bus stops or any utilities. I mean, figuratively, speaking. Just imagine what this sort of find could do for tourism."

Now hang on a minute, this is my garden.

I don't want tourists wandering across my borders.

I don't have enough matching crockery to make tourists tea.

Just then Philip came striding over the ridiculous fence, waving a broom. His face was covered in lacerations.

Philip: "Oi! Gerroff my neighbour's land!"

Penelope sidled behind the opaque 'greenhouse' out of view.

Raymond: "Hello old chap! How's the head? Oh dear, you look a bit cut up about something. Arf, arf, cut up about something..."

Philip: "Shut up, Raymond! It was such a balmy night, I decided to be at one with the earth and sleep under the stars. I just happened to sleep a bit too close to some hedgerow, that's all. Now, what are you doing here?"

Philip turned his attention to Eliza.

Philip: "Do they have your permission to trespass?"

Eliza: "Er, no."

Neither do you, but it doesn't make a blind bit of difference.

Philip waved his broom wildly at them.

Philip: "Get out then, you and the rest of your PHARTS and don't you come back unless you're invited!"

Raymond fanned his hands in an attempt to pacify Philip.

Raymond: "Now calm down, Philip. We're all adults here, except for the child... and the dog... Anyway, we're all in this for the common good."

Philip was going purple with anger and a vein was throbbing in his temple. He was trembling as he brandished the broom at Raymond.

Philip, furiously: "I'm warning you!"

Tom backed away and hid behind Eliza's legs.

Raymond sizing up the situation, nodded curtly.

Raymond: "We've seen enough."

Turning his attention to Eliza.

Raymond, courteously: "We will be on our way, thank you for your time. We'll be in contact again should we wish to undertake further investigation."

Another male from PHARTS, excitedly: "Can we dig a trench, Raymond? I've always wanted to dig a trench!"

Raymond: "We'll see Charles, let's just let the lady and Philip be for now."

The PHARTS gathered together their spades and Penelope huddled close to another person as they made to depart, to try and remain out of Philip's eye line.

She had an ample bottom so it was always going to be a tall order and Philip spotted her immediately.

Philip, apoplectic with rage: "You!! Penelope! I should have known I couldn't trust you – cover Tom's ears, Eliza – you fucketing big arsed, blabber mouthed old barge!"

Fucketing?

Raymond: "Now, now Philip. No need to be personal. It's not Penelope's fault she's got a bottom the size of Suffolk, now is it? She's very good with pre-decimalisation coins. Anyway, we'll not take up any more of your time. Goodbye!"

With that he practically ran off down the path and out of Eliza's back gate.

Tom waved at Raymond's retreating frame.

Tom: "Bye-bye trumpy man!"

As the remainder of the group left, Penelope could be heard talking to another member of the society.

Penelope: "Is my bum really that big, William?"

William: "Put it this way, if you stood for any length of time in my garden, I'd have to plant shade lovers..."

Penelope: "Oh."

The three of them stood at the top of the garden and watched the PHARTS depart and Eliza turned to Philip, who looked a pitiful state.

Eliza: "What really happened to your face?"

Philip gently stroked a cut on his cheek.

Philip: "I did indeed sleep under the stars, my dear girl, only I wasn't facing them. I believe I may have come a cropper in a ditch and fallen face first into a rather unforgiving boundary hedge. Farmer Glynn extricated me at half past ten this morning."

Eliza: "The PHARTS said you were drunk and told old big bum about the booty."

Philip, sighing: "Unusually, the local ale appears to not have been watered down last night, which threw me and I appear to have miscalculated my tolerance threshold. I therefore blame them entirely for me becoming somewhat loose lipped. I shall take the matter up with the landlord when I feel ready to face the hostelry again."

Eliza: "Your helmet's out in the open. When's Mr Regis back?"

Philip: "Next week. Let me check in the tent to make sure they haven't located it."

Philip put down the broom and crawled into the tent.

A few moments later he poked his head out of the flap and put his thumbs up.

Philip: "We're in luck, my helmet remains intact. I put a grow bag over the hole with some courgettes in and it's undisturbed. They must have thought it really was a greenhouse. Stupid PHARTS."

Eliza: "They were looking around the outside of it, there's a freshly dug hole here."

Eliza was pointing to the right of the tent. Philip crawled out of the tent and inspected the hole.

Philip: "That's alright. The only thing they'll find if they keep digging there are your monstrously deep potatoes."

Tom tugged at Eliza's arm.

Tom: "Mummy, I need food. This little blackbird needs his cwumbs."

Eliza: "Yes ok, the action's over for today. I also need a cup of tea."

Philip: "May I take the liberty of buying a padlock for your gate, dear Eliza? I'm stricken with guilt that I put you and Tom in the shocking position of having unwanteds in your garden."

Eliza: "I'll take you up on that, Philip. Yes please."

Philip: "I'll do it this evening. I shall bid you good day, I need to attend to some facial wounds."

Philip picked up his broom and headed off back towards his house, stepping over the ridiculous fence.

Philip, muttering: "So, you want my helmet do you, Raymond? Well, we'll see about that…"

Technically, my helmet.

Well, my landlord's helmet, actually.

Time spent thinking up better acronyms for Pilkington Heritage and Relic Treasury Society: *Twenty-three minutes.*

Time spent penning email to the founding PHART with the suggestion they change their name to the "Wanders Anywhere No Key Ever Required Society": *Thirteen minutes.*

Expectancy of reply: *None.*

Chapter Ten

Quote for the day: *One's dignity may be assaulted, vandalised and cruelly mocked, but it can never be taken away unless it is surrendered. Michael J. Fox*

Dorothy stood back to admire her handiwork and skipped, delightedly in the air. She took in the carefully placed cottage roses mixed in with delicately trimmed and positioned foliage.

Dorothy clapped her hands with pride.

Dorothy, aloud to herself: "I might even win the class competition with this!"

She hugged herself as she took stock of the beauty of her display. What she'd achieved filled her with undiluted joy and she was flooded with a happiness she'd not felt for many years. She looked at the beautiful cut glass vase they stood in; a present from her grandmother many years before.

She leant over and gently traced the engraved pattern on the thick crystal with her forefinger. She smiled fondly as she recalled her patient, kind and encouraging grandmother. It was whom she was named after and it had been perfectly apt as they shared many traits. Dorothy wondered what her grandmother would say if she could see her today, all proud with the display in her beautiful vase; finally taken off the shelf where it had stood for over a decade. They'd shared so many wonderful times before she sadly passed away, the year before Dorothy married Kenneth. It was her who'd taught Dorothy all about floristry, passing on countless tips she'd gained over years of making her own arrangements.

As a result, Dorothy had always loved flower arranging. It totally absorbed her and the delicate art of showing the beautiful array of blooms off to their best advantage filled her with a sense of satisfaction.

She felt vibrant and alive; a long dormant passion had been awakened, along with memories of happy times spent with her grandmother.

Dorothy looked up towards the ceiling and smiled.

Dorothy, wistfully: "You're here aren't you granny? I can feel you. You sent that leaflet, didn't you?"

She'd wanted to become a florist and when she first met Kenneth that had been her dream. She'd told him and when they were dating, he'd listened and even encouraged her. After they were married, however, it seemed to her, her life became less important. Her ambitions no longer mattered. All dreams she had deemed whimsical and unnecessary; she was on this earth to attend to her husband. Her confidence had been eroded over the years; the constant chipping away at her had left her with no interests of her own. She felt like a shell of the person she once was.

Recently, she'd started to look at her life and what she'd become. She wondered if this was all she'd ever be; a servant to her husband. Then, last week, the leaflet about flower arrangement courses dropped through her letterbox. She'd spoken to Joanne next door to see if she'd received one as she knew she liked flowers, but she hadn't. She took it as a sign. A sign she should regain some of her happiness and do something she enjoyed as well as being a good wife. How could it hurt? It was only a hobby.

Just then she heard the key in the front door.

Dorothy, startled: "Huh? Who's that? What time is it?"

She hurriedly ran to look at the mantelpiece clock and upon seeing the time, threw her hands up to her face in horror.

Dorothy: "Oh my goodness! I was so engrossed I didn't realise the time!"

She hastily threw a tea towel over the display and ran out of the lounge; literally bumping into Kenneth in the hall.

Kenneth, winded: "Ooof! Dorothy, must you run through the house?!"

Dorothy, gabbling: "Hello, sorry Kenneth, did you have a good day?"

Kenneth ignored her, threw his briefcase and suit jacket on the chair by the mahogany writing bureau and went to sit in the lounge. Dorothy automatically picked them up and put them in the correct place. When she'd finished, she joined him in the lounge.

Dorothy found him stood, hands on hips with the tea towel in one hand, staring at her flower arrangement.

Dorothy, slightly crestfallen: "Oh, you've seen it already. I was going to do a grand unveiling for you!"

Kenneth, derisively: "For a bunch of flowers?"

Dorothy, proudly: "It's a flower arrangement. Isn't it beautiful? I've spent hours on it."

Kenneth turned to look at her.

Kenneth, flatly: "Why?"

Dorothy, with less certainty: "Because I thought it would be nice."

Kenneth, scornfully: "Nice? What an insipid word 'nice' is."

Kenneth put down the tea towel, turned his back on the display and slumped into his usual chair. He crossed his ankles, put his feet in the air and Dorothy hastily moved the nearby foot stool under them. He put them down and looked up at her expectantly.

Kenneth: "I'll have dinner in here tonight, I want to catch the news."

Dorothy: "Of course, I'll just put it on."

Kenneth straightened in his chair.

Kenneth, icily: "Put it on? You mean it's not ready yet?"

Dorothy felt a prickle under her skin and started to get hot. A feeling of foreboding trickled through her body. She was starting to feel a weight in her chest and involuntarily massaged it.

Dorothy, gabbling: "Well no, I'm sorry Kenneth, I was so engrossed in my display I completely lost track of time. It's only steak, it won't take long."

She hastily backed out of the lounge in an attempt to avoid any further dialogue. She ran into the kitchen and flung open the fridge door to retrieve the ingredients.

Kenneth stood, kicked away the foot stool and followed her.

When Dorothy closed the fridge door, she found him stood in the doorway glaring at her with contempt.

Kenneth, acerbically: "So let me understand this correctly. You've spent a pointless afternoon with a load of dead flowers, whilst I've been at work. Work which ensures you have a roof over your head, clothes to wear and food to eat? And you don't even have the common courtesy to have the food, I have bought, ready for me?"

Dorothy threw the steak haphazardly onto the pan and chucked it under the grill.

Dorothy: "They aren't dead."

Kenneth: "Are they still attached to the plant with which they grew, woman?"

Dorothy, quietly: "No."

Kenneth, sneering at Dorothy: "Then they are as good as dead. A slow decay will encompass them over the next week as they slowly wilt and fester."

Dorothy, sadly: "Must you be quite so disparaging? It's for a competition."

Kenneth, spitting with rage: "Competition? What competition?! Why wasn't I told about this?"

Dorothy, with false bravado: "I'm telling you now. The other week a leaflet came through the door about classes in Billington. I decided I needed a hobby, so I joined. They're running a competition and I think I might win with that display."

Dorothy brushed herself down and busied herself chopping up some potatoes.

Kenneth, mimicking her voice: "Oooh, I'm telling you now."

His eyes bore into her with utter hatred.

Kenneth, caustically: "You are my wife, you don't go 'deciding' anything without my say so, do you understand?"

Dorothy looked at him and a fear enveloped her body, rendering her immobile. She was unable to speak so nodded at him, mutely.

Kenneth strode into the lounge and Dorothy ran after him. He was standing beside the display.

Kenneth: "No wife of mine wastes time, do you hear?"

Dorothy started to cry.

Dorothy: "Yes Kenneth. I'm sorry."

Kenneth: "You think it's alright to not have my dinner ready when I come home?"

Dorothy shook her head pitifully.

Dorothy: "No Kenneth. I'm very sorry."

Kenneth: "So am I."

With that he picked up the display.

Dorothy's eyes widened with horror.

Dorothy, sobbing wildly: "No Kenneth, please! I beg you. I'll never do it again. Please put it down! I've spent all afternoon on it."

She ran over to him and reached over to grasp the vase. His lip curled at her as he held it up above her head and strode towards the French windows and opened them.

Kenneth, stonily: "All the more reason to make you realise how futile it was."

With that, he threw the whole display across the garden; the crystal cut vase smashed against the patio slabs and the once perfectly arranged flowers were strewn amongst the glass fragments, spilt water and earth from the perfectly manicured borders.

Dorothy's legs buckled and she wept uncontrollably at his feet.

Dorothy, between gut wrenching sobs: "My grandmother's vase! How could you?"

Kenneth, dismissively: "Who? Oh her. Well, she's as dead as the flowers, it doesn't matter."

Kenneth roughly stepped over her and went back to sit in his chair.

Kenneth, calmly: "You'd better go and finish dinner. I've waited long enough as it is."

He switched on the television and turned the volume up to drown out Dorothy's baleful sobs.

Poem: *Surrender*

Reflections in your life
Will guide you to a place
Where joy is all around
And your heart is full of grace
A deep peace lies within
Each and everyone
Listen to the voice within
And the lock will be undone.
We all have guidance by our side
And it is shown in many ways
A steering towards a path
And the opportunities it paves
Many have forgotten
The pact they made before
The teachings of life disrupts

What is in their core.
To find yourself again
And the purpose of your life
Surrender
And accept you know it all
It is deeply hidden
Just waiting for your call.

Eliza Wakeley

Chapter Eleven

Quote for the day: *Real knowledge is to know the extent of one's ignorance. Confucius*

Eliza and Lydia were stood in Eliza's kitchen sharing cake and drinking tea. They'd met up to take a newly renovated cupboard to the shop but had got waylaid by the kettle. The door went and Ellington gave a solitary woof.

Eliza wandered over to answer it and was greeted by a highly bronzed Mr Regis.

Eliza: "Blimey, hello Mr Regis. Was it sunny in Margate?"

Mr Regis: "Eh? Was my son in Margaret?"

It's the mortars.

His ears are damaged.

Eliza, hollering: "You're frightfully tanned. Was it hot in Margate?"

Mr Regis held out a pair of very pasty, wrinkled hands.

Mr Regis: "It's only my face. My daughter's just passed her beautification course. She's opened her first shop and was trying out her spraying skills. The wife's not impressed. She was done too and looks like she's been creosoted. She's not been out of the house for three days and the parrot won't talk to her."

Eliza, loudly: "Ohhhh. Are you here to see Philip's helmet?"

Please don't let anyone else hear what I just yelled.

Mr Regis: "I am, ducky. I tried his door but there was no reply. May I come in?"

That's because he spends his life in my garden.

Eliza: "Yes, of course."

Eliza ushered him in. Ellington bounced up to greet him then suddenly dropped like a stone onto his front, cowering. He slunk away into his basket.

Eliza, with concern: "Ellington? What's the matter boy?"

Ellington was quivering in his basket.

Mr Regis: "It's me. My face causes consternation to the animal kingdom. A cat actually hissed at me on the way here and ran across the road to get away. It nearly lost one of its lives care of the dustbin lorry. I'll have to tell my daughter. I think she'll have to invest in a finer nozzle."

Lydia wandered in from the kitchen and dropped her cake on the floor.

Lydia: "Bloody hell, Mr Regis, have you fallen in a furnace?"

Mr Regis: "Eh? Have I fallen on whose face?"

Eliza: "It's fake tan. His daughter's a beautician and has a shop."

Lydia: "Where's the shop?"

Eliza: "Margate."

Lydia: "Remind me never to go."

Mr Regis: "Never go to Margaret? Who is this woman?"

Eliza, shouting: "Is Philip expecting you?"

Mr Regis: "He is, ducky. I believe we are to convene at the back of your garden at eleven. I did try the side gate but it appears to be locked."

Eliza: "Ah yes, Philip did that to stop the PHARTS entering."

Lydia: "PHARTS?"

Eliza: "Pilkington Heritage and Relic Treasury Society."

Mr Regis: "Or bunch of blithering nincompoops, as I like to refer to them."

Eliza: "Don't you get on with the PHARTS?"

Mr Regis: "Eh?"

Louder Eliza.

Eliza: "Don't you like the PHARTS?"

Mr Regis shook his head.

Mr Regis: "I don't know anyone that does. They're a right load of hot air."

Indeed.

Mr Regis continued.

Mr Regis: "Completely hopeless. I used to be the Chair but I stood down after a disagreement about a Roman."

Eliza: "What happened?"

Mr Regis: "It must have been before you moved here; Penelope swore blind she tripped over one on the towpath by the river. She told the mayor and everything. It was quite the scoop. I had the chap from the Billington Gazette literally hounding me

76

morning, noon and night. I struggled to leave the house for fear of the Maserati chasing me."

Lydia shook her head.

Lydia: "Paparazzi."

Mr Regis: "Eh? Bless you, ducky."

Eliza: "What happened next?"

Mr Regis: "I'm very knowledgeable on Romans, hence my eagerness to view Philip's helmet. I knew as soon as I saw the remains Penelope referred to, she was mistaken. They weren't even human. I believe they were of bovine origin. No Roman in history ever had four legs."

He started to chuckle.

Mr Regis: "The silly woman had alerted all and sundry about a dead cow!"

He guffawed loudly and bent double. Standing up, he brushed away a tear of laughter and wiped his hands on his beige, nylon slacks.

Mr Regis, seriously: "However, what with me as PHARTS Chair, I looked a right fool, thanks to her ineptitude and over excitement. She didn't even run the cow past me before announcing it to everyone. She's a liability."

Eliza, loudly: "It was her who told the rest of them about Philip's find."

Mr Regis: "Eh? Pester them about Philip's mind?"

Eliza, sighing: "Doesn't matter. Would you like a cup of tea?"

Eliza did a hand pouring tea in your mouth action.

Mr Regis: "No thank you, ducky. If you'll excuse me, I'll go and find him."

Mr Regis made his way out of the back door and Ellington visibly relaxed and went over to Eliza for a stroke.

Lydia and Eliza went back into the kitchen and they watched out of the window as Mr Regis greeted Philip who was already waiting for him, halfway up Eliza's garden.

Lydia: "I think Philip spends more time in your garden than you do."

Eliza: "I know. I only wish he mowed the lawn rather than digging it up."

The door went again.

Eliza: "Who now?"

Lydia: "I'll get it. Maybe it's that farty bunch. I'll get rid."

Lydia strode out of the kitchen to answer the door and came back a few moments later with a young man in a shiny suit, two sizes too large for him.

Lydia: "I found Tom Hanks from the film Big at the door."

Small man-child with outstretched hand: "Hey, I'm Gaz. I work at the Billington Gazette."

Blimey, I feel old.

Eliza: "Are you on work experience?"

Gaz, offended: "Hey no, I's a journalist."

Lydia: "Of course you are. Do you write your articles in crayon?"

Gaz, slightly miffed at the lack of belief in his profession: "I've met, like, proper famous people. I interviewed the lot from TOWIE, you know."

Lydia: "A true career pinnacle. Your mother must be so proud."

Eliza: "Anyway, Gaz. Why are you here?"

Gaz, glad to not be talking to Lydia: "Some woman rang up and said there's summink in your garden which…"

He looked down at the ringed note pad he was carrying.

Gaz, reading slowly: "Hang on, lemme read what it says here… Some bloke… old thing in garden… could put Pilkington on the map… tourists… make lots of money… meet Royalty… go out with her off Love Island… move to London… buy a boat…"

He trailed off, straightened up and coughed.

Gaz: "Ignore that last bit, the woman went on a bit and I drifted off. Anyway, me boss said to come down 'ere and see what's going down."

I do not want any Maseratis chasing me, thank you very much.

Eliza: "I think you must be mistaken, there's nothing going down or up, for that matter, here. There's absolutely nothing in my garden apart from potatoes."

Gaz visibly looked crestfallen and huffed irritably.

Eliza: "Allow me to show you out."

Gaz, tutting: "Gutted. I thought I was onto something then."

Eliza steered Gaz back towards the front door.

Lydia shouted after him.

Lydia: "Never mind, paper boy. Penelope must have got it wrong."

Gaz stopped in his tracks and turned round.

Oh shit.

Gaz: "Penelope? How did you know it was Penelope who called?"

Lydia, awkwardly: "Ohhhhh."

Gaz: "That's my journalistic skills coming into play, that is. I'm top of my game. Boom!"

Gaz punched the air in victory.

Gaz, authoritatively: "If you'd be so kind to show me to the garden, madam. I'll have a quick squizz to ensure it is just spuds as you say and I'll be on my way."

Lydia: "You're not an extra on The Bill, you stupid boy."

Gaz: "You's probably want to keep your mouth shut, lady. You's been implicated."

Lydia shook her head and rolled her eyes.

Suddenly, there was an almighty commotion as Mr Regis hurtled through Eliza's back door, into the kitchen. Ellington yelped upon sight of him and scuttled to his basket.

Eliza, Lydia and Gaz all ran into the kitchen to see what the matter was.

Eliza: "Whatever's happened, Mr Regis?"

Gaz wrote on his pad. 'Man... sixty odd... mahogany face... spade... back door."

Mr Regis, spluttering: "EVACUATE!! EVACUATE!!"

Philip charged through behind Mr Regis and gasped for air with exertion.

Philip: "Quick! My helmet's going to blow!"

Eliza and Lydia looked on nonplussed and stunned. Gaz carried on note writing.

'... Another man... age? Dunno... unfit... helmet... blow.'

Gaz: "How old are you, helmet man?"

Philip, spluttering: "What the buggering bollocks has it got to do with you, you impertinent child? Get out before you don't make it to puberty."

Gaz: "I ain't no kid. I's a journalist."

Mr Regis: "You!! I recognise you! You were the one who staked out in my rhododendron. It's not bloomed since!"

Philip: "Stop exchanging with the boy. We need to get everyone out, Mr Regis. We need the area cordoned off!"

Mr Regis: "Eh? We need their air-con off? Hmmm, not sure that's a priority, Philip. This, after all, is an emergency."

Philip, exasperatedly: "Everyone out! We have no time to dilly dally."

Philip motioned everyone out.

Eliza "I beg your pardon?"

Lydia: "Now stroll on, this is her house. What is going on?"

Gaz: "Yeah, what's 'appening? I'm in the middle of action. I'm like Bruce Willis, innit. This is so cool!"

Mr Regis, slightly hysterically: "It's not Roman... It's World War Two... Philip's only gone and unearthed a bloody bomb! The silly bastard nearly put his spade through it! We need to call the experts to carry out a controlled explosion."

Eliza: "You what?! A World War Two bomb? In my garden? I've been living with it all this time?!"

Gaz patted Eliza's arm.

Gaz: "Now, now, you's ain't that old, lady. Don't be so harsh on yourself, there's no way you look like you been here since the war. A bit of make-up and it'd knock years off."

Eliza, Lydia, Mr Regis and Philip in unison: "SHUT UP!"

Gaz, blanching: "Whoah! You village folk are, like, hostile."

He went back to his pad and scribbled.

'... bomb... in garden... about to blow up... all killed..."

Gaz stopped writing suddenly.

Gaz, screaming: "There's a bomb! Save yourselves!!"

He turned on his heel and ran out of the front door and down the path.

The remainder of them looked at each other for a moment and nodded. Eliza ran around the house trying to find Norris and located him snoozing on her bed. She grabbed him up and hurtled down the stairs. When Norris laid eyes on Mr Regis, he started squirming madly to get away so Eliza put him up her jumper. Lydia put a lead on Ellington and keeping him a safe distance from Mr Regis, all four of them charged after Gaz down the path.

They ran down the end of the road and Eliza called the police and her landlord to explain the situation.

Eliza: "They're going to get bomb disposal experts down later today to sort it out."

She looked down her jumper at Norris to check he was alright to find him snoozing happily around her midriff.

Eliza looked around.

Eliza: "This is a story, why isn't Gaz still here?"

Lydia: "It's probably time for his nap. Is there anything we need to do?"

Eliza: "No, the police said they will evacuate the area and call the relevant people to diffuse the bomb. I've got to go and open the back gate though, so they have access. My landlord will meet them there."

Philip: "I'll run back, my dear Eliza, and unlock it. If I should have the misfortune of being blown to smithereens, I wish you to know that I hold you in very high esteem and sometimes, just the mere thought of you brings relief."

Urgh!! This I didn't need to know.

Lydia pulled a disapproving face.

Lydia: "What touching final words. Run along, go and get blown up."

Philip: "Will do, I'll be back shortly, hopefully intact."

Philip scuttled off back towards their houses.

Eliza: "Thank you, Mr Regis, you quite possibly saved our lives."

Mr Regis: "Eh? Quite possibly paved your thighs?"

Eliza shrugged in defeat.

Lydia: "Let's drop the animals at mine and then we'll go to the shop. There's nothing much we can do here."

Eliza: "Agreed. I'd rather be in ignorance to what's occurring in my vegetable patch today."

Philip returned puffing profusely and bent over double.

Philip: "I'm not used to physical exertion. I don't know about the bomb finishing me off, running down there and back nearly has."

Philip looked up at the three of them.

Philip: "Might I suggest we keep this to ourselves. I could do without the PHARTS knowing I mistook a bomb for a Roman helmet."

Eliza: "I think you might struggle with that."

Eliza pointed to a police car which was pulling into the road.

Lydia: "Blimey, it's like The Sweeney. He's a bit quick off the mark!"

The police car parked sideways, to block the road.

Philip: "Oh my dear god! They're starting to lock off Pilkington!"

Mr Regis: "I agree old boy, you will be the laughing stock of Pilkington."

Philip looked at Mr Regis and shook his head.

Philip: "Beer, Mr Regis?"

Mr Regis: "Oh, I heard that. Don't mind if I do. I could do with a rest from the wife's face."

Philip: "Excuse us ladies, we're off to imbibe for the rest of the day."

They started to walk off in the direction of the pub.

Eliza shouted after them.

Eliza: "Watch out for unforgiving hedgerows!"

A departing Philip raised his thumb by way of recognition to her comment as he and Mr Regis made their way towards The Anchor.

Eliza and Lydia waved at the nearby police officer and made their way over to him.

A young police officer got out of the car, hastily.

Young constable: "Are you alright ladies? You don't want to be standing around here, it's dangerous. Especially with you in your condition, madam. You look shocking, would you like me to assist you to a bench."

He pointed at Eliza.

Huh?

Oh, that's just charming, that is.

Lydia: "She just needs make-up. I've told her before, but she beats to her own drum that one. I like a man in uniform, what's your name?"

I'm definitely going to stock up on Max Factor at the weekend.

Young constable, blushing: "I'm PC Thorpe. I'm based in Billington."

He waved at Eliza's stomach.

PC Thorpe: "I meant, you're with child. When's it due?"

It's Norris.

Eliza: "In about ten minutes, when I get to my friend's house."

PC Thorpe: "Oh my goodness! There's emergencies everywhere in Pilkington today! I was just attending to an incident in the village when I received the call to come here. Shall I contact my colleagues to assist?"

Eliza: "No, you're ok. I'm only having a cat."

She lifted up her jumper slightly and Norris's tail dropped out.

The police officer looked momentarily shocked then straightened up.

PC Thorpe, importantly: "Police work is a very serious business ladies and I have highly confidential matters in hand which I must attend to. If you'll excuse me."

Lydia: "Such authority too. Well done, you."

PC Thorpe flushed furiously and fiddled with his radio transceiver.

Eliza: "Oh yes, the highly confidential bomb in my garden. I just came over to explain that my landlord will be arriving shortly to liaise with you and the disposal lot."

PC Thorpe: "Oh right, ok. Thank you, madam."

Eliza: "My cat baby and I will be on our way. Good day to you."

Lydia, winking: "Catch you around. I might be tempted to commit a crime so you can tag me."

PC Thorpe dropped his transceiver and laughed nervously.

She can't help herself!

Eliza guided Lydia away and left the police officer fumbling around in the gutter.

Track playing on Lydia's car CD player: *Blown Away. Carrie Underwood*

Chapter Twelve

Sub quote for the day: *Oh, I am very weary, though tears no longer flow; my eyes are tired of weeping, my heart is sick of woe. Anne Bronte*

At the other side of the village, Dorothy wandered into the garden with her half-finished Victoria Sponge and went to crumble it on the bird table.

There was a cough from over the fence. It was her neighbour, Bill, who'd popped his head over.

Neighbour Bill, awkwardly: "Er, hello Dorothy. Are you out here on your own, again?"

Dorothy looked up with surprise and nodded, mutely.

Bill, gently: "I just wondered if everything was alright, my love."

Dorothy straightened up quickly and slapped on an over bright grin. She let out a false, tinkly little laugh.

Dorothy: "I'm fine, fine. Thank you for enquiring."

Bill looked at her with concern etched onto his face.

Bill: "Only we heard a bit of a commotion this morning and Glenys was worried."

Dorothy's stance changed and she looked at him cautiously.

He looked down to his side of the fence to be greeted by his wife, carrying an empty plant pot. She threw it down beside Bill and stepped on it.

Glenys, whispering loudly to Bill: "Is he there?"

Bill shook his head at Glenys.

Glenys: "Good. Help me up Bill, the pot is a bit unsteady. Mind me geraniums."

He hauled his wife up onto the pot and to his right popped up Glenys. They were both poking their heads over the fence looking at Dorothy.

Glenys, babbling: "Hello Dorothy. What a lovely, sunny day. Autumn at its best! Erm, now then, we aren't ones to intrude, are we Bill?"

Bill shook his head, slightly unconvinced.

Glenys, continued quickly at a motionless Dorothy.

Glenys: "As you know, we're not the sort of neighbours who would wish to overstep the boundaries. Live and let live, we say. We're not busy bodies, are we Bill?"

Bill shook his head, still rather unconvinced.

Glenys: "We were worried, that's all. I mean, we thought there may have been an accident. So, we made a decision, didn't we, Bill?"

Bill: "Yes Glenys, you did."

Glenys looked pointedly at Bill.

Glenys: "*We* thought calling the police was the best thing to do. Didn't *we*, Bill?"

Bill, quietly: "Mmmm."

Glenys sighed audibly, glad at having got all of that out of her.

Dorothy who hadn't moved throughout the whole exchange just nodded slowly, expressionless.

Glenys peered over the fence at Dorothy.

Glenys: "You seem alright, all in one piece, ha!"

Dorothy continued to nod slowly, with a slightly glazed look on her face.

Glenys, gabbling: "Well, I am sorry if we intruded. You must have a lot to do. We have, haven't we Bill?"

Bill, surprised: "Have we? I was hoping to watch the cricket."

Glenys: "Yes, that iffy tap in the downstairs' cloakroom needs looking at. Come along, Bill. Let's leave Dorothy to it, she's busy."

Glenys hopped off her pot and from behind the fence gave Bill an imploring look to come away.

Bill: "Oh, oh ok."

Bill turned his attention back to Dorothy.

Bill: "We're sorry if she, I mean, we acted out of turn, Dorothy."

Dorothy stared at him, impassively.

Dorothy, in a monotone: "It is fine, Bill. You go and watch your cricket."

Bill: "Right you are, my love. You take care of yourself. See you soon."

Relieved to get away from the strange atmosphere, he scuttled off after his wife.

Dorothy sighed heavily and turned her attention back to crumbling the cake onto the bird table.

As she stepped away, she narrowly missed treading on a dead blackbird at the foot of the table; victim of a neighbour's cat.

She picked the bird up and stared at it, impassively, in the palm of her hand. She smiled a sad smile and gently stroked his dead, wet little head.

Dorothy looked down at the lifeless bird in her palm and whispered.

Dorothy: "You truly are free now, little bird."

Poem: *Angels*

Angels walk amongst us
So gently do they tread
If we stop to say hello
They will whisper in our head.

Always sharing our journey
They wipe away our tears
They dance with our excitement
And quell our burgeoning fears.

We have our lifetime partners
But often forget they are there
Choosing to feel lost and lonely
In a world that doesn't care.

A quiet voice needs peace to be heard
Some reflective time alone
So we can hear what really matters
And to remember we are never on our own.

Eliza Wakeley.

Chapter Thirteen

Sub quote for the day: *What would life be if we had no courage to attempt anything? Vincent van Gogh*

At Lydia's, they were dropping off the animals and making them comfortable in their temporary abode when there was a call on Eliza's mobile. It was her landlord updating her on the bomb situation.

Eliza put down her mobile.

Eliza: "They've secured the area and have called the disposal people. Apparently, they can't do it where it is so they're making the area safe tonight and carrying out a controlled explosion, tomorrow. If all goes to plan, we'll back home by tomorrow evening."

Lydia: "You and Tom can stay here tonight; we can top and tail."

Lydia thought, momentarily.

Lydia: "Can we do a quick scoot to that new supermarket in Billington to pick up some more pillows, though? How about we go there and then have a cuppa before taking over from Mr Hicks. It'll help us get over the shock of this morning's antics?"

Eliza: "Yeah, why not? Let's give him a quick call to make sure he's happy with that."

Eliza called Mr Hicks who agreed that was fine as long as they picked up some ingredients for him.

List in hand, Eliza and Lydia set off to Billington. They picked up the stuff from the floodlight, immaculate store and lobbed their shopping in the back of Lydia's car.

Lydia: "Blimey, my retinas! It's too bright in there. It's the most unbecoming illumination I've ever stepped into. We'll stick to our usual in future. What about over here?"

Lydia pointed towards Ivor Burger Café in the high street. Eliza nodded in agreement and they made their way to it.

It was very quiet and they were greeted by a sullen looking girl with an empty queue.

Lydia: "You go and sit down, I'll get this. Tea and cake?"

Eliza: "Just tea for me, please."

Lydia nodded and Eliza went and found a table by the window.

Lydia nipped across and leant over the counter to speak to the woman.

Lydia: "Hello, please may I have two teas and a scone."

Sullen girl: "I'm not talking to you until you queue from the right end. There's a sign, down there."

Lydia looked around, incredulously.

Lydia: "Don't be ridiculous. I'm here now and there's no one else is in the queue."

Jobsworthy sullen girl: "Right end or no scone."

Lydia: "Are you kidding me?"

Jobsworth crossed her arms, resolute.

Lydia: "Fine, you stupid non serving scone woman. I'll indulge you in your power trip."

Lydia stepped around the correct way and upon walking down the three feet of the serve over, stood exactly where she was, previously.

Lydia, hands on hips: "There. Happy now?"

Jobsworth shrugged.

Jobsworth: "Can I help you, madam?"

Lydia: "You know you can. I want tea and a scone."

Jobsworth: "We've run out of scones."

Lydia: "God, you're irritating. What have you got then, apart from a bad attitude?"

Jobsworth wafted her hand vaguely towards the serve-over.

Jobsworth: "An array of pastries."

Lydia: "Right. I'll have one array then."

Jobsworth: "We don't have any arrays, just pastries."

Lydia, gritting her teeth: "You also lack any humour, whatsoever. Before I shove the whole bleedin' lot in your face, I shall have one pastry."

Jobsworth slung a rather dried out looking petit pain on a plate and thrust it under Lydia's nose.

Jobsworth: "Is that it?"

Lydia and Jobsworth eyed each other up with mutual dislike.

Lydia: "Apart from enquiring why you felt a customer facing role was suited to you, yes, thank you. You're free to insult your next customer now."

Lydia paid and wandered over to Eliza.

Lydia: "I never thought I'd say this, but I wish we were at the Merrythought. I quite miss Dave."

Eliza: "Oh, I meant to tell you; he's back. Health and Safety have allowed him to reopen. He's taken a course and he said he's binned the J-cloth."

Lydia: "Ah, we'll frequent there again in future, I don't want to contribute to old misery pants wages in here, thank you very much. Belinda's better than her."

Lydia took a bite of her pastry and pulled a face.

Lydia, lobbing the pastry back onto the plate: "That's grim. Come on, drink up and we'll go to the shop."

Eliza nodded in agreement and as they finished their drinks Eliza's mobile rang. It was Margaret.

Eliza: "Hello Margaret. How's things?"

Margaret: "Hello, Eliza. All is fine with me thank you, dear. Geoffrey's finally finished tending to the guttering. It's taken him all of the summer, though in his defence his inner ears are a great cause of discomfort up a ladder. I've been looking at the accounts and I am afraid my call is of a rather serious nature."

Isn't it always?

Eliza: "Oh no. What now?"

Margaret: "To be blunt dear, you're not making enough sales. You need to start making more profit or you'll be in a rather large pickle."

Eliza: "It has been very quiet of late, I'm not sure what's happened. How serious is it?"

Margaret: "To be blunt, losses of this extent cannot be maintained for your business to survive."

Very serious, then.

95

Eliza: "Oh no. I can't bear the thought of losing all that money I put in."

Margaret: "You need to turn the tide, my dear, and quickly. Statistically speaking half of all businesses fail within the first five years due to poor business strategies and planning."

Eliza: "Ok, thank you. I'll have a look into what's going on and see if we can do something and fast.

Eliza despondently put down her phone and looked at Lydia, who was looking at her enquiringly.

Eliza: "We're in rapid decline and have almost become a statistic."

Lydia: "Not a good one by the sounds of it."

Eliza: "No Lydia, a decidedly bad one."

Articles read about the demise of new businesses: *One and a bit as too depressing.*

Chapter Fourteen

Sub quote for the day: *Three things cannot be long hidden: the sun, the moon, and the truth. Buddha*

Eliza and Lydia wandered into their shop, to be greeted by a subdued Mr Hicks.

Eliza: "Is everything alright, Mr Hicks?"

Mr Hicks: "I had a visit this morning from Kenneth Cuthbert; Dorothy's husband."

Mr Hicks wiped his brow with concern.

Eliza: "Really? What did he want? He's never been in here before."

Lydia: "No, he doesn't strike me as a fair-trade kind of man."

Mr Hicks: "Indeed, Lydia. There isn't much fair about him."

Mr Hicks sighed.

Mr Hicks: "He came to inform you, but in your absence, me, that there won't be a coffee morning tomorrow."

Lydia visibly sagged.

Lydia: "Oh thank god for that."

Mr Hicks looked at her, sharply.

Mr Hicks: "You created the event, if you don't like the woman, you shouldn't make plans with her. The only loser in this is Dorothy."

Lydia: "Calm down, I didn't say I didn't like her. Anyway, what do you mean?"

Mr Hicks: "I don't wish to gossip about people's private lives. God knows I've been subject of it enough when Patricia left me. Dorothy needs true friends not lip service."

Lydia: "Yeah, yeah, alright. You be her friend; you seem to like her so much."

Mr Hicks sighed, heavily and was about to say something else.

I sense trouble.

I need to change the subject.

Eliza, shrilly: "I have a bomb in my garden. Isn't that nice?"

Mr Hicks looked at Eliza, completely stumped.

Yeah, that stopped you in your tracks, didn't it?

Lydia: "It's going to be blown up tomorrow."

Mr Hicks: "Oh!"

Eliza: "We also bought your ingredients."

Eliza huffed as she plonked two bags of bread making ingredients onto the counter.

Mr Hicks: "Ah, thank you. If it's ok with you, I'll attend to my baking. Excuse me ladies."

Mr Hicks picked up the bags and went into the kitchen.

Lydia: "What do you make of the whole Dorothy thing, Eli?"

Eliza: "I don't honestly know. I've not met Kenneth really; I only know him as the bigwig who employs most of the people in Pilkington."

Lydia: "Yeah, he seems a bit full of his own importance. Big fish, small pond syndrome. He likes the power he wields."

Lydia paused and a dawning look spread across her face.

Lydia: "Ohhh."

Eliza: "What?"

Lydia waved her hands expansively.

Lydia: "I've just had the most marvellous brainwave. God, I'm a genius!"

Lydia held her breath, pulled up her limited frame and addressed the empty shop.

Who are you looking at?

Eliza looked around.

No one – just me and the imaginary audience.

Lydia, importantly: "I am going to become Dorothy Cuthbert's friend. Yes, I. Not a fly by night sort of 'give me the gossip' then leave sort of friend. A proper friend. Her confident."

Her confidante, I think you'll find is the correct term... but do continue.

Lydia looked at Eliza square in the eyes.

Oooh serious face alert. Pay attention and put your features in a 'taking it all in' position.

Lydia: "Are you in pain?"

Eliza: "Er, no. I don't think so, why?"

Lydia: "You were frowning so hard your eyebrows nearly met."

My 'taking it all in' face might need some work. I'll just nod.

Eliza: "No, no I'm fine. Do continue. You were her *confidante*."

You just couldn't help correcting her could you Eli. Tut.

Lydia: "Oh yes... Your face put me off... Just think, Eli, Kenneth has so much influence. If I'm pally with his wife it'll hold us in good stead and he might even take us on. He's all about brand management and promotions. Perhaps your hippiness is rubbing off on me; maybe it's a sign and the fates are throwing us a lucky charm. Kenneth came into the shop today; he's never done that before. Perhaps, Dorothy told him about how good it is and he wants to promote it. He was probably checking out how good we are... Now then, don't worry, you'll always be my best friend Eli, I want you to know that. I am doing this for us. I have a dream for our future. I'm going to take Dorothy on..."

Lydia addressed the empty shop again, grandly.

Lydia: "I, Lydia Harriet Perkins, will change our lives! I will save our shop!"

Crikey, I wasn't prepared for a rousing speech.

Eliza nodded and started to clap.

Eliza: "Bravo! In your capacity as new bezzie, can you try and encourage her to curb her trifle eating in the morning? I'm worried about her faculties after having too much of that. How she didn't scald her innards with that red hot tea the other week, I'll never know."

Lydia was warming to her theme.

Lydia: "I shall. That'll be my first assignment. I'll also take her shopping and teach her how to apply make-up. She's like a project. I'll remove all the bad bits and will reinvent her as a new woman."

Eliza: "Indeed. You do appear to be treating her much like that knackered out old dresser we had in last week. Are you going to flog her for eight hundred quid at the end of it too?"

Lydia: "I'll do better than that. I shall present her back to her influential husband, as a new improved version. He'll be delighted! God knows how she let herself get the way she has but I'll sort her out. I'll start today."

Right you are.

Eliza: "In the meantime, I'll run the shop, shall I?"

Lydia: "Would you mind, darling? I'll pick the kids up from school and we'll meet you back at mine when you've locked up. I'll make us spag bol; Tom's favourite. Laters taters."

With that, Lydia breezed out of the shop again.

Eliza busied herself dusting stock when a realisation came across her.

Ohhhh, flipping flip-flops!

I forgot to pick up Cheddar Chicken.

Tom will go mental.

I might have to sedate him.

Time spent in front of mirror perfecting "taking it all in" face: *Seven minutes twelve seconds.*

Chapter Fifteen

Sub sub sub quote for the day: *Don't walk in front of me, I may not follow. Don't walk behind me, I may not lead. Just walk beside me and be my friend. Anonymous*

Lydia strolled along to Dorothy's house and after psyching herself up for a moment on the driveway, she knocked on her door.

Dorothy sat in the lounge looking out at Lydia flexing her arms outside the bay window and wondered what had brought her here. She hadn't been invited and tomorrow had been cancelled.

Why would someone so busy and with so many friends bother to come round her house, she thought.

The doorbell went again.

Dorothy remained seated and wondered.

She looked up to the ceiling and whispered.

Dorothy: "Is this you granny? Are you helping me? If you are, make her knock one more time. If she does, I'll open it."

Dorothy breathed lightly and waited.

She watched as Lydia stepped back from the front door, hands on hips as she looked around.

Dorothy remained stock still; scared to move.

Lydia started to walk back up the driveway towards the road when suddenly she stopped and looked back over her shoulder towards the house. She paused, momentarily, then suddenly turned round and strode up, purposefully, towards the front door again.

This time she gave it an almighty thump.

Dorothy jumped up from her chair.

Dorothy: "Oh granny! I'm coming!"

Dorothy ran, joyously, towards the front door and flung it open.

Lydia, taken aback: "Shit me!!"

Lydia gathered herself.

Lydia: "I mean... Good afternoon."

Dorothy grabbed Lydia's arm, breathlessly.

Dorothy: "Lydia! Why did you come back and knock again?"

Lydia stared at the vice like grip Dorothy had her in.

Lydia: "Eh? Oh, erm, I dunno. Something just made me think you were there. Call it my sixth sense, ha ha!"

Dorothy: "I do indeed believe it was a sixth sense."

Lydia pulled her arms back to release Dorothy's grasp.

Lydia: "Okaaay."

There was an awkward pause as Lydia stood on the doorstep and Dorothy stood in the doorway.

Lydia: "Erm, I got the message about tomorrow. I'm sorry to hear about that."

Dorothy looked at her feet.

Dorothy, sadly: "I'm sorry too, Lydia. Kenneth saw it on the calendar and wasn't happy. It's a terrible shame; I was making you Victoria Sponge too."

Lydia: "Don't worry about it, Dorothy."

Lydia breathed in deeply and started to gabble.

Lydia: "Right... I was wondering... You can say no if you want, but I thought it might be nice, but say no if you'd rather not... I expect you're tripping over people asking... but if you'd like to go out shopping or something together. Perhaps we could get you a make-over or something fun."

Lydia exhaled quickly.

Lydia, under her breath: "There I did it..."

Dorothy looked up in utter astonishment and her mouth fell slack. Her eyes welled up and Lydia shifted uncomfortably.

Lydia: "Oh now don't be getting all upset, Dorothy, it was only an idea."

Dorothy: "No, no! I would absolutely love to spend time with you."

Dorothy searched Lydia's face, carefully.

Dorothy: "You want to be my friend?"

Lydia shrugged.

Lydia: "Er yes, why not? I can't say I fancy having all our conversations on the doorstep, though."

Dorothy: "Oh my goodness! I'm so sorry, Lydia. My manners! I've not had the best of days up until now, please forgive me."

Lydia, simply: "You're forgiven."

Lydia started to ferret around in her handbag.

Lydia: "Here's my number, give me yours too and let me know when you're free and we'll go out for coffee -

give you a break from all that cake making. How does that sound?"

Dorothy: "It sounds to me that you are heaven sent."

Lydia: "Blimey, ok. So, we'll do that then. Shall we sort it for next week?"

Dorothy scuttled into the hallway and scribbled her mobile number on it and handed it to Lydia.

Dorothy: "Sometimes one needs altruism to ignite a dormant emotion. Thank you, Lydia."

Lydia looked at her blankly for a moment.

Lydia: "Yeah, indeed. There's nothing worse than dormant emotions, they just clog up your system, much like blackheads do pores."

Dorothy: "You're most correct. They do clog up your whole being."

Lydia: "Yeah well, don't worry, we'll sort out your blackheads - emotional and otherwise. See you next week."

Lydia made a hasty exit and once out of sight let out a huge sigh.

She made off down the road and texted Eliza.

Lydia's text: "First assignment complete. Contact made. I fear I may have taken on a bigger challenge than I thought. I'm starting to wonder if she's actually a bit loopy. I don't think she's a shoot-you-in-the-head sort of loopy more a bit off-the-scale-talking-gibberish sort of loopy. Do you think that's mendable with decent make-up and a listening ear? xx"

Poem: *Isolation*

I am high in a tower

Locked from the world
Shall I jump, my body throw
Would anyone care?
If my wings did not work
And I ended up, broken
On the earth below.

Detached from the world
No one can see my tears
A solitary existence
Just me and my fears.
The world carries on around me
Oblivious to my pain
I keep up the pretence
And I wonder if my life can start again
Hope is the glimmer
The spark to my flame
A knowing if I became stronger
There's a new path for me to claim.

Eliza Wakeley

Chapter Sixteen

Forgotten how many subs, quote for the day: *You can learn many things from children. How much patience you have, for instance. Franklin P. Jones*

Later that evening back at Lydia's, Eliza was tucking a wailing Tom into his makeshift bed on the settee.

Tom: "Whaaah mummy, Cheddar Chicken he not here, he be missing me!"

Think fast.

Eliza: "He's fine, he's taken a trip to Blackpool to see the illuminations."

Tom: "What are illuminashons?"

Eliza: "Lights. There's the seaside too, he might be going for a paddle."

Tom: "It dark, Cheddar Chicken, he not like lights and he can't swim. He don't have a cozzie."

Lydia wandered into the room after tucking Freya into bed.

Lydia: "What's up, Tom?"

Tom: "Cheddar Chicken, he gone paddling in a pool without his trunks."

Lydia looked at a loss.

Lydia: "Oh. He's quite the adventurer, isn't he? Would Heatman do for tonight, instead? He's a superhero and warms little boys' beds."

Tom's eyes widened.

Tom: "Oooh, I like superheroes. Yes please!"

Lydia winked at Eliza and left the room.

She came back a couple of minutes later with a hot water bottle which she tucked in with him and snuggled him down.

Ooh, I want Heatman.

Lydia, with authority: "Heatman demands that you go to sleep in two minutes or he turns into Iceman and chills your blood. You'll forever be a statue, locked in an ice body."

She leant over him and let out a maniacal laugh.

Lydia: "Mwhahhhahhhaaah."

Blimey. Stroll on. He's four, Lydia!

Tom's bottom lip shot out and he started to wail.

Tom: "Whaaaaaah!"

Lydia looked helplessly at Eliza.

Lydia: "Bit much?"

Eliza, nodding: "Bit much."

Lydia, shrugging: "Soz."

Eliza patted Tom down into bed.

Eliza: "He doesn't really, Tom, he just makes your big toe a bit chilly. Now go to sleep."

Tom, calming down: "Ok mummy, I sleep with Heatman. Cheddar Chicken he ok, isn't he? He might borrow wellies."

Eliza: "Yes Tom. He'll be fine."

If he doesn't get blown up...

Lydia left the room and gestured 'tea' to Eliza and she gave the thumbs up.

Eliza: "Now, night Tom."

Eliza started to creep out of the room when suddenly he sat bolt upright.

Oh, what now!

Tom: "Mummy? What flag am I?"

Erm...

Placate the child.

Eliza: "You're not a flag, Tom. You're a beacon. A beacon of joy and happiness."

Tom: "No, I'm a flag. Which one?"

Ok, indulge.

Eliza looked at his haphazardly slung together nightwear.

Eliza: "You've got blue and white on, so Scottish?"

Tom, patiently: "No mummy, letter in book bag says about me being a flag."

Bugger that book bag! Bloody harbourer of all manner of unwanted information.

Eliza: "Ohhh, a letter you say? I may have missed that."

What with there being a bomb in the garden and Lydia taking on a human project in the shape of Dorothy.

Eliza: "No worries, when is it?"

Tom burst into tears.

Tom: "Tomorrow!! I have to be a flag!"

Really? Don't these teachers have a national curriculum to follow these days?

Eliza sighed.

Eliza: "It's not mandatory, Tom. It's a suggestion by a primary school teacher to liven up her otherwise tedious day full of unruly children."

Tom: "Ummm, mummy, Miss Gardner, she tell you off."

Eliza: "Do I look bothered? She's about twelve; I'm old enough to be her mother. A point of fact I don't wish to dwell on, quite frankly. Anyway, if she does tell me off, I'll just send her to her room. Now go to sleep."

Tom started wailing again.

Oh, for goodness' sake.

Eliza: "Tom, there's famine, war and decimation of crops thanks to global warming and don't even get me started on the orangutans and palm oil. You not dressing up as a flag doesn't register on the Richter scale, in all honesty."

That's it, launch into a diatribe about world catastrophes.

Why not lob in Ebola and an asteroid impact whilst you're at it? Really settle him down for the night.

And you said Iceman was a bit strong.

Tom, wiping his eyes: "What's the Richter scale?"

Eliza: "Earthquakes – which are also a bit more important than four-year-olds dressed up as flags, now stop talking and go to sleep or Heatman will make your toes cold."

Tom: "Do we have earthquakes here?"

Eliza: "Well, not in Pilkington, I don't think we're on any tectonic plates. They must have some down the road, though, because a couple of years ago in Billington there was a shudder and peoples' wardrobe doors involuntarily opened."

Tom, wide eyed: "Really? We not go there again."

Eliza: "We need to go to Billington, it's where the supermarket is."

Tom: "I don't want any electronic plates, we got enough normal ones in the cupboard. We click and they drop. I saw advert about it. We do that. Man in van, he bring food."

Eliza: "Stop talking. Go to sleep."

Tom: "I have more words to use up."

Eliza: "Put them in tomorrow's word bucket. You'll have extra then."

Tom: "Ok, we can have an extra-long talk about Batman."

Eliza: "Marvellous, I can hardly wait. Night love, Meet you by the fountain in Dreamland."

Tom: "I might be a bit late; I'm going to get Cheddar Chicken from the black pool first. Night night, mummy."

Evening research carried out: *Amassing of statistical data relating to the likelihood of house obliteration due to unearthed World War Two bombs.*

Second piece of research carried out: *Long term emotional effects to children under the age of five as a result of being made aware of the state of the planet.*

Chapter Seventeen

Quote for the day: *You cannot shake hands with a clenched fist. Indira Gandhi*

Dorothy sat gazing intently at the photograph. The corners were bent through years of holding but the essence remained as powerful as the day it was taken. She looked at her grandmother's face smiling down at her and hers beaming up. The expression of love for each other tangible to anyone who ever looked at the image. It was as if it could be delicately touched. An impromptu moment; captured on camera to be cherished forever. No one except for Dorothy did ever look at the photograph; it was her memory and she wouldn't allow the life she had found herself in now tarnish it. As Dorothy stared at their faces, a deep feeling of loss and injustice at the world overwhelmed her and silent tears ran down her cheeks.

Dorothy whispered to the elderly face on the photograph smiling at her younger self.

Dorothy: "Why did you have to leave me? Why couldn't you have stayed? I need you granny. I've always needed you."

She wiped away tears with the sleeve of her jumper and gently touched her grandmother's face. It was so familiar, yet untouchable. She knew every wrinkle and pore on her face. She recalled her grandmother's delicate, bony fingers as they deftly cut the stems on freshly cut flowers and smiled as she replayed in her mind her grandmother's easy, relaxed tinkle of a laugh. How cruel life was to take that away; to deny the world her beauty and existence.

Some days she was able to look at the photograph and smile. She'd speak to it and tell her grandmother her plans for the day. On other occasions, like today, it rendered Dorothy immobile with grief and loss.

Dorothy wept, lost in sorrow and she gulped back her words.

Dorothy: "I wish I could turn back the clock. I wish I could have said all the things I never said... I don't think I ever told you how much I love you. I'm lost without you. I wish I had the chance to touch your face and to hold your hand again. I'd give anything to just touch you and speak to you one more time. To say all the things, I never said before."

Dorothy placed the photograph carefully on her lap and wiped her eyes. A familiar pain had returned and she massaged her stomach. The physical ache born out of emotional anguish.

She looked around her empty lounge and took in her surroundings in a detached manner. She had an immaculate house on the best road in a lovely village. Outwardly, she looked like she had it all. Financially, she could have anything she ever wanted but here she was at eleven o'clock on a sunny autumn morning, slumped in an armchair looking at a battered photograph from years ago; engulfed by a tide of desolation.

She placed the treasured picture on the arm of the chair and went to put the kettle on. She paused at the drinks cabinet and furtively looked around.

Dorothy, sadly: "Why are you looking around you stupid woman? There's just you here. There's always just you here. You and your memories and misery."

She opened the door of the cabinet, took out a bottle of vodka, placed it on top and looked at it.

Dorothy spoke aloud, again.

Dorothy: "You could, you know. You could just make the pain end. Once and for all. No one would miss you."

She looked to the ceiling.

Dorothy: "I could be with you granny. Where I belong."

Dorothy sighed heavily and looked out of her French windows. She threw her hand to her mouth.

Dorothy: "Oh my goodness! I've forgotten to feed the birds!"

She hurried from the lounge, fetched the bread crusts she'd put aside from the kitchen and went and crumbled them onto the bird table.

As she was walking back into the lounge there was a ring on the doorbell.

Dorothy stopped in her tracks, puzzled.

Who would want to turn up at her house unannounced?

Her initial instinct was to ignore it.

The ringing went on.

Dorothy huffed, pulled her cardigan around herself and went to open it.

She was greeted by a very jovial Lydia.

Lydia, chirruping: "Morning!"

Lydia peered at Dorothy.

Lydia: "Blimey, are you alright?"

Dorothy stood in the doorway stunned at the cheery, unexpected visitor.

Dorothy: "Huh?"

Lydia wafted her hand across her face.

Lydia: "Not wishing to be rude or anything but I think you might have quite a lot of snot smeared around your face."

Dorothy: "Oh."

Dorothy half-heartedly wiped her nose with her hand.

Lydia: "No matter, I'm here now. I've got a wet wipe in my handbag – I'll sort you out."

Lydia breezed past Dorothy into the hallway.

Dorothy stepped back in surprise and stammered.

Dorothy: "Am... I, erm... expecting you?"

Lydia looked up from rummaging in her handbag.

Lydia: "Not formally, no, but we are friends now and friends turn up for a cup of tea."

Dorothy: "Do they?"

Lydia: "Yes, they do. I'll put the kettle on. Here, wipe your chops."

Lydia handed Dorothy a wet wipe and she dutifully cleaned her face. Lydia held her hand out and Dorothy silently handed the wet wipe back to Lydia which she then put in the bin.

Lydia made the tea and, remembering the scalding hot glugging from previously, put a bit of cold tap water in Dorothy's. Dorothy, meanwhile, looked on silently – completely unaccustomed to people other than her and Kenneth in her household.

Lydia, poshly: "Shall we adjourn to the drawing room, ma'am?"

Dorothy mutely nodded and trailed behind Lydia.

As Lydia put the drinks down, she clocked the bottle of vodka on top of the open drinks cabinet and looked at Dorothy as she put the drinks down.

Lydia, with concern: "'Allo 'allo. You're not having a tipple, are you?"

Dorothy waved her hands in denial.

Dorothy: "Oh, good heavens no!"

Lydia searched Dorothy's face, unsure whether to believe her.

Dorothy: "I was cleaning."

Lydia was able to believe that so nodded, satisfied with the reply.

Lydia: "You need to stop doing that, Dorothy. Life passes you by whilst you've got a mop in your hand. There are more important things to be doing."

Dorothy: "Is there? What are they?"

Lydia looked aghast.

Lydia: "Well, there's make-up for a start. Clothes… Men, obviously – but I suppose you've got one of them. A very influential one at that, by all accounts."

Dorothy: "Who? Kenneth?"

Lydia: "Yes, of course Kenneth. He's top of his promotional and branding game, isn't he?"

Dorothy: "I suppose so."

Lydia: "He makes unknowns into household names, doesn't he?"

Dorothy: "Yes, I suppose so."

Lydia sighed, slightly peeved.

She looked over to Dorothy's chair at the photograph perched on the arm.

Lydia: "Is that you?"

Dorothy followed Lydia's gaze and protectively snatched up the photo and put it in her cardigan pocket.

Dorothy: "Oh it's nothing. A silly old photo. Tell me about what you've been up to."

Lydia ignored Dorothy's question.

Lydia: "It doesn't look like nothing. Can I see it?"

Dorothy paused and looked cautiously at Lydia. Lydia raised her eyebrows and held her hand out.

Dorothy breathed in and exhaled heavily. She put her hand into her pocket and held the photo out for Lydia to see but didn't let go.

Lydia looked closely at the photograph.

Lydia, smiling broadly: "Oh Dorothy! You look absolutely beautiful, so happy! Who is the lady you're looking up at? She's like you!!"

Dorothy looked at the photo with Lydia.

Dorothy: "She's Dorothy too. She's my grandmother."

Lydia: "You look so similar! Oh Dorothy, I can feel how close you are."

Dorothy, sadly: "Were."

Lydia looked across quickly at Dorothy, sensing her heartache.

Lydia: "Oh Dorothy, when was this photograph taken?"

Dorothy: "About fifteen years ago. We'd been out for the day and this was taken in our favourite restaurant in the evening."

Dorothy smiled, pleased at finally having someone to share her nostalgia with and placed the photograph back on the arm of the chair.

Dorothy drifted off, lost in her own thoughts.

Dorothy: "We'd been to a flower show. Granny was very keen. She taught me and shared her love of the outside with me. We had Dauphinoise potatoes that night. Granny called them "dolphin nose," can you believe?! She was so funny. I know all the Latin for plants thanks to her. She was my life. I looked up to her for everything."

Lydia smiled.

Lydia: "That's lovely!"

Dorothy, simply: "Then she died."

Lydia frowned and looked at the desolate Dorothy, staring at the faded photograph.

Lydia: "Oh Dorothy."

Dorothy, quietly: "I think a part of me left that day too, Lydia."

Lydia touched Dorothy's hand gently and Dorothy looked at it, impassively.

Lydia: "Have you spoken to anyone about this?"

Dorothy kept her gaze on Lydia's hand placed on hers but didn't move it.

Dorothy: "About what?"

Lydia: "About how you feel? How it still makes you feel. What about Kenneth?"

Dorothy looked up and spat with derision.

Dorothy: "No. Kenneth doesn't care to get involved in that side of my life."

Lydia: "What side? That is your life, isn't it? Your grandmother and how her death has affected you."

Dorothy: "Well you would think, wouldn't you?"

Lydia puffed out her cheeks, aware she had touched a deep nerve.

Lydia: "Are you alright, Dorothy? I mean, properly alright. I might be a bit out of my depth here. Perhaps you should go and see someone."

Dorothy gently removed Lydia's hand from hers and composed herself.

Dorothy, politely: "I'm fine, Lydia, but thank you for your concern."

Lydia, sensing the shift in mood, downed her tea and searched around for something else to talk about.

Dorothy watched Lydia's discomfort.

Dorothy, candidly: "Would you like to leave now?"

Lydia: "Er no, not unless you want me to."

Dorothy raised her eyebrows with surprise.

Dorothy: "Oh, I presumed you'd want to go home now. I'm not the best company, am I?"

Lydia sighed.

Lydia: "You're alright, Dorothy. You're troubled that's all. We all have times of upset. We find ourselves in situations which we can't understand or deal with."

Dorothy: "You don't seem to have any troubles, Lydia. You appear to be a wonderful butterfly; free and beautiful."

Lydia snorted.

Lydia: "Yeah, right! I'm full of insecurities. I just don't eat trifle in the morning to deal with it. I get clothes, make-up and, between you and I, quite a few boyfriends instead to make me feel better about myself. In truth, the man I married was a bully and put simply, didn't love me back. Rejection like that stays with you, Doroth..."

Lydia stopped herself, realising she'd gone into a rambling monologue.

Dorothy and Lydia looked at each other in silence. The silence stretched out as they sat there staring at each other.

Just then a key went into the front door.

Dorothy gathered herself quickly, brushed herself down and stood.

Dorothy, nervously: "Oh my god! It's Kenneth! You must go!"

Lydia looked around, bewildered.

Lydia: "Eh? Why?"

Kenneth came through the front door and hearing voices in the lounge, strode in with a face like thunder.

Dorothy, nervously: "Ah! You're home unexpectedly, Kenneth! This is my friend, Lydia."

Upon seeing Lydia, he changed suddenly and planted a disingenuous smile on his face.

Kenneth: "Oh, company. How unexpected. Hello Lydia."

Kenneth held out his hand. Lydia involuntarily shivered and shook his.

Lydia: "Hello. Nice to meet you."

Kenneth: "Nice. Hmmm, I'm sure it is. I'm surprised you're not in your little shop."

Dorothy: "Lydia was just going back to it, weren't you, Lydia?"

Dorothy's eyes widened.

Lydia: "Er yes. I only popped by as I was in the area."

Kenneth: "I wouldn't have thought our road was your area but it always helps to pick up ideas on what decent furniture looks like, doesn't it, my dear?"

Lydia: "Oh. Er..."

Lydia stood and went towards the door and Dorothy ran and opened the door ahead of her.

Dorothy, whispering in Lydia's ear: "I'll text you."

Lydia nodded, mutely, feeling intensely awkward at the situation surrounding her.

Lydia walked out of the house in silence and Dorothy shut the door quickly behind her.

Lydia turned round and felt a wave of unease. She didn't want to leave Dorothy in that situation. She had a very bad feeling and it was a familiar one to her. A feeling that made her instantly protective of Dorothy.

Lydia walked back to her car and sat in the driver's seat not wanting to drive away.

Lydia: "Oh Dorothy, you poor woman. Perhaps we are more alike than I thought."

Poem: *Loss*

As I brush your cheek
And stroke your hair
I imagine that you're still there.
All your laughter and wit
Now withered and gone
Never to be heard
Like the end of bird song.

Free from the shackles
Of a life that was led
You're now free
But I'm the shell you left.

Stop the clock and turn back the hands
Time the cruel taker
The shifter of sands.

Eliza Wakeley

Chapter Eighteen

Sub quote for the day: *It is a man's own mind, not his enemy or foe that lures him to evil ways. Buddha*

Dorothy went back into the lounge where Kenneth was standing, vodka bottle in hand.

Kenneth: "So this is what you and your little tart get up to when I'm at work, is it?"

Dorothy: "She's not a tart! She's a lovely person and no, we haven't touched it. I was cleaning."

Kenneth sneered at Dorothy.

Kenneth: "Of course you were."

He looked over to the chair where the photograph was perched.

Dorothy followed his gaze and instantly went over to snatch it up.

Kenneth beat her to it and grabbed the photograph, roughly.

Dorothy: "Please Kenneth, give me that! I implore you!"

Kenneth looked at the photograph and back at Dorothy with his lip curled.

Kenneth: "You looked better then. Not like the jaded old hag I've ended up with now. Your dead grandmother looks more appealing than you, quite frankly."

Dorothy, sadly: "You're an unkind man, Kenneth. Please give me my photograph. God knows I don't have many memories to cherish. Let me have that one."

Kenneth: "Living in the past is what's made you the mess you are. It's no good for you, woman. You need to let it go."

His eyes bore into hers as he took the photograph between his thumbs and forefingers and held it in front of her face.

Dorothy threw herself at him and grabbed desperately for the photograph but he kept it just out of her reach.

Dorothy, sobbing uncontrollably: "NO!! PLEASE! I beg you, don't Kenneth!"

He continued to stare at her whilst he slowly and deliberately tore the photograph into two.

Kenneth: "It's for your own good. I have a business to run. I haven't got time to keep checking up on you."

Dorothy crumpled into a heap on the carpet and he proceeded to rip the photograph into small pieces and let them fall on her head.

He brushed his hands on his thighs and stepped back from Dorothy, lying on the floor, covered in fragments of her cherished photograph.

Kenneth: "I've got to get back to the office. I only came back to collect my laptop. I have an important meeting; you and your behaviour are making me forget things. It has to stop, do you hear?"

He looked down at the inconsolable Dorothy and tutted.

Kenneth: "I'll be back at six. I expect dinner to be waiting."

Without another word, he fetched his laptop and left the house.

Lydia slunk down in her seat and watched Kenneth close the front door and head towards his car. He stopped as he was about to get in and wandered over to her.

Lydia, between gritted teeth: "Shit."

Kenneth and Lydia eyed each other up and he motioned to her to wind down her window.

He smiled at her, disarmingly.

Kenneth: "Ah my dear, you're still here. Do you have car trouble?"

Lydia: "Er no. I was just er, making a call. It's finished now so I'll be off."

She went to turn the ignition.

Kenneth: "Oh well, it's quite fortuitous, perhaps, that you did. Your little shop is quite endearing, in its own way. I was wondering if you were seeking any assistance with regard to its marketplace awareness. I see you're a friend of my wife and I value her character judgement. Perhaps you'd like to put together your marketing budget and run it by my secretary, see if we can help you at all. Hmmm? What do you think?"

Lydia raised her eyes in surprise at the turn of conversation.

Lydia: "Oh, oh, ok. I'll have a word with Eli... I mean my business partner and we'll get back to you."

Kenneth: "Indeed, dear girl, you do that. Run along now and speak to her."

He waited as she turned the key and made off down the road.

Kenneth turned on his heel and got into his car, shaking his head, derisively.

Kenneth: "Stupid girl."

Number of wet wipes used by Lydia to clean her dashboard whilst sitting outside the Cuthbert's house: *Four.*

Chapter Nineteen

Sub quote for the day (It's turning into an attention seeker's social media feed there's that many today): *One does not make friends. One recognises them. Garth Henrichs*

Lydia got back to the shop and flung her bag on the counter.

Eliza: "How'd it go?"

Lydia: "Unsettling. I'm exhausted."

Eliza: "I'll put the kettle on."

Lydia followed behind her to the back of the shop where Mr Hicks was making a batch of gingerbread men.

Eliza: "So in what way unsettling?"

Lydia: "She's very troubled."

Eliza: "This does not come as any surprise, Lydia. The careful stacking of cushions is testament to that fact. No one does that if they're fully capacitated. I even went home and gathered all my cushions from around the house and arranged them on the lounge settee to see if I could make mine look like hers... I couldn't. They just looked like I was in the process of moving house."

Those cushions have stayed with me.

Lydia looked at her, blankly.

Lydia, muttering: "I'm surrounded by fruit cakes."

She shook her head in dismay.

Lydia: "It's her granny what's done it."

Eliza: "Her granny does the cushions for her? Older people must have the knack."

Lydia huffed, irritably.

Lydia: "No, you silly bint. I mean, the granny that looks like her is what troubles her."

Eliza: "Mmm, it must be unnerving having an older replica. A sort of vision into your future."

Lydia: "She's dead."

Eliza: "Flip that really is the future."

Mr Hicks looked up from his gingerbread man cutting.

Mr Hicks: "How did you get on to the discussion of her grandmother, Lydia?"

Lydia was pleased to have a change of person to talk to and turned her attention to Mr Hicks.

Lydia: "She had a photo of them. Oh, Mr Hicks, it was lovely. She looked truly content in it. Not the shambles she is now... No disrespect or anything."

Mr Hicks: "Life can leave its scars, Lydia. Emotional can become physical as they etch their path."

Lydia: "Yeah well, that's a big old path, Mr Hicks. It's more of a bypass."

Mr Hicks sighed, sadly.

Mr Hicks: "This photo, when was it?"

Lydia: "She said it was fifteen years ago. They'd had dolphin nose potatoes."

Mr Hicks laughed, nodded and got back on with his gingerbread cutting.

Eliza: "So do you think you'll be successful in your mission?"

Lydia: "It was all a bit easy, actually. Kenneth came home. I'm not too sure about him, he has a very discomforting manner."

Mr Hicks stopped cutting and looked up.

Lydia continued.

Lydia: "I left pretty sharpish after he turned up but he came up to me after, as I'd stayed in the car, and asked if we wanted help promoting the shop. Tadarr! Mission complete. How good am I?"

Mr Hicks put down his cutter and put his hands on his hips.

Oh no, I sense trouble in the kitchens...

Mr Hicks: "Is that the reason why you befriended Dorothy; for your own commercial ends, Lydia?"

Be careful how you answer this one, Lydia. He could blow.

Lydia looked at Mr Hicks, then Eliza and clocking Eliza's wary face, worded her next sentence carefully.

Lydia: "I would not put it quite so crudely, Mr Hicks. It would be an added bonus to have some cheap advertising for the shop through new contacts we've made, but I genuinely feel something for Dorothy. I didn't think I would as I thought she was just crackers but I want to help her, if I can."

Mr Hicks considered her reply.

Mr Hicks: "If you wish to be her friend, Lydia, bear in mind she keeps her own counsel and you need to respect that."

Lydia: "She keeps the council? Like she's the head of it?! No wonder she's not got any potholes outside her house and I did note there are copious amounts of hanging baskets and mowed verges down her road."

Mr Hicks shook his head and picked up his cutter again.

Eliza: "I might have found out why we're struggling. I was reading an article when you were out. Apparently, the bottom's fallen out of shabby chic chairs. It's all about contemporary now and properly painted."

Lydia: "Really? Oh, we're buggered, then. There's no way I can paint a dresser properly. We really do need the mighty Kenneth's help."

Mr Hicks: "Without wishing to butt in on your business strategies. May I be so bold as to suggest you wait until hell freezes over before enlisting the help of that man?"

Oh, he really doesn't like Kenneth.

Lydia was about to open her mouth but Eliza cut across.

Eliza: "We take your opinions on board, Mr Hicks. Don't we, Lydia? We need to think of a way of raising the shop profile and making it more profitable."

Mr Hicks: "Would it help you if I assisted in some marketing? I'd rather you didn't ask for Kenneth's involvement. My shop was quite popular in its day... before Patricia..."

His voice trailed off.

I sense emotion.

Intervene.

Eliza: "That would be lovely, Mr Hicks. Let's all put our heads together and draw up some ideas."

Lists made containing marketing ideas: *Three.*

Ideas on list that hold any viable marketing opportunities: *None.*

Airplanes made out of list paper: *Six.*

Stock items nearly broken by plane test flights: *Four.*

Chapter Twenty

Late afternoon quote for the day: *Don't let schooling interfere with your education. Mark Twain*

Eliza was waiting in the playground at pick up when Tom came running out with a broad grin.

Tom: "Mummy, mummy! I win star!"

He was jumping up and down with excitement.

Eliza: "Oh, lovely. What did you do?"

Tom: "I won the best flag t shirt."

Blimey, they must have had slim pickings.

She turned her attention to Tom and gave him a hug.

Eliza: "That's wonderful, if a bit unexpected. You see, I didn't let you down, did I?"

Tom: "No mummy, Miss Gardner say it the best Canada flag she ever seen."

Eh?

Eliza: "Welsh, love."

Tom, shaking his head: "No. Canada."

Eliza: "Since when did Canada have a dragon in the middle?"

Tom: "A dragon in Canada? I thought they lived in caves. She say it a leaf."

Tom pulled up his coat to reveal an oversized white t shirt which reached down to his knees. On the front was a rather indecipherable red felt tipped doodle.

Lydia bent down and peered at it closely.

Lydia: "Well, if it was the Welsh flag, you should have put green on it, like grass. If it was the Canadian flag, you missed the red side bits. I agree with Miss Sippy-Cup though, it looks more like a maple leaf than a dragon."

Eliza: "Oh, I do beg your pardon, I wasn't aware your specialised subject was flags of the world. It was hastily done and I used my best white T shirt as it was the only thing to hand. I did have other things on my mind."

Tom: "What other things?"

Lydia: "You had a bomb in your garden but the men blew it up."

Really? Did you have to be quite so honest?!

Tom's eyes widened and his mouth dropped open.

Tom: "A BOMB?! As in kerpow kerpow films?"

Eliza, sighing: "Something like that."

Tom: "Coooool! Can I take it to show and tell?"

Eliza: "No, it's gone now and hopefully with it that blummin' forensic tent."

Tom: "What's a foreign sick tent?"

Freya came across the playground and lobbed her bags at Lydia. Catching the end of the conversation she butted in, knowledgeably.

Freya: "It's where you go on holiday when you've got a funny tummy. You mustn't eat the ice cubes."

Tom: "Oh."

I think it's time to leave now.

I'm quite concerned about his upbringing.

I might need to get a book from the library and see how normal people raise children.

Eliza: "Right then, I fancy it's time to go home for a nice cup of tea, don't you?"

Tom: "I need to see Cheddar Chicken. Make sure men not blow him up."

Lydia: "Ah he'll be ok, Tom. Anyway, there's always Heatman as a stand in."

Lydia bent down and laughed sinisterly.

Lydia: "Mwahaaahaaah."

Tom stepped back slightly with dismay.

Tom: "You a bit scary with that, Auntie Wydia. I'd like it if you didn't do that again, me old china."

Lydia, shrugging: "Soz."

Freya: "She is scary, Tom. You don't have to live with her."

Lydia scrunched her nose up at Freya and she returned the gesture.

Tom: "Oh mummy, I nearly forgot. I made you present as fank you for t shirt."

Awww, my thoughtful baby.

I don't need a book from the library.

He's turning out fully adjusted and fine.

Tom scrabbled about in his book bag and triumphantly pulled out a lolly stick with some paper stuck to it.

Tom: "Tadarr!!"

Oh. What is that?

Think fast...

Eliza: "Erm. Is it a flag?"

Tom: "Yes, your very own one. But it's not any old flag. It's a flag in the shape of a pair of orange pants. Your very own pants flag, mummy."

As you were... back to the library.

Eliza: "Thank you. Words fail me son."

Tom: "I thought they might..."

Books picked up at library relating to child psychology: *Three.*

Child psychology books promptly put back in favour of 'How to make Cakes in Under Ten Minutes' book: *Three.*

Chapter Twenty-one

Quote for the day: *The struggle of my life created empathy - I could relate to pain, being abandoned, having people not love me. Oprah Winfrey*

It was now late November and Lydia had been spending more time with Dorothy during the days and Eliza had been staffing the shop as well as trying to renovate furniture in the evenings. Margaret had made it plain that the financial situation with the shop was looking very dire indeed but Eliza and Lydia seemed at a loss how things had turned so sour, so quickly. They were also at a loss how to make it better. Lydia had pinned her hopes on Kenneth coming up trumps with marketing if she made his wife into a walking goddess and Eliza was pinning her hopes on the ether. Something she called out to frequently in the hope the financial fairy was listening.

One Monday morning in the shop, Eliza was busy dusting and reorganising ornaments whilst Lydia and Mr Hicks were pondering.

Lydia: "What if we do a BOGOF thing?"

Mr Hicks: "I don't think insulting the customers is the way forward, Lydia. You need to connect with them and make them feel at ease in the surroundings. Encouragement leads to sales. Years of shifting poppy seed bloomers taught me that."

Lydia: "No, you bakering fool – you buy one, you get one free."

Mr Hicks: "Oh, I see. They buy one dresser get another one free? I don't fancy that'll catch on. There's a lot of cottages in this village, I don't think they'd fit two in."

Lydia harrumphed.

Lydia: "That was my suggestion. Yours now, Mr I-am-a-customer's-best-friend Hicks."

Mr Hicks: "Well, I have been having a little deliberate. What about an open day and I could provide a selection of baked products by way of enticement?"

Lydia: "You mean leave cheese straw arrows along the high street pavement to lead people into the shop? It's about as good as my free dresser idea."

Eliza looked up from her dusting.

Eliza: "Ooh, Mr Hicks, that's a brilliant idea. How about we have a craft making day for kids, they can be kept amused whilst their parents have a look around and, hopefully, buy stuff. We could do special offers."

Eliza put down her cloth and straightened up.

Ooh, ooh ideas are flowing freely.

My chakras must be free of debris.

Eliza, excitedly: "... And we could display the children's crafts. We could hold a competition for the best and give the winner a prize. We could call it the "Illusions of Grandeur Crafts Kids Competition." We should advertise it in the paper."

Mr Hicks: "Oh Eliza, inspired! You clever lady!"

Lydia: "Tut, it's on a par with my BOGOF, I think, but fair enough."

Mr Hicks: "Would you like me to still provide baked products?"

Eliza: "Of course, Mr Hicks!"

Mr Hicks's face lit up with an idea.

Mr Hicks: "Ohhh! I'd be delighted, if you'd allow me ladies, to bake the prize. How about I make an Illusions of Grandeur Crafts winner's cake. It'll keep costs low as I'd be happy to provide the ingredients."

Eliza: "Wonderful!"

Mr Hicks: "It's been a long time since I did a bespoke cake. I used to be quite known for them, you know. People came from as far as the other side of Billington to buy their birthday cakes from me. I feel quite invigorated at the prospect."

Eliza: "Awww, thank you Mr Hicks. We're very grateful, aren't we Lydia?"

Lydia: "Yeah, don't make it better than my Black Forest Gateau, though."

She winked at Eliza.

Eliza: "We need to choose a good day – Christmas is around the corner so we could promote gift ideas."

Mr Hicks: "Two ticks, ladies. I'll run and get my calendar."

Mr Hicks ran off upstairs.

Eliza: "Isn't it nice to see him excited? I never knew he could be so animated."

Lydia: "Yes, it's a shame he became so downtrodden. People do that. They squash the soul with their hob nail boots."

Eliza raised her eyebrows at Lydia.

Okaaay.

Mr Hicks came back, slightly out of breath.

Mr Hicks: "Now then, we ought to make it a Saturday."

Eliza: "Start of the Christmas holidays?"

Lydia and Mr Hicks nodded with approval.

Eliza: "How about we let the kids come in throughout the first week to do their craft things. We can put them on display at the end of each day and then on the Saturday have the competition. Prolong the joy and have the offers going all week."

Mr Hicks nodded.

Mr Hicks: "Good idea. Maximum exposure. This is very good, ladies."

Eliza: "So from the first Saturday to the second weekend, we'll all be on hand to promote the shop and hold the craft things from nine to five? Agreed?"

Lydia looked unsure.

Eliza cocked her head at her.

Eliza: "Team effort, Lydia. Agreed?"

Lydia sighed.

Lydia: "Yes, yes agreed. Only I do have other things on but I suppose I could reschedule them."

Eliza was about to speak but Mr Hicks stepped in quickly.

Mr Hicks: "Brilliant. Everyone knows for a business to survive you need dedication and drive."

Lydia: "Yeah and no vermin in the loaves."

Mr Hicks visibly blanched and Eliza gasped.

Eliza: "Lydia! Don't be so unkind! Mr Hicks is going out of his way to help us. Say sorry!"

Lydia, flatly: "Sorry."

Mr Hicks nodded briefly.

Mr Hicks to Eliza: "I've got some things to do upstairs for a while as you're both here to watch the shop. Do excuse me."

Eliza: "Yes of course, see you later and thank you."

Mr Hicks excused himself quickly and left Eliza staring at Lydia.

Lydia: "What?"

Eliza: "What's the matter with you?"

Lydia sighed heavily and flumped down in a Lloyd Loom chair.

Lydia: "I'm concerned about something. I've not been sleeping properly."

Eliza: "There's no need to be horrible, though, is there? Mr Hicks goes out of his way to help us."

Lydia: "I know. I've lost my filter. I'm distracted and it just comes out. I think these things all the time but generally I can stop them before they reach my voice box. I hope it's not permanent."

Eliza: "Me an' all or we'll lose all friends and customers. What are you concerned about?"

Lydia: "Dorothy."

Eh?

Eliza furrowed her brow.

Eliza: "Your new best friend, Dorothy?"

Lydia: "Yeah. I was doing the washing up the other night and I started thinking back to when I was living with Roy."

Eliza: "Oh dear. What brought that on?"

Lydia: "I hadn't thought about that for ages and I wondered why it had suddenly come back into my mind and I realised. Kenneth fills me with the same feeling I had when Roy used to come home drunk. A feeling of dread."

Eliza: "Oh."

Lydia: "I also replayed that time the other month when Kenneth turned up and offered his help with our shop and, do you know, I think that he duped me. I think he wanted me to leave and not go back in to see Dorothy and then I remembered that time at Freya's birthday when Roy did a similar thing to you."

Eliza cocked her head to the ceiling trying to recall the situation.

Eliza: "Oh, the time he said the birthday party was cancelled because you had a headache?"

Lydia: "I had a headache, alright. Thanks to him. But yes, then. He didn't want you near me, did he? He didn't want you to see what he'd done. I think Kenneth wanted me away too. Then I thought 'Oh my god. She's me!'"

Eliza digested this revelation and her eyes widened.

Lydia: "Well, I can apply make-up better and I don't wear cardigans all the time."

Lydia leant forward.

Lydia: "What if he hits her and she has to wear them?"

Eliza exhaled heavily.

Eliza: "Now be careful Lydia, you can't jump to conclusions just because her husband's a bit creepy and she wears pullovers. You can't let your imagination run away with you."

Lydia: "Shall I go to the police?"

Eliza: "You what?! Hang on, you have no proof other than a feeling of discomfort. She's not said anything has she? Surely, she'd tell someone."

Lydia: "I didn't."

Eliza: "Oh."

Lydia: "I'm worried about her, Eli. What if she's going through what I did?"

Eliza: "Well, you need to talk to her. Befriend her properly if you want to help her but please don't be rash."

Lydia shrugged.

Lydia: "I don't know how she can still be with such a horrible man."

Eliza: "I wondered the same when you were with Roy. She must love him."

Lydia: "How can she love him?"

Eliza: "You tell me."

Lydia looked up at Eliza and shook her head sadly.

Lydia: "When you look at it from the outside, it makes for a whole different picture. Saying it out loud, it seems preposterous that anyone could love someone who systematically destroys every ounce of happiness and steals their joy of life. I felt worthless. If I hadn't had you to lean on, I think I'd still be there now. I'd had my courage beaten out of me."

Eliza: "No person has the right to make any other feel worthless, Lydia. We are equal beings who should live in harmony and stand shoulder to shoulder with all other living creatures."

I should have recorded that. Mum would combust with joy.

Lydia: "Er yes, quite. Some more equal than others though, eh? I don't want to stand next to a blob fish. They're grim looking things."

I need to broach a little something that has popped into my mind.

Eliza: "Do you still call Roy and hang up?"

Lydia shifted awkwardly.

Lydia: "Well, not since I had the washing up revelation. Something happened to my mind-set by the time I got to the saucepans."

Well, that's got to be a good thing. Every cloud and all that.

Eliza: "So, what are you going to do?"

Lydia: "I'll do as you suggest. Be there for her. I know from experience you need help and support. She keeps the council according to Mr Hicks, so she must have some contacts."

Pardon?

Eliza: "Oh ok. Just be careful, please. She strikes me as somewhat delicate."

Mr Hicks had come downstairs and was standing, unseen, in the kitchens by the door to the shop.

When he'd heard that the conversation had turned to Dorothy he'd stopped to covertly listen. He sighed sadly and tapped the ends of his fingers together in contemplation. After a few moments he nodded in silent resolution and went back upstairs to fetch his coat.

Mr Hicks breezed into the shop, putting his coat on as Lydia was getting up from the Lloyd Loom chair.

Lydia: "I'm very sorry Mr Hicks, I didn't mean to offend you. I'm not quite myself at the moment."

Mr Hicks, kindly: "You're forgiven, Lydia."

He directed his gaze to Eliza.

Mr Hicks: "I'm going to be out for the rest of the day, if that's agreeable. I have a few errands to run."

Eliza: "Oh, yes fine. Thank you, Mr Hicks. I'll get on and put an advert in the paper for the craft thing. We should take a photo of us all to go with it."

Mr Hicks: "I'm on the hoof today, I'm afraid, so it will have to wait."

Lydia: "Yeah and I've got bags the size of suitcases thanks to my lack of sleep. Can we use an old one?"

Mr Hicks, on the way out of the door: "How about that one your mother took Eliza, when you opened the shop? You both looked wonderful in that. See you later."

Mr Hicks waved and left the shop.

Lydia: "He's in a hurry all of a sudden."

Eliza: "That's probably because you offended him."

Lydia pulled a face.

Lydia: "I need to address all this so I can get some sleep and take control of my mouth faculties again."

Eliza: "Good plan. What are you going to do?"

Lydia: "I haven't a clue but I might need to go shopping for the mists to clear."

Here we go...

Eliza: "I'm watching the shop for the rest of the day then, yes?"

Lydia: "Oh, would you? Darling, you are a marvel. Thank you."

Eliza tutted.

Lydia: "You're doing it for Dorothy, not me."

Eliza: "Oh shut your face and go shopping."

Lydia: "I'm gone. Ciao, my little bambino of loveliness."

Yeah, yeah. Clear off. Leave me to run our dwindling business.

Time spent Googling the phrase "Dorothy Cuthbert runs the Pilkington Parish Council": *Thirty seconds.*

Results: *None.*

Chapter Twenty-two

Quote for the day: *Natural beauty takes at least two hours in front of a mirror. Pamela Anderson*

Lydia parked up in Billington's multi storey car park and wandered towards Duvalle's, the department store.

Duvalle's was a family run store with the feel of a bygone age. The second floor contained overflowing wooden cupboards full of dusty sewing patterns showing women in fifties style dresses wearing jaunty hats. Next to these were cabinets of decade old ribbon wheels, wool, and numerous floral fabrics.

Lydia sniffed with disapproval as she swept past a couple of elderly women who were debating floral curtain fabric on her way to the beauty department.

She looked around and presented herself to a young woman who looked as if her face was trying out all available make-up products in one go. She was studiously texting on her mobile.

Lydia coughed to get her attention.

The young woman looked up with disinterest.

Disinterested texting girl: "Yeah? Can I help you?"

Lydia: "You can indeed, wearer of the alarmingly long eyelashes."

The disinterested texting girl sighed and put down her phone.

Slightly irritated by customer interrupting her texting, girl: "What can I do for you?"

Lydia waved her hands around her face.

Lydia: "What are you going to do about this?"

Just-received-a-text-but-can't-reply-to-it-because-of-a-customer, girl: "Huh?"

Lydia: "My face. It needs help. I've not slept for days and everything's sagging towards me tits. I have bags and I swear..."

Lydia looked furtively around then whispered to the girl.

Lydia: "I'm getting jowls."

The girl gasped in horror and put her hand to her mouth.

Lydia: "I know. You have to stop it. You and your enormous eye lashes. Are you up for the challenge?"

The girl nodded and cracked her knuckles.

Lydia: "What's your name?"

Girl, cricking her neck and stretching in preparation for battle: "Sasha."

Lydia: "Qualifications?"

Sasha: "Top false eyelash putter-onner 2018 as awarded by Sheila - owner of Bold and Beautiful of Billington and winner of the fastest fake tanner at this year's Biscuit Brown Convention."

Lydia nodded with approval.

Sasha was pinging on some latex gloves.

Just then there was a pining from an oversize bag behind the counter.

Sasha: "Hang on. That'll be Prince Harry."

Lydia looked around bemused.

Sasha bent down and opened the zip on the bag and a little pointed face with massive ears popped out.

Lydia: "Ohhh, it's a bat thing."

Sasha: "It's a Chorkie. A cross between a Yorkshire terrier and a Chihuahua. Innit cute?"

Lydia: "Are you allowed to bring your dog in here?"

Sasha: "Yeah, my dad owns this place. I can do what I want."

She put Prince Harry in his bag on the counter facing Lydia.

Sasha motioned for Lydia to perch on a stool near the make-up counter.

Sasha: "He likes to see the before and after. I'm like a master at work."

Lydia looked a bit unsure at having a canine audience at such close proximity but let it go and allowed Sasha to pin her hair back and make a start on her make over.

Lydia: "So you're called Sasha Duvalle? How very exotic."

Exotic Sasha Duvalle: "Yeah, I thought so. My real name is Donna but Sasha's me stage name."

Lydia: "Stage?"

Donna, I mean, Sasha: "Yeah."

She looked around and whispered to Lydia.

Sasha: "I do talking to men. You know..."

She raised her eyebrows.

Lydia thought for a moment and then the penny dropped.

Lydia: "Oh, that sort of talking? Oh, I see."

Sasha carried on with her work and Lydia pondered for a moment.

Lydia: "Does it pay well?"

Sasha: "What this? Nah, that's why I talk to men. It bought me Prince Harry, that did, and my tanning course. I've got regulars. Men are a funny old bunch. I've got one who wants me to talk about hammer drills. I know eff all about DIY but my dad's got a Reader's Digest book on home decorating and I just read lumps of that out to him. He phones every week after The One Show."

Sasha stood back to admire her handiwork. She nodded with approval and went back in for a second round.

Lydia looked a bit disappointed.

Lydia: "Don't they ever want to talk about their willies?"

Sasha: "Oh yeah, and some are right into their testicles. It's a mixed ball bag. Ha ha, I'm quite funny too. I've got it all going on, haven't I?"

Lydia, nodding: "Well, you do certainly appear to have."

They sat in silence for a few minutes whilst Sasha went about her work.

Eventually, she stood back and looked at Prince Harry who yapped with approval.

Sasha: "Prince Harry says you're finished. 'Ere have a look."

Sasha fetched a magnifying mirror and thrust it in front of Lydia.

Lydia: "Yikes!"

Sasha: "Oh hang on, I'll reduce you. You can't see the wrinkles so much then."

Sasha swivelled the mirror and returned it to Lydia's now fully made-up face.

Lydia gasped.

Lydia: "Oooh, I say. That's quite... erm... vibrant."

Sasha: "Do you mean your eye shadow? It's my trademark. Peacock feather eyes."

Lydia stared transfixed at her reflection.

Lydia: "It's quite bold for day wear, if I may say."

Sasha: "Bold's the new black. No one gets anywhere by looking bland."

Lydia: "No, well. Quite."

Sasha: "You're quite pretty and you've not got a bad figure for your age. Some blokes like an older woman; you could talk to them on a laptop. My friend, Sapphire, bought a Ford Focus doing it. They send her presents to a PO Box. She's got that many love balls she could build a Newton's Cradle with them."

Lydia: "I'm not that old, actually. I've just had a stressful few weeks. Anyway, Sapphire? Really?"

Sasha: "No, not really. She's called Laura."

Lydia: "I like the name Laura."

Sasha: "Yeah, I know but it doesn't say cock, does it?"

Lydia: "No, I suppose not. I'm called Lydia."

Sasha: "Oh that says cock. What's your real name?"

Lydia, looking quite put out: "Lydia."

Sasha looked at Prince Harry who yapped.

Sasha: "You should do it. You're a born natural. Even Prince Harry agrees."

Lydia: "Thank you, I'll bear that in mind."

Sasha delved into her voluminous handbag behind Prince Harry's bottom and pulled out a card.

Sasha: "This is me. Call me if you want any contacts."

Lydia: "Thank you."

Lydia put the card in her pocket and hopped off the stool.

Sasha: "Do you want any of the products I've used today?"

Lydia: "How much is the mascara?"

Sasha: "Nineteen ninety-nine."

Lydia: "Blimey! What's so special about it?"

Sasha: "Dunno."

Sasha read the marketing blurb on the box.

Sasha: "It don't clump. Do you want it?"

Lydia: "I don't think so, thanks."

Sasha shrugged, put down the mascara in exchange for her phone and started reading her texts.

Lydia, sensing the consultation was now over: "Which way to the ladies' toilets?"

Sasha didn't look up and pointed vaguely to the right.

Lydia: "Thank you. Good day to you and you, Prince Harry."

Prince Harry yapped his good tidings from the bag.

Lydia scurried off, threw herself in the toilets and promptly washed her face. When she'd dried it using toilet paper, she took the pink diamante encrusted card out of her coat pocket and looked at it.

Lydia, thinking to herself: "Hmmm, I know quite a lot about hammer drills and ball bags…"

Track playing on Duvalle's in-house radio: *Man! I Feel Like A Woman. Shania Twain*

Chapter Twenty-three

Quote for the day: *To the world you may be just one person, but to one person you may be the world. Brandi Snyder*

Eliza scrolled back through the photos on her camera and found the one Mr Hicks had referred to which had been taken on opening day. She downloaded it and attached it to the email she had penned to the local paper. She'd spoken to a woman in the marketing department at the Billington Gazette and had secured a half page advert for next week's issue.

Right, that's that done.

Business advertising...Tick.

Now what?

Hmmmm.

She looked around furtively,

I have a bit of spare time...

How about I do another casual little search for Jude.

There can't be many Judes in Billington.

She typed 'Jude Billington' in the search engine and hit return.

All manner of peculiar results including Jude Law came up but none of her Jude.

She typed in 'good looking, crinkly laughter lines Jude.'

Merr, old men faces.

A lot of images of elderly men were the result.

She typed in 'Jude big willy.'

Oh Bejeeezus!

Close your eyes, Eli!

A lot of very disturbing images came up and she hit the back button quickly.

I hope to god my computer doesn't get stolen.

They'll think I'm looking for porn at two in the afternoon.

People will say, 'instead of watching Homes under the Hammer she was on the internet looking at willies. It's no wonder her business was struggling.'

I need to stop.

I'm turning into a weird stalker.

Eliza huffed, despondently.

Futile search for the man of my dreams carried out… Tick.

Perhaps I should go back on multitudeofmates.com and just try and find another one.

I tried with Henry and he was lovely but he wasn't my lovely.

I'm ruined.

I'll be a mental old hag with cats and no sex.

I'll go and have a look to see if I've had any messages.

She typed in www.multitudeofmates.com and logged into her account.

She'd received a few and after deleting all bar one due to their dodgy profile picture backdrops she opened up BRADPITT3.

I wonder what happened to Brad Pitt number two.

Eliza did a search for BRADPITT2 and a geriatric man with a full beard and dyed black hair came up. He was holding a trombone and his profile strap line was "Potholing's the game, finding uncharted tunnels my aim."

Ah, he went barmy.

She turned her attention back to Brad Pitt the Third. His message went like this:

BRADPITT3: Howdy, U have eyes that cud calm a bellicose rhino.

I'm sorry...

Re-read it, I must have made that up.

Trombone Brad has knocked me off kilter with his tunnel hunting.

Eliza re-read the message.

How odd is that?

He can't type 'you' or 'could' fully, yet uses the word bellicose in an opening gambit.

I bet Jude would spell words properly.

And he wouldn't say 'Howdy'.

... Or use the word bellicose in a greeting.

She typed a reply to BRADPITT3.

SHAKESPEARESISTER1: Thank you for passing on your thoughts. It's handy to know that if I ever go on safari my eyeballs would stun the wildlife into a stupor. I'm very busy these days as I've just been hired as a human cannonball and my estimated destination this evening is Pontefract. Good luck finding someone, though you might want to start typing your words in full if you message anyone over the age of eighteen. Goodbye.

Reply to message from random no hoper... Tick.

Eliza sat at her computer and opened her blog "The Adventures of an Incompetent Mother."

I'm not an incompetent mother anymore as I've kept Tom alive and functioning long enough to go to school.

She put a line through it and renamed it "The Adventures of a Love-struck Damsel." She stared at it a bit longer then put a line through it and typed "The Adventures of a Struggling Shop Owner." She then put a line through that and renamed it "The Adventures of a Failure."

A few minutes later Eliza switched off her computer and went in search of Ellington and Norris for a cuddle. She found them sleeping two storey in Ellington's bed so she snuggled up beside them and rested her head on Norris's snoozing tummy. He squirmed slightly and started purring and kneading his paws into Ellington's ribcage.

I'll definitely end up with a menagerie with a tea cosy on my head.

I won't even be surprised if I end up holding a trombone in my multitudeofmates profile picture.

Time spent researching tea cosy prices: *Ten minutes.*

Number of times uttered "Oh, that's a nice one. That'd suit me.": *Seven.*

Chapter Twenty-four

Quote for the day: *A lie can travel halfway around the world while the truth is putting on its shoes. Mark Twain*

Eliza and Lydia stood in the shop and looked at the Billington Gazette.

Eliza: "Well, that should do the trick. It's a great advert and article. I had no idea they were going to make it so prominent."

Lydia peered at the photograph accompanying the piece.

Lydia: "Mr Hicks was right; we look lovely in that. I'd just had my hair done ahead of the opening."

The shop door clattered open and they looked up to be greeted by the rotund man Eliza recognised from the ottoman auction.

The man raised his eyebrows with surprise and acknowledgement.

Eliza: "Oh hello, it's you. I remember you from the auction."

Rotund man: "Ohhh, I thought you looked familiar in the picture. You're the crazy woman who was in the bin a few months back."

Eliza straightened up to try and gain some air of authority.

Eliza: "Indeed. You drowned my dreams. What can I do for you today, sir?"

Rotund man was feverishly looking around the shop.

Rotund man: "I saw your piece in the local paper today."

Lydia: "Oh, you're a bit early. It doesn't start until Christmas; didn't it say that in the paper?"

Lydia looked back down at the paper to scan it the advert.

Rotund man: "That's as may be, the craft thing isn't why I'm here. May I peruse?"

Eliza and Lydia nodded.

Eliza: "Of course, be our guest."

Rotund man grunted and started looking along all the shelves.

Eliza and Lydia looked at each other.

Eliza, whispering: "That advert paid off quicker than we expected. One hour in and we've already gained a new customer."

Lydia: "He does seem to be looking very keenly."

They watched as rotund man moved items to see the stock behind them.

Eliza cleared her throat.

Eliza: "Are you looking for something in particular?"

Rotund man looked sharply at her.

Rotund man: "Erm, sort of. A book."

Eliza: "Oh! We have our selection of quality pre-loved books over here."

Eliza walked over to a bookcase which housed a display of leather-bound books.

Rotund man scanned them and tutted.

Rotund man: "Is that it? Have you got any more?"

Eliza: "Er, no, but if you're looking for something in particular, we're happy to see if we can obtain it. We search far and wide to find that special item for our customers. Nothing is too much trouble, is it Lydia?"

Lydia: "Eh? Oh no. We scour the internet for hours looking for cheap stuff."

That's it. Sell us.

Eliza: "As long as it's ethical, of course. Isn't that right, Lydia?"

Lydia: "Oh yeah, we're big on fair-trade and all that. It needs to be cheap but they need to be cheerful about it or it affects Eli's karma."

Rotund man rolled his eyes and looked at Lydia, carefully.

Rotund man: "You look different from the photo in the paper."

Lydia looked aghast.

Lydia: "Well, really. I've not been sleeping, that's all."

Rotund man walked over to the counter and pulled the newspaper towards him and stared at the photo.

Rotund man: "No, no. Your hair's much longer now."

He looked at them, suspiciously.

Rotund man: "When was this photograph taken? It's not recent, is it?"

Lydia put her hands on her hips.

Lydia: "Well, I don't see how that really matters. What are you going to do? Report us to the newspaper regulation board for misrepresentation of current hairstyles?"

He shook his head.

Rotund man: "Jesus, you're both as mental as each other. I mean, the stock on the display behind you in the photograph. It's all been sold now then, has it?"

Eliza: "Eh? What stock?"

Eliza and Lydia snatched the paper back off the man and stared at it.

Behind the smiling pair was the first dresser they'd renovated and visible was an array of artefacts, haphazardly displayed on the shelves.

Eliza: "Oh flip, probably. I don't even remember half that stuff, do you Lydia?"

Lydia scrunched her nose up and shook her head.

Lydia: "Nah, that was nearly two years ago."

Rotund man: "Two years?!"

Lydia: "You're annoying me now."

Customer service at its best.

Brilliant.

Eliza: "She doesn't mean it, it's her humour."

Rotund man: "Is it? Right well, I've not found what I'm looking for so I'll be on my way."

Eliza: "If we can be of any help to you in the future, please don't hesitate to visit again."

Rotund man raised an eyebrow, sceptically.

Rotund man: "Hmmm."

His mobile rang and he picked it up. On the way out of the door he could be heard saying: "Nah, it's gone. Bet it sold for a fiver considering the nous on the pair that run it..."

The door rattled behind him as he carried on speaking to the caller.

Eliza and Lydia looked at each other with confusion and stared at the paper.

Lydia: "What are we looking at?"

Eliza, shrugging: "Don't know."

Lydia: "I don't quite understand what happened then."

Eliza: "Me neither but he looked at the photograph. There must be a clue."

They both stared at the paper for a few minutes.

Eliza: "Anything?"

Lydia: "Nope. None the wiser, except thinking I might go back to that hairstyle in case he reports us to the Out-of-date Picture Association."

Is there such a thing?

Probably, and there's sure to be a fine.

Eliza: "I'll put the kettle on."

Lydia: "I'll book an appointment at Fringe Benefits."

Eliza nodded.

Eliza: "I'll see if Mr Hicks has left any biscuits out the back."

Eliza wandered out to the kitchens and left Lydia on the phone making her appointment.

Meanwhile, across the other side of Billington, Henry was at work in the auction house and was sitting down to his elevenses with his weekly copy of the Billington Gazette.

He turned the page and looked at the section advertising Eliza and Lydia's shop competition. Suddenly, he spat his mouthful of tea out all over Eliza's face. He quickly mopped the spillage with his sleeve and looked carefully at the page. He reached over the far side of his desk and picked up his magnifying glass and looked closely at the paper.

He exhaled loudly.

Henry: "Well! I'll be buggered. Surely not!"

He picked up his phone and searched out the number for Illusions of Grandeur Crafts and quickly dialled it.

Henry: "Bums. It's engaged."

He rapped his fingers on the desk for a moment in contemplation, then jumped up, downed the remainder of his tea, and threw on his coat from the back of his chair.

On the way out of his little office he called out to a woman who was labelling items for the next auction.

Henry: "I'm just off out for a bit. I've got my phone if you need me."

The woman waved in acknowledgement and went back to her labels.

Henry jumped into his car and set off for Pilkington.

Minutes spent on government website trying to find laws about time limit of photographs used in media publications: *Six and a half.*

Chapter Twenty-five

Sub quote for the day: *Real knowledge is to know the extent of one's ignorance. Confucius*

Twenty minutes later, Henry pushed through the door of Illusions of Grandeur Crafts to be greeted with a wide-eyed Lydia who was stood behind the counter, speaking to two burly men.

Lydia: "I don't know who you are but I'm not accepting a fine. I'm having my hair done on Tuesday and no one will be any the wiser."

Man one: "What? I ain't bovvered wiv yer hair. I wanna look around the place."

Man two: "C'mon Nigel, let's stop the small talk and 'ave a gander."

Nigel nodded and they started looking along the shelves.

Lydia clocked Henry and smiled, coquettishly at him.

Henry rushed up to the counter.

Henry, breathlessly: "I had to come and see you."

Lydia blushed furiously and batted her eyelashes at him.

Lydia: "On a Thursday? In the middle of the day? How frightfully gallant!"

Henry: "Eh?"

Henry looked slightly wrong-footed then bent over the counter towards Lydia.

Henry, whispering: "Erm... These men, do you know them?"

Lydia shook her head.

Henry nodded wisely.

Henry: "May I?"

Lydia shrugged and nodded, not wise at all to the situation.

She watched as Henry went over to the two men and spoke quietly to them.

One of the men pulled out a ripped section from the paper and showed him.

Henry shook his head and a couple of moments later the men left the shop without another word.

Henry came back to the counter.

Lydia: "Oooh, you dealt with them so masterfully. Would you like a jammy dodger?"

Lydia proffered a tin of biscuits at him but he shook his head.

Henry: "I can't stop. It's just... I saw your picture in the paper and dropped everything to come over."

Lydia gasped.

Lydia: "Oh my god, this is so romantic. I feel quite faint!"

Eliza strode back into the shop with a pint of milk.

Eliza: "Oh! Hello Henry. How are you?"

Lydia started gabbling.

Lydia: "He had to come and see me. I didn't do anything Eli, I promise, but he was powerless to his urges. What can I say? Sometimes a man only has to look at me and he's head over heels. He saw my picture in the paper and dropped everything. On a Thursday, too! Nothing normally happens on a Thursday."

Eliza stood in the doorway, stumped.

Henry stood by the counter, stumped.

Henry: "You what? I'm talking about the book."

Lydia was crestfallen.

Lydia: "What fucking book?!"

Eliza walked across the shop and put the milk on the counter.

Eliza: "Not you an' all. Everyone's looking for books today."

Henry: "Yes and they won't be the only ones."

He went over to the counter and pulled across the paper. He wiped jammy dodger crumbs off the photograph and pointed to the second shelf down on the dresser behind Eliza's head.

Henry: "That is what they're looking for."

Eliza and Lydia peered millimetres away from the page.

Eliza: "A stuffed badger?"

Henry: "Next to the badger."

A look of recollection crossed Lydia's face.

Lydia: "Oh that?! I donated that old thing. My Uncle Terry left me that when he died. I wanted his Art Deco lamp so was quite pissed off when all I got was a crappy book. It didn't go with my minimalist décor.

Books are very last year. It's all about electronic literature now."

Henry stared at her in amazement.

Henry: "Did you know it's a Charles Dickens?"

Lydia tutted.

Lydia: "I did know actually, as he'd written something and signed it. I can't believe he'd actually doodled and defaced one of his own books. It upset me; I need pristine in my life - not dusty old books with dead author scribbles on them."

Henry put his hands up to his face and puffed breathlessly.

Henry's voice went up a pitch.

Henry: "Signed you say? Oh, dear me."

He pulled up the Lloyd Loom chair and flumped into it.

Henry, urgently: "Where is it?"

Eliza and Lydia shrugged.

Eliza and Lydia in unison: "I dunno."

Henry, quietly and deliberately: "Please. Think. I'll ask again... Where is it?"

Lydia: "I told you. I don't know!! Eli? Do you know where it is?"

Eliza: "No, but I'm sensing it might be quite important. Henry looks a bit pale."

Lydia: "Meh. Dickens Schmickens. It's hardly Fifty Shades, is it?"

Eliza took in Henry's pallor.

Eliza: "Is it important, Henry?"

Henry nodded in a state of shock.

Henry: "If I'm not mistaken it's a cloth bound Charles Dickens novel, Hard Times; possibly a first edition. If it's a signed as Lydia says and with an inscription it'll be worth a fortune."

Eliza and Lydia stood stock still, completely dumbfounded.

Lydia: "You're having a laugh, aren't you?!"

Eliza: "Oh my god! Hard Times is worth a fortune? What sort of fortune? Holiday in Spain or new house fortune?"

Henry: "New house fortune."

Eliza and Lydia looked agog at each other.

Flipping flip-flops!

Henry: "Now focus... Where is it? Did you sell it? You need to check your records. We need to know if you still have it."

Eliza: "We keep a record of every item we sell on a stock sheet."

Lydia looked surprised at Eliza.

Lydia: "Do we?"

Eliza: "Yes. We write it on that ring bound pad under the counter."

Lydia: "Oh. I wondered what that was for. I've been drawing on it."

Really??

Eliza looked at Lydia with dismay.

Henry wiped his brow in exasperation.

Just then another newcomer entered the shop.

Newcomer: "Hello. I've come for a look around. I saw your advert."

Lydia: "The book's gone now piss off."

The newcomer stepped back with shock.

Newcomer: "I was going to buy a cabinet for my dining room but if this is the welcome extended to new customers, I'll perhaps nip to IKEA instead."

We'll not stay open till the end of the week at this rate.

Eliza: "Sorry, she's on a high dosage of medication. They misjudged it as she's lost weight and she's hallucinating today. I caught her eating loom bands earlier. Henry's just going to take her out the back for a sit down, aren't you, Henry?"

Henry dragged his bones up from the Lloyd Loom chair and nodded.

Henry to Lydia: "Come on, out the back you or we'll have to send back your medal for exemplary customer service."

Lydia allowed herself to be guided out to the kitchens by Henry.

She looked up at him bashfully as he touched her elbow and he looked down at her and gulped, loudly.

Eliza managed to salvage the situation and ten minutes later, the customer went off happily with a unit painted in Tuscan sun for his dining room.

Eliza hollered towards the kitchens.

Eliza: "You can come out now!"

A couple of minutes later a red-faced Lydia came back into the shop and Henry was tucking in his shirt.

'Allo. Something's been occurring.

Eliza looked at them both suspiciously and put her hands on her hips.

Eliza to Lydia: "Have you been doing a Goldilocks?"

Lydia, indignantly: "No! I most certainly have not!"

Henry looked at them both, perplexed.

Lydia: "We were thinking, weren't we Henry?"

Now I know you're lying.

Henry: "Er, yes... Indeed. You need to find out what happened to that book. I'm pleased I caught you to tell you. Be careful, you may get a lot of interest with dealers wanting to pick it up on the cheap, so just say it was a fake to get rid of them until we know the score. I must go; I've left Jessica in charge of labelling. Let me know of any developments and if you find it, please promise to use my auction house to sell it. The exposure would be brilliant!"

He dashed off and the door rattled behind him.

Eliza and Lydia turned their attentions back to the paper and stared at the photograph.

Eliza: "We need to find that book. It'll save us."

Lydia: "I quite like Uncle Terry now. I've been calling him for years since the time I nearly choked on a foil covered coin in his Christmas pudding. He has redeemed himself."

Lydia looked to the ceiling.

Lydia: "Terry! It's me. Where's your old book gone?"

Eliza: "Well it's not going to be up there, is it?"

Lydia: "I'm waiting for a sign. Terry was into all that; he did the runes."

Eliza: "I'll ask mum, see if she can help with her team of ethereal pixies."

Lydia: "Good call."

Eliza: "I suppose we could also go through the sales records for the past two years. If I sold it there'll be a note."

Lydia: "Sounds a bit boring."

Eliza nodded.

Eliza: "Shall we just ask for divine intervention instead?"

Lydia: "Yeah, lets."

Positive affirmations thought up to enlist the help of the cosmos to find Hard Times: *Thirty-eight.*

Glances at stock sheet records: *None.*

Chapter Twenty-six

Quote for the day: *Everything has beauty, but not everyone sees it. Confucius*

Mr Hicks looked at the photograph plonked in front of him.

Eliza: "Now then, you see my left ear? Do you know what happened to it?"

Mr Hicks: "Your ear? You've lost your ear? Oh, my dear, that's most unfortunate."

Do I look like the sort of person who would mislay a body part?

Eliza, patiently: "No, Mr Hicks. Behind my ear."

Mr Hicks looked at the photograph again.

Mr Hicks: "The badger? I sold it last year to a lover of taxidermy. Quite pleased I was too. It had a very unnerving look to it and used to watch me across the shop with its beady little eyes. I used to put a bobble hat on it so it couldn't stare at me whilst I was doing my Sudoku."

You put a bobble hat on a stuffed badger?

Eliza, slightly less patiently: "Not the badger, Mr Hicks, the book."

Mr Hicks looked closely again at the photograph.

Mr Hicks: "The big old worn out looking one?"

Eliza: "Yes. The big old worn out looking one that's worth a fortune."

Mr Hicks looked at her, shocked

Mr Hicks: "Oh really!? Are you sure?"

Eliza: "Yes. Henry, the oracle on dead people's paraphernalia, says it's a Charles Dickens and perhaps a first edition."

Mr Hicks: "Crikey! Well, I'm sorry I can't assist, my dear. My level of expertise lies in yeast products. I'm afraid I don't recall this item."

Just then, Lydia came bowling into the shop laden with shopping bags and a new hairstyle.

Gawd, blimey!

Eliza: "Whoah! I mean... Whoooh! You've had your hair done."

Oh my god. Did she turn her head at a salient moment and the hairdresser cut the wrong lump off?

Lydia threw her shopping bags on the floor and flattened down her hair.

Lydia: "I have. I'm not sure about it, if I'm honest. It's meant to be edgy."

It's wonky. Not edgy.

Don't stare Eli.

It's hard not to, I know, but be strong.

Eliza: "There's something happening with the top which is slightly bothersome."

Lydia leant against the counter next to Eliza.

Lydia: "I had a new girl; she's just finished her NVQ. As you know, I was going to go like the photograph so that we wouldn't be fined, but she had it and it looked dead funky on her. I asked for it on a whim. I think she called it a discomforted bob."

You're not wrong, there.

Eliza: "Disconnected. It's called a disconnected bob."

Lydia: "Yeah, one of them."

Think of something nice to say.

Eliza: "Well, it certainly evokes a response."

Mr Hicks patted Lydia's hand.

Mr Hicks: "Never mind dear, it'll grow."

Lydia: "Shut up."

Mr Hicks looked a bit hurt and wandered off to the kitchens.

Lydia turned round and lifted her coat to reveal her bottom.

Lydia: "Does my bum look big in this?"

She's having a crisis.

It does seem to have ballooned, though.

Maybe she's been eating cake on the quiet.

Lie.

Eliza: "No! Of course not. It's as pert and beautiful as a nubile teenager's."

Lydia tutted.

Lydia: "Shit. I'll have to get some more padding then. I've got special pants on; it's like sitting on a rubber ring. I could sit for hours on a concrete slab and not get piles wearing these."

Okaaay.

Eliza: "Have you hit your head?"

Lydia: "Eh? No, big bums are the new black. If you haven't got a big bum, you're not worth knowing."

Eliza: "Oh."

Eliza rubbed her bottom in contemplation.

That's me friendless then.

Lydia: "I'm thinking I might start taking selfies but I need to be match fit first."

Eliza: "What's brought this on?"

Lydia: "I'm reinventing myself and moving on. It's all that thinking I've been doing. It's been quite good actually. Cathartic."

Well, that's debatable.

You've got a wonky dysfunctional bob and a big arse as a result.

Eliza: "What thinking have you been doing, then?"

Lydia: "Well, because of Dorothy, I've been thinking about Roy and all the shit he put me through and how I was still hanging on to him. It made me think, why am I doing that? It's like I've opened a door which I'd not ventured through. Obviously not an actual door. I don't have a fear of doors. Though, I'm not a lover of revolving doors. I never know when to get out. I lack confidence in a revolving door… Also, saying that, I wouldn't willingly open a cellar door. There's always dodgy things in cellars, they're always dark for a start…"

Lydia looked to the ceiling, lost in thought, and carried on.

Lydia: "It's like I was in the cellar with Roy and wasn't able to walk up the stairs out to the light… Anyway, I asked myself, do I want him back? The reply was no.

So, I'm regenerating myself as a new woman. I have walked out of the Roy cellar and into a new clean, white feng shui'ed room."

Oh, she's had a Roy epiphany and gone all new age.

I feel her pain. This happened to me with Lewis.

She'll be chanting next and clearing her chakras.

Eliza: "I quite liked the old one."

Lydia waved her hands, expansively.

Lydia: "The new me won't take any crap. I read this article about being happy with yourself so that you can find the right man for you. I'm doing that. I'm also thinking of having my colours done next week. I think my problem is I dress in 'winter' but I'm probably a 'summer' with a hint of 'autumn'. Maybe just the odd leaf – a horse chestnut or something."

Hmmm.

Well, isn't this all fine and dandy?

Eliza: "Well, that's all lovely. For fear of bringing reality back to the new room you've wandered into, you do recall we're struggling with the shop and are in the midst of trying to find your book and run a craft competition to drum up income or we'll be shopless?"

Lydia: "Yes, yes. The new me can handle all that boring stuff, too. I won't let humdrum define me. I am an empowered, free woman. I am independent and won't be dictated to by any man ever again!"

Boring? Humdrum?

The shop has been left in the cellar with Roy!

Eliza: "Do I feature in the big bottomed white room?"

Lydia: "Oh, of course darling! You are my past, present and future. My base tone in a new world of technicolour."

Eliza: "I thought it was a white room?"

I can't keep up.

Lydia: "It's a white room awaiting a future of colour. I need to save Dorothy and take her with me. She's part of the rainbow."

Eliza: "How about you just concentrate on yourself and see if Dorothy wants to be involved in the rainbow."

Just then Dorothy came bustling into the shop.

Lydia: "Hello Dorothy! We were just talking about you!"

Dorothy looked hesitant.

Dorothy, nervously: "Oh! Have you? What have you been saying?"

She pulled her coat around herself.

Ooh she looks a bit twitchy.

Think neutral and think fast.

Eliza: "Nothing bad, Dorothy. Lydia was saying she's going to have her colours done and wondered if you wanted yours done too?"

Lydia: "Yeah, I think I might be summer with a bit of fallen autumn leaf. Would you like to come with me?"

Lily with mulch.

That's an interesting combination.

Dorothy visibly relaxed.

Dorothy: "Oh I see. That's very kind of you, Lydia, but I was done a few years ago. I'm spring. My favourite flower is a snowdrop so it is quite apt."

Dorothy looked carefully at Lydia and smiled.

Dorothy: "What a wonderfully radical hairstyle, Lydia! You've got such a delightful face, you can carry any style off, even one which would look simply hideous on anyone else."

Lydia instinctively ran her fingers through her hair.

Lydia: "Oh."

Eliza: "Yeah, lovely, isn't it? This is her white room hairdo. She got herself a big bum to go with it."

Dorothy looked at her nonplussed.

Lydia: "Ignore her. What brings you to our little shop today, Dorothy?"

Dorothy: "I'm on my way to the garden centre and wondered if you'd like to come to with me? I need to replace some flowers in my borders."

Lydia: "Oooh, what a splendid idea! We can go to that Whitegate Flower Emporium. Shall I get some perineums to plonk outside the shop – make it a bit more welcoming?

Perineums?!

Welcome to Illusions of Grandeur Crafts. You can't miss us – we're the ones with a row of cocks in a pot at the entrance.

Dorothy coughed.

Eliza: "Perennials. She means perennials, Dorothy."

Dorothy, laughing: "Oh, my goodness. That is a relief!"

Eliza: "It might not convey upcycled furniture to the passing customer."

Dorothy: "No indeed! What would the ladies of Pilkington say about that?!"

Lydia put her hands on her hips, unhappy to be out of the loop.

Lydia: "What are you on about? But yes, I'd love to come with you Dorothy. Shall we go now?"

Dorothy: "I don't think it's the time of year for perennials but we might find some nice winter pansies. Would you like to come, Eliza?"

Eliza, pointedly: "I'd love to but someone needs to man the shop."

Lydia: "Yes, yes darling. I'll treat it as a marketing mission. I'll claim mileage."

Eliza: "Don't go too wild with your flower purchases. Margaret is insistent we start turning a profit or we're going to have to take a severe cut in pay."

Eliza looked purposefully at Lydia's shopping bags and Lydia followed her gaze.

Lydia: "Don't worry, darling. I have it all under control. Trust me."

This comes from a person who's just had a run in with Edward Scissorhands, has two halves of Edam stuck to her arse and is about to plant a knob display outside our shop.

We're doomed.

Amount of tissues wedged in pants to see what a big bottom felt like: *Complete box.*

Feeling when sitting down on new bottom: *Extreme comfort.*

Chapter Twenty-seven

Quote for the day: *Be yourself; everyone else is already taken. Oscar Wilde*

Tom came running across the playground at the end of school and leapt into the arms of an awaiting Eliza.

Eliza: "Hello darling! You're very chirpy."

Tom: "Hello mummy! I've got something to show you!"

Tom ferreted about in his book bag and pulled out a pencil case.

Tom: "'Ere, sniff that! What does that smell of?"

Eliza bent down and Tom shoved it under her nose.

Eliza: "Erm... plastic."

Tom shook his head, solemnly.

Tom: "No, mummy. That's the smell of success."

Oh!

Tom: "I win ten stars this term and got this from Miss Gardner as reward for goodness."

Eliza: "Oh! How wonderful! Clever boy, Tom."

Tom: "I excited. It's the end of term."

Eliza: "I know! Great, isn't it?"

Tom: "Yeah... What does that mean?"

Eliza: "It means two weeks off school and Father Christmas comes."

Tom's eyes widened.

Tom: "Really?! Yayyyy!!"

Eliza: "We're doing that craft competition in the shop this week. Will you help run it with us?"

Tom: "Can I bring my new pencil case?"

Eliza: "You can."

Tom: "Can I bring Postman Pat?"

Eliza: "You can."

Tom: "Can I bring chocolate?"

For goodness' sake.

Eliza, sighing: "Uh huh."

Tom: "Then yes. I will help you."

Eliza, sarcastically: "Thank you."

Tom: "My pleasure. Happy to be of assistance, me old treacle."

Lydia came into the playground with a strange gait – half run, half waddle.

Eliza, Tom, and a fair few other people watched her entrance with a bemused expression.

Lydia reached Eliza and Tom and puffed with exertion.

Lydia: "Sorry I'm late. Has Freya come out yet?"

Eliza: "No. Are you alright?"

Lydia, whispering to Eliza: "It's these fucking pants. My fake arse keeps dropping. I can't wait to get 'em off."

Tom meanwhile was wandering around to the rear of Lydia and he dropped his book bag with surprise.

Tom: "Auntie Wydia! Your bottom is massive!! It blown up like a balloon."

Freya came out with her eyes fixed on Lydia's hair.

Freya: "What's happened to your hair?!"

Before Lydia could reply Tom yanked her by the arm and gesticulated wildly at Lydia's bottom.

Freya: "Whoah! That's humungous! What have you done to yourself?"

Uh oh. Bullying in the playground.

Lydia's about to cry.

I need to step in.

Eliza: "Mummy's had an allergic reaction."

Freya's face turned from derision to horror.

Freya: "Are you alright, mummy?"

Eliza: "She sat on a wasps' nest and they all stung her bottom. She needs to go home and sit in a cold bath. It will be back to normal by tomorrow, won't it Lydia?"

Lydia: "Flippin' right it will. I'm sticking with my own, at least that's slipping down naturally."

Freya, seriously: "I'm not sure about your hair, mummy."

Lydia: "No. It was a bit of an impulse buy. I think I might consider extensions."

Freya nodded.

Freya: "I think that might be wise."

Lydia: "I'm reinventing myself; it's trial and error. The bum is an error and my disaffected bob is turning into a trial."

Freya gave Lydia a hug.

Freya: "You're beautiful mummy, just as you are. You don't need anything else."

Awww.

Tom: "Oh, I don't know about that, Freya."

It had to be my son, didn't it?

Eliza: "Tom!"

Tom: "What? She look better wiv make-up."

Eliza: "Anyway, are you and Freya going to meet us at the shop early tomorrow to help set up?"

Lydia: "We will be there, my little pastel tone. Panic not, darling."

Eliza: "Good. Come on Tom."

Lydia signalled for Freya to stand behind her on the way out.

Lydia: "You take my rear till we get to the car. I can't take the stares."

Freya: "Gotcha."

They set off out of the playground with Freya announcing to anyone who would listen.

Freya: "Move along, there's nothing to see here. She's just got an allergic bottom."

Lydia whispered to Eliza.

Lydia: "Humiliation doesn't quite cover it."

Eliza: "No, but neither would a size twenty pair of trousers."

They got out of the playground and split up as they went their respective ways.

Tom, waving: "Bye Auntie Big Bum!"

Lydia: "Yes, yes. Goodbye."

Lydia could be heard telling Freya as Eliza and Tom departed.

Lydia: "I'm going to walk out of the white room and back in again. I've had a bum start."

Ain't that the truth?

Pretend bottom order that was placed online as a result of tissue dry run: *Cancelled.*

No amount of comfort is worth that much humiliation.

***

Dorothy dashed through the front door and threw her handbag on the hallway bureau and nervously glanced at the clock. She'd been out most of the afternoon and she admonished herself for allowing time to run away with her. She'd had a wonderful few hours and felt more carefree than she had in years. It was a pause in the miserable existence that had become her life with Kenneth.

She ran into the kitchen to throw the dinner into the oven and then started scurrying around the house; straightening cushions and checking each room was as it should be.

She hurried back into the hall and dragged her bag off the bureau. With it, she accidently knocked a folder which had been perched on top. The folder dropped to the floor, scattering its contents.

Dorothy muttered under her breath and bent down to pick up the documents. There were bank statements and letters from what she recognised as Kenneth's solicitor and also from his firm of accountants.

She straightened them up and a name caught her eye as it wasn't Cuthbert Promotions Ltd. She leafed through the documents and saw they all related to this unknown company.

Dorothy rubbed her chest with anxiety as a weight suddenly pressed against her ribcage. She looked troubled and skim read the letter from the accountants. The business had been incorporated earlier that year.

She looked at the name of the company again and read through the paperwork.

A few minutes later she decided she'd read enough and replaced the documents in the folder. As she stood to put them back onto the bureau, something clicked in her. A steely resolve flooded through her body and she took a deep breath. This time Kenneth had gone too far.

This time it wasn't just about her.

Chapter Twenty-eight

Quote for the day: *Cows are my passion. What I have ever sighed for has been to retreat to a Swiss farm and live entirely surrounded by cows - and china. Charles Dickens*

Eliza and Tom were tidying up the craft stuff from small renovated tables when Lydia breezed in.

Eliza: "Oh, finally! You took your flip-flopping time!"

Lydia: "Sorry darling. I had to have these put in and Freya decided to go to Roy's again."

She flicked her now shoulder length hair laden with extensions.

Eliza: "Oh! Now that's better. It's way less distracting."

Lydia looked around the shop.

Lydia: "It's not very busy in here. Where's Mr Hicks?"

Eliza shook her head.

Eliza: "It's not been a roaring success today, has it Tom? Mr Hicks said he had something to attend to at about midday and we've not seen him since."

Tom: "I been doing doodles all day on me own. I gonna win the craft competition."

Eliza: "You can't, Tom, you're related to the management."

Tom's bottom lip shot out.

Tom: "That not my fault! I an artist. I a natural, gwandma says."

Eliza turned her attention to Lydia.

Eliza: "Regrettably, we've had a lot of, what I can only assume are book dealers, and not a lot of craft taker-uppers. Still, we've got the rest of the week."

Just then a very short, wiry looking man with a pale face came into the shop.

Eliza whispered to Lydia.

Eliza: "You wait, it'll be another book enquiry..."

Lydia: "Don't worry, I'll deal with him."

Lydia turned her attention to the wiry man.

Lydia: "Can I be of service to you, sir?"

Wiry man stepped back slightly, caught off guard and cocked his head, enquiringly, at Lydia.

Wiry man: "Erm... Pwaps."

Lydia straightened up and looked cautiously at the wiry man.

Wiry man looked at her, equally cautiously.

Eliza continued oblivious.

Eliza: "What is it you're looking for?"

Wiry man turned his attention to Eliza.

Wiry man: "I am Fwederwick Wobinson. I deal with interwesting and ware antiqwities."

Lydia gulped loudly and hissed at Eliza.

Lydia: "I'm off out the back."

As she made a hasty retreat, Fwederwick called after her.

Fwederwick: "Clawabelle?"

Eliza and Tom looked nonplussed at Lydia and then at Fwederwick.

Lydia, shrilly: "No! Goodbye. I have urgent matters to attend to!"

Fwederwick didn't look convinced but shrugged and turned his attention back to Eliza.

Fwederwick: "I saw what could be a particuwally ware book in your midst."

Eliza: "Oh, that. It's not here, unfortunately, but never mind. At least it's brought in a lot of attention. Whilst you're here would you like to have a look around and see if anything else takes your fancy?"

Fwederwick smiled and wiped a bit of spit from the corners of his mouth.

Fwederwick: "No, no. I only deal with items of worth."

Cheeky bastard!

Eliza: "Oh well, off you go then. I'll shut the door behind you."

Eliza ushered him out and slammed the door unnecessarily loudly after him and turned the "closed" sign round.

She sighed, heavily.

Eliza: "Well, that wasn't the best day was it, Tom?"

Tom harrumphed.

Tom: "No and now I found out I can't win. I not happy. I could have been at play barn wiv gwandma."

Eliza: "I'll call her later and ask if she's free for a couple of days during the rest of this week, ok?"

Tom: "Ok."

Eliza hollered out to the kitchens.

Eliza: "He's gone!"

Lydia came running out looking flushed.

Lydia: "Oh thank god."

Eliza looked enquiringly at Lydia.

Lydia: "Ok, I'll tell you. But you promise not to judge."

This sounds dubious.

I probably will judge. There's little to prevent that.

Just lie.

Eliza: "Of course not! Just bear in mind Tom is here with tender ears."

Tom rubbed his ears and pulled on them a bit.

Tom, muttering: "They not tender, they fine."

Eliza: "Hang on."

Eliza hastily plonked him down in front of a paper mâché mask and dragged over a pot full of felt tip pens.

Eliza: "Make me a mask, Tom."

Tom: "Only if I get a present. Creativity costs."

Eliza: "I'll buy you a bar of chocolate on the way home. Now go and flourish the pens."

Tom nodded and pulled up his sleeves, ready for action.

Once settled, Eliza ushered Lydia back out towards the kitchens.

Eliza: "Well?"

Lydia put her hands on her hips.

Lydia: "Ok. I met Sasha; she works in the department store in Billington. She's got a dog in a bag and massive eyelashes. They're quite astonishing. They touch her cheeks when she blinks. Anyway, she does calls to people… you know…calls…"

Lydia nodded by way of gap filling.

Eliza: "PPI calls?"

Lydia rolled her eyes.

Lydia: "No… Calls. 'What would you like me to do?' sort of calls."

Eliza: "Would you like new double-glazing calls?"

Lydia visibly slumped with irritation and widened her eyes.

Lydia: "I offer a service to lonely people."

Eliza: "You've joined the Samaritans?"

Lydia: "Nooo. Slightly more… erm… intimate."

The penny's dropped.

Eliza: "Filthy calls?!"

Lydia: "No! I just let men indulge in their fantasies whilst I do the ironing."

Eliza: "Filthy calls then."

Lydia shook her head.

Lydia: "More of a sex Samaritan, darling. Anyway, I'd recognise that speech impediment anywhere!"

Lydia pulled a face.

Lydia, continuing: "He likes feet. I have to tell him I'm wearing gladiator sandals when he calls."

Eliza thought for a moment.

Eliza: "Your porn name is a cow."

Lydia: "Pardon?"

Eliza: "Clarabelle. You've named yourself after a cow!"

She started laughing and Lydia's mouth dropped open.

Lydia: "I haven't, have I?! Oh god! That's because of that stupid Sasha girl with her big batty eyelashes and doleful expression. She must have subliminally influenced me."

She tutted loudly and thought for a moment.

Lydia: "Do you know, I did wonder why men kept asking about the size of my udders."

Eliza: "No whey. You'll have to tell them to mooove along."

Lydia: "Oh ha de ha. Aren't we full of the cow puns?"

Eliza: "You deserve a pat on the back for doing that."

Lydia: "Shut up now."

Eliza: "Sorry. I'll not milk it."

I could go on all day.

Lydia ignored her.

Lydia: "It makes good money. It's bought my pretend hair. You should think about it; what with the business being in trouble. I decided I needed a plan B in case it doesn't pick up."

Eliza: "Oh stroll on. I couldn't talk to men about their dubious predilections."

Lydia: "You shouldn't be so judgmental. A lot of the time they're just bored."

Eliza: "Then they should take up Scrabble. It's good for the mind and expands one's vocabulary."

Lydia: "Fair enough, little Miss Prim. You need to get a man, have a good old seeing to and lighten up. Are you still on multitudeofmates.com?"

Eliza: "I have the odd peruse but my heart isn't in it."

Lydia: "I tell you what. Why don't we go out for a night? Take our minds off the shop, the book, and the fact I'm a seductive cow."

Eliza: "Oh yes! What a wonderful idea."

Lydia: "Let's sort it for next Saturday evening. We'll go to Billington; you can show me the pole dancing club."

Eliza: "I'd rather not. I've got a bit of a beef with that place.

Lydia: "Seriously. Shut up."

Eliza: "Sorry."

Lydia: "Next week. We'll dress up nicely but I'll leave my bum at home."

Eliza: "Good plan. Do you fancy a cuppa?"

Lydia: "Yes please, then I'll be off."

Eliza: "De-calf-inated with cream?"

Lydia: "That's it. I'm leaving now; stick your drink. I'm off to change my porn name."

Lydia whisked off and kissed Tom on the head on the way out.

She called back to Eliza.

Lydia: "I'll be by first light on Monday, darling. You have my word."

Eliza, hollering back: "You'd better be or I'll be right cheesed off!"

Lydia, calling through a closing door: "You're not funny!"

Eliza wandered out of the kitchens, back into the shop to find Tom covered in black felt tip.

He proudly held up a completely black mask.

Tom: "Tadarr!"

Eliza: "I thought you were an artist."

Tom: "I am."

Eliza: "What is it?"

Tom: "It's Darth Vader."

He held it up to his face and breathed heavily.

Tom, using his best Darth Vader voice: "I find your lack of faith disturbing."

He put the mask down.

Tom: "See."

Eliza: "Oh yes, sorry; very good. Come on, let's go and get some chocolate."

Tom put the mask back to his face and breathed loudly.

Tom, in a deep voice: "As you wish."

I'm surrounded by madness.

It's a wonder I'm not a fruitcake.

Amount of liquid soap used trying to remove black felt tip from child: *Half a bottle.*

Chapter Twenty-nine

Quote for the day: *When everything seems to be going against you, remember that the airplane takes off against the wind, not with it. Henry Ford*

It was four o'clock on the final Saturday of the 'Illusions of Grandeur Crafts Kids Competition' and Eliza and Lydia were busy framing up and exhibiting the entrants' offerings. They displayed them all along the shelves of a dresser. Freya had taken the opportunity to stay at Roy's again and Tom was pottering about handing artwork to Eliza.

Tom: "This one's wubbish mummy. Don't let that one win. It look like it done by a child."

Quite.

Mr Hicks was in the kitchens adding the final flourishing touches to his bespoke winner's cake. He'd been busy all day beavering away.

Eliza: "He's been singing a lot today. I've never heard him sing before."

Lydia: "I know. He's happy, lost in a world of sponge."

A woman and two eager children came into the shop and she called across to Eliza.

Woman with eager children: "Has the judging started?"

Eliza: "No."

Woman with eager children: "I do hope we win. I would love to win Mr Hicks's cake."

Eliza: "Ah, he'll be delighted to hear that. He's spent all day making it."

Woman with eager children: "We were very sorry when he closed. It's a shame his wonderful bakery was replaced with this shop."

Oh charming.

The woman with eager children carried on oblivious to the offence she was causing.

Woman with eager children: "We all said, Pilkington doesn't need a knick knack shop. Plus, it's never open when it's meant to be. How many times do you two shut up shop, willy-nilly? There's a wonderful reclamation and shabby chic store the other side of Billington that's just opened up. That's where we'll all go to when we want pre-loved furniture. Pilkington, however, will always need cake."

Hang on… there's another shop like ours not far away?

Our shop's not open when it's meant to be?

I bet that's because of Mr Hicks and his Bunty exploits.

Eliza: "There's another shop opened like ours?"

Lydia started to sidle away from the counter and surreptitiously backed into the kitchens.

Woman with eager children: "Yes of course! You get some of your stock from them."

Eh?

The woman pointed to a bedside cabinet which Lydia had renovated.

Woman with eager children: "That cabinet. It's part of their new range."

Eliza: "No, no. That's a one off. It was renovated by Lydia, wasn't it Lydia…. Lydia?"

Eliza looked around to find Lydia was nowhere in sight.

The woman with eager children went over to the cabinet, lifted the price tag, and puffed loudly.

Woman with eager children, who were now slumped bored: "Huffff... And theirs is thirty pounds cheaper than yours!"

Eliza: "I think you must be mistaken. What's the name of this shop?"

Woman with bored children: "It's..."

Their conversation was halted as a number of other women and children came clattering into the shop.

A random newcomer: "Are we too late to see if we've won the cake?"

Woman with now very bored children: "No, the judging's not taken place yet."

Random newcomer: "Ooh good. I do hope my Josh's effort has won. I would love to try one of Mr Hicks's cakes again."

Woman with extremely bored children who were starting to become unruly: "I know, that's the reason why we're here. Isn't it a shame he doesn't do it anymore?"

Random newcomer: "A dreadful pity. The only reason I bought a sideboard from here is because it contained six floury baps and a cream horn."

Woman with children who Eliza was in danger of shouting at: "I know, Marjorie. He's sorely missed. I am still annoyed at Mrs Reynolds for kicking up such a stink about the dead mouse she found that time in her bloomer."

Random newcomer, who we now know is Marjorie: "It's thanks to her, Gwen, we have this place instead of our village bakery. She always was a drama queen. Do you remember the hoo-hah she caused when the ice cream van mounted the kerb and squashed her front borders? I mean, her garden is hardly Kew, now is it? I've seen her buy plants off the market."

Gwen, the woman with children of whom Eliza has given the dead eye to, shook her head: "I said to my Adrian, we need to deal with troublemakers effectively. I've not invited her to Bridge since."

I'm stunned into silence.

I thought our shop had been well received.

It turns out they only visited because there was a chance they could still get some of Mr Hicks's baked products.

The others murmured and nodded.

The door clattered again and in rushed Brian.

Eliza: "Brian?!"

Brian: "Hello poppet! I'm not too late for the judging, am I?"

Eliza: "No, what are you doing here?"

Brian: "Lydia told me Mr Hicks was making a cake as a prize. Clive and I used to lust after them; they're out of this world. I almost nicked a kid just so I could enter!"

Just then Lydia came blustering out.

Lydia: "Judging time! Mr Hicks has made a phenomenal cake for the winner! Hello Brian! You made it!"

Brian: "I wouldn't have missed the chance to see a Mr Hicks special!"

Have I been living in a bubble?

Shops which stock the same furniture?

Mr Hicks the cake legend?

Why am I not aware of any of this?!

They all hushed and Mr Hicks came out of the kitchen holding a bulging silver foil tray with a tea towel over it.

He placed it carefully on the counter and smiled at the assembled group.

Lydia: "Which one's the winner, Eli?"

Eliza looked at the crafted efforts and shrugged.

Eliza: "Brian? You're impartial. Who's the winner?"

Brian jumped with glee and clapped his hands.

Brian: "Oooh thank you! I like judging responsibility – it empowers me. Now let's have a look…"

Brian rolled his sleeves up, went along to the dresser and started looking carefully at them.

Brian, murmuring: "Hmmm, good content and build-up of colours. I particularly like the red splashes. Most effective."

A little boy piped up.

Little boy: "That was when Alfie knocked over the poster paint."

Brian grasped his chin and continued along the line.

Brian: "I'm not sure about this completely black mask. Whoever's child did this is very disturbed."

Oh, that'll be my child.

Tom, with his best Darth Vader voice: "You underestimate the power of the Dark Side."

Eliza hastily put her hand over his mouth.

Eliza: "Ignore that, move along."

Brian carried on staring at the entries for a few moments longer.

Brian swung round and waved to the group expansively.

Brian: "I have made my decision."

He looked around the shop, dramatically.

Brian: "... There can only be one winner..."

Lydia: "Yes, yes. Crack on with it, there's a pet."

Brian looked at her sharply.

Brian: "Shush. I'm building tension."

He went back to addressing the shop.

Brian: "I am a thousand percent confident in my choice..."

Technically that's not possible.

He turned round and grabbed a frame from the dresser and held it aloft.

Brian: "Congratulations! This is the winning entry!"

Gwen leapt in the air with delight.

Gwen: "My Connor did that! I get the cake! Yay!"

Tom huffed with irritation.

Mr Hicks took off the tea towel to reveal the cake he'd made and the whole group gasped with amazement.

Tom and all the other children: "Whoaaaaah!"

The cake was two tiered and leaning against the white iced bottom was a paint palette made of white royal icing with primary colour blobs of icing splatted on it. The top tier was sponge in the shape of a paint pot which had been positioned to look as if it had fallen over and had a river of coloured icing dribbling down the side of the cake, on to the silver tray below. The label on the fallen paint pot had "Illusions of Grandeur Crafts Kid's Competition Winner" written on it with black icing.

Eliza: "Oh my god Mr Hicks, it's incredible!"

Brian: "Oh my heavens man, you're wasted standing in your pants eating toast! You were born to cook. Where's my phone? I must take a picture to show Clive. Carlos will literally weep when he sees it. His cakes are cack, by comparison."

The rest of the group started to clap and Mr Hicks blushed furiously.

Mr Hicks: "Please, stop. It was a pleasure to make. I'm delighted it's been so well received."

Lydia: "Mr Hicks, I had no idea you had any talent."

Mr Hicks: "I did say I was known for my cakes."

Brian: "My restaurant is crying out for your abilities. We get a lot of birthday bookings; would you consider making them for my customers?"

Mr Hicks: "Oh well, I don't really know... I've retired, really. I do have to admit, though, making this has made me very happy."

Lydia: "You're telling me. You've been singing the first three bars of Nessun Dorma all day."

Mr Hicks: "Sorry."

Lydia: "You're ok, it was worth it."

The shop door clattered open and in fell Gaz from the Billington Gazette.

Gaz: "Hi peeps. I'm not too late, am I? My boss says some competition is occurring and I was to cover it."

Eliza: "Really? Oh brilliant!"

Gwen: "Mr Hicks, I am truly honoured to be the recipient of such a fondant masterpiece."

Then she knelt slightly and bowed her head.

Lydia: "Calm down, it's only a cake, and anyway Connor won it, not you."

Connor: "Yeah mummy. My artwork won the competition. It's my cake."

Gwen gave him a look and he gulped, loudly.

Connor: "I might give you a slice, though."

Mr Hicks: "Oh please, stop. Let's not forget how good Lydia is at baking – she won this year's show with her Black Forest Gateau."

Lydia: "Oh well, let's not dwell on that, eh? This is your moment... Ahem."

Gaz made his way to the front of the group.

Gaz: "Wowsers, now that's a cake! Who dunnit?"

Mr Hicks raised his hand.

Gaz got out his ringed notepad.

Gaz: "Name?"

Mr Hicks: "Mr Hicks."

Gaz: "Age?"

Mr Hicks: "Er... old enough."

Gaz looked up from his pad, stared at him and wrote "old" on his notepad.

Gaz: "What's your relationship with the owners of this..."

He looked around.

Gaz: "Junk shop."

Eliza and Lydia both coughed.

Let me at him!

Mr Hicks, smoothly: "It's a craft shop and a lovely one at that. I am a friend of the owners."

Thank you, Mr Hicks for correcting him so eloquently.

Gwen pushed herself forward and nestled up to Gaz. He squirmed, awkwardly, and tried to step back but was stopped by a rather large chest of drawers.

Gwen: "Oh, Mr Hicks is too modest. He is the most talented baker this village has ever had the pleasure of knowing. His wife, however, was terrible at window displays. Portugal is the best place for her. I expect they aren't worried if their chocolate éclairs are displayed in the midday sun... She also used to cheat at Whist; I can't be doing with cheats. It's an awful shame he let the bakery go to this furniture pair. Fair trade? I don't call the prices very fair. If they were looking to ingratiate themselves with the village, they should have used the residents' crafts; there's a lot of talent in Pilkington. I'm marvellous at dry stone walling and Marjorie, here, makes the most aesthetically pleasing wind-chimes from bicycle pumps, don't you Marjorie?"

Marjorie flushed and nodded, bashfully.

Gaz looked around for help but everyone was stood agog at Gwen.

Brian found his voice first.

Brian, breezily: "Right!! Let's get some lovely photos for the Gazette then, shall we?"

Mr Hicks rubbed his chin.

Mr Hicks, muttering: "I wondered why my éclairs never sold. Fancy putting them in the window. Silly woman. She went on a course and everything."

Brian turned his attention to Gaz, grabbed his hand and yanked him away from Gwen.

Brian, hissing at Gaz: "Ignore everything that woman has just said. She drinks turps and we'll sue."

Gaz nodded, grateful to be away from having her ample bust pushed up against him.

Gaz: "Yeah man. She's like a word machine gun. Ratatatat. I can't be getting any of that on my pad. I ain't no PA."

Brian patted his hand.

Brian: "Eliza, you think up something for laddio here to put in the article."

Eliza nodded and went over to Connor to get his full name and details.

Gaz: "Cheers. I'm out tonight and need to get this out of the way. Hang on... I recognise you two."

He pointed at Eliza.

Gaz: "You's the lady with a bomb."

Eliza looked up from her note taking.

Eliza: "I am. Ex bomb. Had you stuck around you'd have known that."

Gaz shrugged, noncommittally.

Gaz: "I ain't getting blown up; job or no job. I's got responsibilities. I's got gerbils."

Brian guffawed.

Brian: "Come on John Simpson, let's get your snaps."

Gaz got his camera out of his case.

Gaz: "I want the winning kid, his art thing and the cake."

Connor dutifully picked up his framed artwork, stood by the cake and did a thumbs up.

Gwen: "Mouth open Connor, please! You look like you've got a mouthful of marbles when you smile with your mouth shut."

She looked at Marjorie.

Gwen: "He gets that from Adrian's side. That family are a right ugly bunch."

Connor promptly opened his mouth with a grin wide enough to fit in a baguette sideways and Gaz took a few photographs then ushered Mr Hicks in.

Gaz: "Old baker man, I'll have one with you by your cake."

Mr Hicks: "What about Eliza and Lydia? It's their shop and competition, after all."

Gaz tutted.

Gaz: "I s'pose. Come on then bomb woman and flicky hair, you can be in it an' all."

He signalled to Mr Hicks, Eliza and Lydia to stand behind the counter by the cake and took some more pictures.

Gaz: "Right that'll do; I's got places to be. Gimme yer words and I'll ask me boss to bung it in next week's issue."

Gaz flipped over the pages of his ring pad, shoved his camera back in its case then held his hand out to Eliza and she handed him her hastily written article which he stuffed in his pocket.

Gaz headed towards the door.

Gaz, waving: "I'm off... Yippee-Ki-Yay Mother Fu..."

All the adults screaming in unison: "GET OUT!!!"

Gaz tripped out of the door in shock and shook his head.

Gaz, mumbling: "Man, you village sort are so hostile."

Once Gaz had left, all attention turned back to Mr Hicks's wonderful prize. A triumphant Gwen took ownership of the cake, much to the dismay of Connor, and left promptly afterwards without even a passing goodbye to Eliza or Lydia. The remaining customers dwindled over the course of the next fifteen minutes, leaving Eliza, Lydia, Brian and Tom with Mr Hicks standing in the shop.

Brian: "Right, I must be away too; we've got a busy one tonight. Apparently, someone famous has booked. I left Carlos hollering at Clive about the lack of peppers."

Lydia: "I need to be off as well; I need to prepare for our night out. I've only got three hours."

Just as Lydia and Brian were leaving, they bumped into Dorothy who was hurrying towards the shop.

Lydia: "Hello Dorothy! I'm afraid I'm just on my way out. I have a face to prepare. Can we reconvene Monday or something?"

Dorothy: "Eh? Oh no, my dear, I'm not here to see you, though, it's always a delight to see your beautiful face."

Lydia: "Oh. Fair enough."

Dorothy: "Have I missed the cake?"

Brian: "You have. It was the most remarkable cake I've seen in years. It'll be in the paper next week, though."

Dorothy looked upset.

Dorothy: "Bother and damnation. Excuse me, I need to see someone."

She blustered past them and into the shop and bumped into Eliza and Tom who were just locking up.

Eliza: "Hello Dorothy! What brings you here? We've just closed, I'm afraid."

Dorothy: "Hello dear, is Mr Hicks in?"

Eliza opened the door wide and hollered towards the kitchens.

Eliza: "Mr Hic..."

Mr Hicks emerged from the back of the shop, smiling.

Tom tugged at Eliza.

Tom: "Mummy, I wanna go home. Me plates of wheat hurt."

Eliza: "Meat. Plates of meat. If you insist on using rhyming slang, at least get it right."

Tom: "I a child. I'm learning a second language."

I can see it now on his CV.

Languages spoken: English, Cockney and French.

Eliza: "Yes love, it is right up there with Spanish and Sanskrit. Come on, let's go home."

Eliza called into the shop behind her.

Eliza: "I've left it on the latch, Mr Hicks, if you'd be so kind to do the honours."

Mr Hicks did a thumbs up so Eliza shut the door behind Dorothy and set off home.

Dorothy stood, awkwardly, in the middle of the shop and wrung her hands, nervously.

Dorothy, stammering: "I'm so sorry... I was delayed... I had to finish the ironing... I'm mortified I missed your special moment."

Mr Hicks went over to Dorothy and laid a gentle hand on her shoulder to calm her down.

Mr Hicks: "Shhh, it is fine. I'll make more."

Dorothy looked up at him with expectant eyes.

Dorothy: "Really? Will you?"

Mr Hicks thought for a moment.

Mr Hicks: "Yes actually, I think I will. I'd forgotten how absorbing the whole activity was; I've missed it."

Dorothy's eyes lit up.

Dorothy: "That's wonderful!"

Mr Hicks: "On one condition, however."

Dorothy: "Oh, what's that?"

Mr Hicks: "You continue with your flower arranging."

Dorothy's face fell.

Dorothy, sadly: "Oh... I don't know. I don't have granny's vase anymore..."

Mr Hicks looked at her with concern.

Mr Hicks: "What happened to it?"

Dorothy, quietly: "Oh, oh. It got smashed."

Dorothy slumped in the Lloyd Loom chair and looked sorrowfully at her lap.

Dorothy: "I miss her. I've not seen her for so long."

Mr Hicks knelt and placed his hands gently on her knees.

Mr Hicks: "I know. Your Dot was a lovely woman."

Dorothy looked up from her lap and stared at Mr Hicks. She falteringly lifted her hand and lightly traced a finger down his cheek.

Mr Hicks caught his breath at her touch.

Dorothy: "She held you in very great regard. I should have listened to her."

Mr Hicks looked squarely at her.

Mr Hicks, quietly: "Listen to her now."

Dorothy and Mr Hicks remained, motionless, both scarcely breathing, looking at each other.

Mr Hicks broke the silence and spoke at barely a whisper.

Mr Hicks: "Be happy, Dorothy. It's all I've ever wanted."

There was a pause.

Dorothy, simply: "I don't know how to be anymore."

Mr Hicks sighed, heavily.

Mr Hicks: "I know. We've had our fill of heart ache but we're still alive. We're still here. You and I are, after all these years and everything that's happened, still standing. We still have passion in our hearts. We still have the ability to make our hearts sing, if we'd let them."

Dorothy, lost in her thoughts: "... like the sound of bird song..."

Mr Hicks: "Ye..."

All of a sudden, the rousing march of 'When the Saints go Marching In' started blaring out of Dorothy's handbag and they both jumped, startled.

Dorothy: "Oh... Oh... It's my mobile."

Dorothy gathered herself and scrabbled around in her bag.

She picked up her phone, breathlessly.

Dorothy: "... Hello? Oh yes, I know, I was called away. I'll come back now and do it... Sorry... Yes, I understand... I'll be as quick as I can..."

She hit end on the call and jumped up from the chair, leaving a knelt Mr Hicks looking up at her.

Dorothy's whole being had changed and she spoke in a staccato monotone.

Dorothy: "That was Kenneth. I have to go. I've left the iron out."

Without any further ado she brushed herself down and left the shop.

Mr Hicks remained in the middle of the shop on his knees and watched as she hurried out of the door and rush down the road.

He put his head in his hands and rested his face on the still warm seat and let out an anguished cry as he wept loudly into the cushion.

Poem: *Sanctuary*

Take me to a place
Warm, peaceful and calm
Take me to that place...

I sit back
And admire the view
I see the clouds scud by
Though there's only a few.

The air is pure
And the sky is bright
The sun warms my face
I feel full of light.

I inhale deeply
Invigorating every cell
It takes me to the place
I remember so well.

A place of knowledge
And of peace
Being in the now
All worries they do cease.

Drifting, peaceful and without a care
I am in that place
An inner oasis we all share.

Eliza Wakeley

Chapter Thirty

Sub quote for the day: *All you need is love. John Lennon*

Later that evening, Eliza opened the front door to her mother.

Eliza: "Hi, mum."

Eliza's mother: "Hello, Sparrow. Where's my little Tommy?"

I'm fine, thanks.

She looked around over Eliza's shoulder.

Tom came running up to her and scooted under Eliza's arm to get a hug.

Eliza's mother scooped him up and planted big kisses on his forehead. She placed him down and smiled fondly at him before letting herself be led by Tom into the house.

Eliza's mother: "'Ere, shall we carry on with that game we started on Thursday?"

Tom: "Yay! Come on. I pwepare the counters for us."

Eliza's mother and Tom darted off to his room to carry on with their board game.

Yes, it was a spectacular day, thank you for asking.

Eliza followed them upstairs to Tom's room and kissed him.

Eliza: "I've left food and all sorts out for you both. I won't be late."

Eliza's mother: "Don't you worry about us, love. You have a nice time. Let your hair down."

Tom: "I'll only get gwandma to text you if I get a decent score ok, mummy?"

Eliza: "Good idea. Let's not celebrate mediocrity. That's the problem with society these days."

Eliza went into her bedroom and weighed up the two choices of footwear she'd hooked out for the evening; her trusty boots or some bought-on-a-whim high heeled strappy shoes which had remained in their box since she bought them.

She slung on her boots and looked at her reflection in her cheval mirror.

Hmmm.

Nice. Comfy.

Have I slid in my slippered feet towards comfy footwear on a night out?

Eliza looked at a snoozing Ellington who was sprawled sideways, beside the bed.

Eliza: "What do you think, Ellington?"

Ellington raised his head in surprise at the sound of his name, looked at her and yawned.

Even the dog finds the ensemble uninspiring.

She took them off and strapped up her new shoes.

Oooh!

Eliza: "What do you think to these, Ellington?"

Ellington sensing a new scent got up and sniffed her feet. He started wagging his tail and roughly put his front paw on one in an attempt to bring it towards him.

Eliza: "Oi! Gerroff!"

Ellington then wandered over to the empty box, flumped down and started chewing the corner of the cardboard.

Well, they received more of a response.

I'll wear these.

Plus, I can't take them back now as Ellington has decided to eat their packaging.

There was a tooting of a horn outside the house and Eliza kissed Ellington and left him chomping on the box. She scooted downstairs, opened the front door and waved to the driver before hollering up the stairs.

Eliza: "The taxi's here. See you later mum!"

Eliza's mother's voice drifted down the stairs from Tom's room.

Eliza's mother: "Have fun!"

She threw her coat on, picked up her keys and started to run down the path. Four strides in, she lost her balance and grabbed onto the hedge.

Oh bums! I've forgotten how to walk in heels!

I need to take myself in hand.

It'll be elasticated waist bands and fleeces next.

Eliza cautiously aimed for the car, grabbing foliage on the way past.

Lydia was already in the taxi and she looked Eliza up and down as she gratefully clambered into the car.

Lydia: "Hello, darling, you look wonderful. You really should try more often."

Oh charming.

Eliza: "Thank you for the back handed compliment."

Eliza peered in the half light at Lydia who was done up to the nines.

Eliza: "Wow! You look stunning! Your eyes look amazing."

Lydia: "Thank you. They're called peacock feather eyes. I've got a new mascara. It cost twenty quid can you believe? If I'm not offered a modelling contract the instant I leave this taxi, I'll be very disappointed."

Eliza: "Blummin' heck! Twenty quid for mascara?!"

Lydia: "Beauty costs. It's all part of my new white room regime."

Eliza: "Cow calling must pay well."

Lydia: "It's like a bleedin' call centre in my lounge. I've run out of things to iron. I've even taken to pressing my pants; I must be a natural."

Eliza: "Who'd have known?"

Lydia: "I know. One never knows where one's talent lies."

They asked the driver to drop them off outside a pub in the centre of Billington.

Lydia: "Let's make this our first venue."

Eliza: "Ok. Please don't let me get drunk."

Lydia: "Yeah, yeah. Whatevs."

Eliza watched as Lydia strode up to the bar and men unashamedly stared at her.

What must it be like to engender that reaction just by walking into a room?

Eliza trailed up the rear, holding on to backs of chairs in order to maintain upright, and the same men smiled at her.

Ah, they think if they smile at me, it'll be a way to Lydia.

Little do they know if they ring the cow bell, she'll talk to them as much as they like.

A couple of minutes later, Lydia turned round and thrust a glass in Eliza's hand.

Lydia: "Surfer here bought us a drink."

She nudged a teenager who was sporting long floppy hair and was wearing shorts with espadrilles and a hoodie.

Surfer boy: "Yo."

Yo? What sort of greeting is that to another fully functioning adult?

Eliza: "Oh."

I can't even respond.

I'm out of my depth already.

Just drink your drink, Eli.

Eliza swigged a mouthful of her drink and gasped as it went down her pipes.

Eliza: "Blimey! That's strong!"

Lydia: "It's a big 'un. Make the most of a freebie, eh?!"

She's practised in the art of receiving drinks.

Surfer boy shoved forward one of his friends and he smiled awkwardly at Eliza.

Oh, really??

You look like you ride a skateboard.

Skateboard boy: "Yo."

Oh, another yo boy.

How simply charming.

Eliza: "Yes indeed, yo, and other such teenage colloquialisms."

Skateboard boy's brow furrowed then he smiled again at her.

Skateboard boy: "Hey! You're clever. Clever's sick."

Sick?

He'll be saying OMG next.

Where's my drink?

Eliza downed her drink and shot a look at Lydia but she was oblivious as surfer boy was showing her something on his phone.

Skateboard boy: "Do you want to have my number?"

Ooh they make them bold these days.

Eliza: "In case I need babysitter or my lawn mowed?"

Skateboard boy rubbed the meagre stubble on his chin.

Skateboard boy: "Nah, you misunderstand. Do you want to go somewhere with me?"

To the park?

Eliza: "It's very kind of you child, but no. I'm having a picnic with a Gruffalo."

Skateboard boy laughed.

Skateboard boy: "Ha! I love that book."

Eliza: "I thought you might. Do you read it before you go to sleep?"

A look of dawning crept across his face.

Skateboard boy: "Ah, I see what you're getting at. It's because you're old, innit?"

How very dare you!

Eliza spluttered and skateboard boy continued.

Skateboard boy: "You're ok, I like the mature woman and you look like you know a thing or two."

Oh, do I now?!

I don't know whether to be offended or flattered.

When did I cross the line from normal woman to older?

I have suddenly become acutely aware that vast swathes of the population are younger than me. I'm not happy about this. I might need to start hanging around bingo halls and garden centres in a bid to feel a bit better about myself.

Oh, he's still talking...

Skateboard boy: "Yeah man, get the mood right; the lights, the music, the am-bee-ance. It don't matter the age. It's all about the skills, you know?"

He started swaying his hips in what Eliza presumed to be a provocative manner.

I feel a fervent desire to hit you.

You're lucky I'm passive thanks to years of hippy chakra remodelling or you'd be in serious danger of a slap.

I need to stop conversing with an underling.

I've got Tom if I want to talk about Lego and Batman.

She tugged on Lydia's arm.

Lydia looked across from her conversation with surfer boy.

Eliza: "Can we move along, please?"

Lydia: "Eh? Oh, yes, definitely."

She turned to surfer boy.

Lydia: "Thanks for the drink and for showing me your phone game; truly gripping. But we must be on our way, I believe men whose balls have dropped require our attention."

Lydia downed the remainder of her drink, threw her glass on the bar, and whisked off out of the door.

Eliza was left stood with the pair of them.

Uh oh. I feel the need to leave things on a more polite tone.

That's my upbringing again.

I seriously need to have some sort of aversion therapy.

Eliza: "We're not really on the pull. We're just out for a bit of liquid relief as our shop has hit hard times and we can't find Hard Times which would, by all accounts, ease our ... erm ..."

I'm rambling.

Both surfer and skateboard boy were staring at her blankly.

I've gabbled them into a trance.

Surfer boy, breaking the lull: "… Hard times?"

Eliza: "Indeed… Goodbye."

Make a break for it.

Eliza waved half-heartedly at them both as she scuttled out after Lydia. She saw her frame striding confidently down the road.

Eliza: "Oi, slow down! I can't walk in me shoes! I've got to hold onto everything in grabbing distance in order to remain vertical!"

Eliza caught up with her as she was striding out towards the next bar in the street.

Eliza, puffing: "Blimey that was a bit rude!"

Lydia: "Eh? Ah, forget it. They need to get used to rejection. I'm teaching them a valuable life lesson."

Eliza: "Do I look like I've slept around?"

Lydia turned around mid-step to Eliza.

Lydia: "Are you kidding me?! Who said that?"

Eliza: "One of the yo-yos said I look like I know a thing or two about… you know."

Eliza widened her eyes, looked towards her nether regions, and wafted her hands in front of her pelvic area.

Lydia: "You can't even say sex, let alone look like you do it. Come on you silly bint, let's go in here."

Lydia dragged Eliza by the arm into the next bar. It was full of middle-aged men and they all looked up as they walked in.

Be careful what you wish for.

We've single-handedly reduced the average age in here by twenty years.

Lydia, whispering to Eliza: "Ooh, this must be what cowboys feel like when they walk into the saloon in a new town."

Eliza, whispering back: "I feel ill at ease. I think I preferred the children's club."

Lydia: "Just one and we'll move on."

Lydia strode confidently to the bar and Eliza scurried up and stood next to her.

Eliza: "I'll get these."

Lydia: "Ok... What?"

Lydia felt a tap on her shoulder and swung her head round.

A tall man in his late fifties with a goatee beard and bald head smiled enigmatically at her.

Eliza followed Lydia's gaze.

Aren't they a bit outdated? I thought goatees went out in the noughties.

It's all about the big beards these days.

Grizzly Adams would get the girl if he went out on a Friday night, make no mistake.

Goatee beard: "Lydia?"

He had a deep voice like treacle and it made Eliza's stomach lurch slightly.

Oooh, he's very manly. All grrrr.

I'll overlook the outdated beard on account of the voice.

Eliza looked at Lydia and saw that she was staring up at him and had gone the colour of a pillar box.

Lydia, shrilly: "Tony?"

The man smiled, nodded, and stared deep into her eyes.

Perhaps Tony: "Ah, my Lydia. Ma grande petite mort."

Oooh, foreign.

He's really rather bewitching in a highly unexpected way.

I feel a bit quivery.

Lydia groaned and continued to stare, transfixed at the man.

Eliza nudged her and Lydia shook herself out of her stupor.

Lydia cleared her throat.

Lydia, with a voice travelling up and down several octaves: "Eli, this is Tony. We used to be... er... friends."

Tony gently ran a finger down Lydia's arm and she jumped like a cat on a hot tin roof.

Definitely Tony: "Ahhh, I believe it was slightly more than friends."

Lydia, quickly: "Yes well, whatever."

Oh, crikey.

He's not what she normally goes for. He's not remotely good looking.

But there is definitely something very debilitating about him.

He exudes sexual power.

I've never encountered someone so seductive before.

I almost feel compelled to take my clothes off right here and now.

Maybe he's a real-life master man; like in those books.

Perhaps he makes normal women who are happily doing their washing up one minute, suddenly feel the need to whip off their rubber gloves and sprawl spread-eagle on the worktop.

Tony: "Are you married?"

Both Eliza and Lydia shook their heads, mutely.

Tony winked at Eliza and smiled a beguiling grin at Lydia.

Oh, he meant Lydia.

Stupid me.

Of course, he did.

Tony licked his lips, suggestively, and leant towards them both.

Tony, slowly and quietly: "How fortunate. Two beautiful ladies available in one night. What more could any man wish for?"

I do believe my innards have just turned to jelly and have left my body.

It's the manner with which he commands.

I would never in a million years do what he's intimating, it's just the way he says it.

I think he could be saying what he's putting in a sandwich and it'd have the same effect.

Perhaps, even just the word.

Eliza: "Can you say sandwich, please?"

Tony looked somewhat surprised and raised one eyebrow.

Tony: "As the lady wishes… Sandwich."

Yep, I was right.

It's anything he says.

Eliza: "Thank you. I was just checking something."

Tony stood back and sighed heavily.

Tony: "I am otherwise detained this evening so I must leave you to make your own conviviality. Isn't life inconvenient sometimes?"

Eliza and Lydia both nodded at him.

He turned his attention to Lydia.

Tony: "Seeing you again brings back many happy memories… till we meet again."

He picked up Lydia's hand and kissed the back of it, gently.

Tony: "Bonne soiree, ma grande petite mort."

Tony swept away from them back to a booth where he was sitting, hidden behind a pillar.

I can't cope.

He's too much.

Eliza: "I need a drink."

Lydia exhaled a massive sigh.

Lydia: "Ditto. Make it a double."

Eliza motioned to the bartender and he lined up two drinks for them which they both took a gulp of.

This is the last one.

It's not good for my chakras drinking like this.

They moved to a table and flumped into a couple of chairs.

Eliza: "Who is he?"

Lydia: "He was my first love."

Eh?

Eliza: "I thought Alex was your first love."

Lydia: "Oh yeah, I forgot about him. I've had lots of first loves."

Eliza: "That one was a bit potent."

Lydia: "You're telling me. He's spellbinding even now. As a young woman I was buggered."

Oh.

Eliza pulled a face.

Lydia: "Not literally, you silly mare. I mean, I didn't stand a chance. I was completely under his charm."

Eliza: "Why did it end?"

Lydia: "I had a visit from his wife."

Ohhh.

Lydia: "I knew he had one but she had just been the word 'wife' until I met her. She then became a person. She was lovely and I realised I couldn't continue, no matter how intoxicating he was… is."

Eliza: "Did she stay with him?"

Lydia: "I don't know. Tony and I were meant to meet up to go for a weekend away to Great Yarmouth; she paid me a visit the day before we were due to go. I felt so awful, I didn't show up. He tried calling me for months after but I ignored his calls. It was a tough one to get over but even though it was the right thing to do, I've regretted standing him up. I met Roy not long after and, as you know, the rest is history. I can't be around him for long, I might not be held responsible for my actions. Can we drink up and move along please, darling?"

Eliza: "I agree. I nearly disrobed there and then… Down the hatch."

They downed their drinks and Eliza patted her chest and tried, but failed, to let out a lady like burp.

Eliza: "I think we are the sort of people I've read articles about. Perfectly normal women during the week then they go out and drink a bottle of vodka on a Saturday night."

I'm being a bit generous with the 'perfectly normal' bit.

Lydia: "I blame men. They're invariably the reason why women end up face down in the gutter with their dresses up round their ears and a pair of perfectly good shoes, ruined."

I'd be quite grateful to have these ruined.

The balls of my feet are killing me.

I am beyond the period in my life where uncomfortable footwear is acceptable.

Eliza: "Indeed. Where to next?"

Lydia: "Take me to Vertigo."

Eliza: "Ok, but for god's sake don't let me anywhere near the pole."

Lydia: "Understood."

Amount of regret at wearing ridiculous footwear: *Total.*

Chapter Thirty-one

Sub sub quote for the day: *I couldn't repair your brakes, so I made your horn louder. Steven Wright*

They turned the corner to the road where Vertigo was and were greeted with a massive queue.

Lydia: "Good heavens! Have we mistakenly ended up in Ibiza?!"

Eliza and Lydia looked at each other and shrugged.

Eliza: "It wasn't anywhere near this busy last time I came."

Eliza took in the array of looks sported by the occupants waiting in the queue. You could see the styles that had been attempted but it was safe to say it was all a bit bargain basement. Many a magazine had been pored over and styles emulated but on a budget.

I've wandered into the land of make believe!

Fake tan, eyelashes, fingernails, eyebrows, bosoms, extensions and pouts!

When all that comes off at the end of the night it must fill a room!

If this keeps up walk in wardrobes will become walk in body part rooms.

They'll swing open the doors to reveal mannequins with stuck on extras. There'll be ones for different looks. Wednesday would be big bum and boob day with individual false eyelashes... Thursday is no boob day with full eyelashes and shellac nails.

They joined the end of the queue and Lydia tapped the shoulder of the girl in front of them. Her ample bust was spilling over a very unforgiving red body-con dress. She was wearing platform shoes so high her feet resembled hooves. She topped the look off with massive henna red hair, which framed a face full of cheap make-up and over lined lips.

Why would you do that?

We can all see you've got a thin top lip like the rest of us.

You look like a caricature.

Jessica Rabbit – the bankrupt years.

Lydia: "Hello. Why is it so busy?"

Jessica Rabbit blinked eyelashes that narrowly missed sweeping the pavement.

Jessica Rabbit wannabe: "Derrr! It's because of Barney. He's doing a PA."

Barney the Dinosaur is visiting Vertigo?

I can't imagine he'd cope with the pole very well.

He's got quite a paunch on him.

Lydia: "Oh, I don't like him very much. He's a bit full of himself."

Eliza: "I know, but he teaches children quite well. Tom loves him."

Lydia: "Does he? I didn't know he had any educational merit, whatsoever."

Eliza: "Oh yes. Tom learnt all about Irish country dancing from him."

The girl in front looked round at her in astonishment.

Jessica Rabbit wannabe: "Barney does Irish country dancing?"

Eliza: "Yes. His legs are a bit short to get his knees up so he just jiggles about a bit on the side-lines. He has a troupe of girls doing the arms-by-their-sides jumpy bit."

The girl looked at her friend and they pulled out their phones, got YouTube up and whilst waiting in the queue, did a search for a clip.

Jessica Rabbit wannabe: "Bugger me, Becca. I've got to see this."

Becca: "God yeah, Jade. I thought I knew all there was about Barney."

They waited a couple more minutes in the queue when Eliza felt a tap on her arm.

Tapper of Eliza's arm: "Eli?"

Eliza: "Yes. Oh! Hello Neville!"

Stood beside her was Neville in top to toe khaki.

Neville: "How brilliant to see you again! You look as gorgeous as ever. You're brave coming back here, after last time!"

Eliza: "Indeed. I'm not going near the pole; Lydia wants to pay a visit."

Lydia: "Hi plate licker. How's the doll collecting going?"

Neville, correcting her: "Memorabilia. I've had success with a couple more items, thank you. I've had to put them in the loft now, though, as I've run out of wall space."

He looked up and down the line of people waiting to enter the club.

Neville: "Would you like me to get you in?"

Eliza and Lydia looked at each other and grinned.

Eliza and Lydia, in unison: "Yes please!"

Jessica Rabbit (who we now know is called Jade) turned round and curled her over-emphasised top lip.

Eliza ignored her and looked at Neville.

Eliza: "How can you do that?"

Neville: "I'm dating one of the resident podium dancers now. I only nipped out to get her some plasters as her shoes are killing her. I did tell her to wear them around the house for the day so they'd stretch but she said four-inch stilettos would damage the lino."

Eliza: "Does she yodel?"

Neville rubbed his hands with glee.

Neville: "Like a professional! She's also very good off-piste. Nothing is out of bounds!"

Eliza: "Well, lucky old you. You certainly came up trumps there."

Neville: "I have indeed. Have you met anyone else?"

Eliza: "No. I'm still on my own."

Neville: "Perhaps you might catch Barney's eye."

Oh, that's just lovely.

You get a sex charged dancing skier and I get a purple dinosaur.

Lydia coughed and nudged Eliza.

Lydia: "Bored now. Can we go in, please?"

Eliza: "Oh sorry, yes. Thanks Neville."

He started to lead the way and Jade caught her eye.

Eliza: "Neville! This girl and her friend are with us too. Can they come in as well, please?"

Neville turned round.

Neville: "Huh? Oh, I s'pose, but let's get you in quick before Ramone goes on the door. He's a bit petty minded."

Jade and Becca jumped with excitement, did a thumbs up at Eliza and hurried along behind them.

As they jumped the queue Becca and Jade looked at the waiting line with superiority.

Becca: "This is the best night ever!"

Jade: "I know! If we get to talk to him, shall we ask him to do Riverdance?"

Becca: "God yeah. Wait!! Stop a minute...!"

All five of them stopped in their tracks.

Neville, Eliza, Lydia and Jade: "What?!"

Becca, in a sing song voice: "Selfie time!!"

Jade: "Yay!!"

Neville, Eliza and Lydia: "Eh?"

Becca and Jade struck a well-practised pose and pouted for Becca's held aloft mobile.

Lydia put her hands on her hips.

Lydia: "Oh, for goodness' sake. This is your fault, Eli; picking up a couple of strays."

Eliza: "Sorry. I was feeling charitable."

Neville: "Hurry up or I'll get into trouble!"

Neville got to the front door, had a word with the woman at the entrance and a couple of moments waved them through.

Once inside, Becca and Jade said thank you and raced off to find Barney.

Neville: "I'll try and catch up with you later. I must give my beloved these."

He held up the plasters.

Eliza: "'Ere Neville, please can I have a couple before you go?"

Neville: "Of course, gorgeous. Here you are."

Neville handed her a couple of plasters and rushed off to find his girlfriend.

Eliza and Lydia looked around and took in the place. It was absolutely packed. Most of the guys were stood around the bar area and most of the women had gravitated towards the right-hand corner where groups of scantily clad girls were pushing each other and bouncers were stood in front of a stage, facing them.

Lydia: "Must be for Barney. Drink?"

I feel uneasy with the number of strangers packed in such a confined area.

I'm happiest in a wide-open field or beach.

Either I'm turning very anti-social or I have spread my wings and have become a true hippy.

I would definitely find flip flops more appealing than these efforts, that's for sure.

Eliza nodded.

Eliza: "Drink."

A man nudged her on the way past and she nearly lost her balance. She looked at his parting frame and snarled with irritation.

Close your eyes sober fairy.

I feel the need to numb the antagonism which is starting to flow through my veins. I'm not able to cope with people in such close proximity.

Would a true hippy punch a bystander for no more reason than being in the vicinity?

I think I need to recognise I require a bit more personal development before I'm the Dalai Lama.

Lydia had pushed her way to the front of the bar and was gesturing at the bartender.

Eliza stood rooted to the spot willing her drink to come quickly.

What shall I do whilst I'm waiting?

Oooh, I like this song.

I'll have a little dance.

That frees the mind and the limbs.

Eliza started swaying to the beat of the track. Her head began to bob about, then it worked down to her arms and they started jiggling. Then she started wiggling her bottom.

Oh yeah. This is perking me up.

Get my hips moooving!

As Eliza got more into the beat, she looked to what a girl over to her right was doing.

Oooh, I can do that.

I have happy feet.

Eliza studiously copied the girl and then let rip with her own moves as the track built to a crescendo.

Lydia pushed her way back from the bar and stared, wide-eyed at a flailing Eliza.

Lydia: "Jeezus woman! Are you having a turn?!"

Eh?

Eliza: "You want me to turn?"

Eliza jumped up in the air and attempted a three-hundred-and-sixty-degree mid-air turn.

She failed. This, however, did not prevent her from having another go.

I know what I did wrong. I didn't find my spot.

Eliza fixed her stare on the podium dancer and then had another attempt at doing a mid-air turn, this time she whipped her head round halfway to fix her eyes on the podium dancer again.

Ooh that hurt a bit. I might have done a bit of damage to my neck.

That may require a bit more practice.

I'll try and do a few mid-air turns a night before I go to bed.

The music sped up in tempo and Eliza went back to her manic dancing.

Oooh I've got happy hands to match my feet!

Lydia, stood back to avoid being whacked in the face by Eliza's thrashing arms.

Lydia: "What the hell are you doing?"

Eliza: "I'm lost in the groove!"

Lydia shook her head in dismay.

Lydia: "Do you want to borrow my sat nav so you can find your way back to the beat?"

Lydia pulled at her and thrust her drink in her face.

Lydia: "Stop doing that, it's upsetting me. Drink this."

Eliza: "Eh? Oh ok. I am a bit puffed and I think I may have inadvertently given myself whiplash."

All of a sudden, the music stopped and an almighty racket started blaring out of the speakers. A DJ started speaking at a level so loud, the words rolled into one in.

Do you have to have it so loud?

We are literally feet away from you, man!

We don't all want tinnitus for the rest of our lives!

Eliza: "What's the man on the microphone saying?"

Lydia concentrated.

Lydia: "...something... television... something else... Barney... some other indistinguishable utterings... give it up for... "

All of a sudden there was utter mayhem as scores of girls screamed at the top of their lungs.

Lydia: "Shit me! Have some decorum for fuck's sake women!!"

Eliza: "All this for a bleedin' dinosaur?!"

Lydia looked at Eliza with bemusement then a look of realisation crept across her face and she started laughing.

Lydia: "You silly mare! Barney from 'Bright Lights of Bolton' is here. He's the fit one who takes his shirt off at every given opportunity; not Barney the bloody dinosaur!!"

Ohhhh.

That makes a bit more sense.

Bright Lights of Bolton?

Eliza: "What's 'Bright Lights of Bolton?'"

Lydia: "Do you live in a cave, darling? It's that reality show about this group of men who are bricklayers. It follows their everyday lives."

How thrilling.

Eliza: "How does that make worthy television? I can go down that new estate in Billington and watch that."

Lydia: "They go out with women who have completely new bodies thanks to plastic surgery. They all cry a lot, go to the gym a lot and get engaged, unengaged and pregnant a lot. They build a few houses and Barney takes his shirt off, even in sub-zero temperatures, to pour concrete foundations. It's won industry awards."

Shoot me now.

I have no place in this world.

All of a sudden there was a BOOM and from behind a black curtain pranced on a guy in his early twenties with an oiled bare chest. He had rolled up jeans and sandals on. He smiled at the assembled crowd and revealed neon white teeth.

He looks like he's just come ashore.

I was not aware that Bolton was on the coast.

Ooh, he's got Greek Gary teeth.

I wonder if he also had them done at the same place 'what done, Jordan's.'

He arrogantly stood in the middle of the stage posing and nodded at his audience.

He lifted up a microphone and hollered into it.

Barney: "Yeah, this is why you come! Feast and enjoy! It's all about the Barney!! Built like a bear, hugs like a bear and makes lurvvve like a bear…"

Lydia muttered under breath at Eliza.

Lydia: "… Shits in the woods like a bear…"

Eliza muttered back at Lydia.

Eliza: "… Steals your picnic like a bear…"

How does a bear actually make love?

I don't suppose he has the faintest idea.

Him with his geographically incorrect attire and ridiculous teeth.

No-one in Bolton has the requirement for teeth like that.

Honestly, what a complete idiot.

The DJ spoke up.

DJ: "Yeah, let's hear it for Barney from BLOB!"

All the girls screamed with excitement.

Barney piped up again whilst still maintaining his pose.

Barney: "Yeah man. I'm your Barney from BLOB, laydeees!"

BLOB?

Eliza looked with confusion at Lydia.

Lydia: "Bright Lights of Bolton. They shorten it so stupid people can spell it."

Well, that wasn't very well thought out.

This must be what an alien would feel like.

I feel completely thrown by what is happening in front of my eyes.

Am I the only sane person in this room?

Lydia took in Eliza's nonplussed look.

Lydia: "Drink up, chicken. It's a different world to the one in which we dwell."

Eliza nodded and knocked back her drink.

Vertigo will be the death of me.

Eliza stumbled slightly and was steadied by a young guy next to her who was staring appreciatively at the overconfident posturing of Barney.

Steadying Guy: "Ooh, whoopsy daisies. You nearly went there, love."

Eliza: "Sorry, I've had a couple and I'm not good on heels."

Steadying Guy nodded at Barney.

Steadying Guy: "He's something else, isn't he?"

Eliza: "Indeed. He does rather love himself."

He nudged her and leant in, conspiratorially.

Steadying Guy: "I read about him in the paper. He's a bear alright; he sounds like he's got a right old temper on him. Apparently, he punched a milkman in the face for delivering semi instead of skimmed. I blame years of steroid abuse. He does, however, have the best pectoral muscles I've ever clapped eyes on. I'm in touch with my feminine side so I can say that without feeling any loss of masculinity. Alpha males don't get the women; men that make the bed and cook do. Men should be wary wearing a frock, though. I can tell you from experience, that's pushing the envelope for many women."

He stood aside and presented himself to them and continued.

Steadying Guy: "You'd never know from looking at me but I knit. It calms the mind and keeps the fingers nimble. It also generates blankets for the homeless; so it's worthy, as well as relaxing."

Eliza and Lydia stared; slack jawed at him whilst he wittered on.

Lydia nudged Eliza.

Lydia: "Drink?"

Eliza nodded then announced to anyone within earshot.

Eliza: "I need a wee."

Lydia: "Ok, darling. I'll make this one a coke then meet you by the bogs."

They both completely ignored Steadying Knitting Guy and went their separate ways. As Eliza made her way to the toilets, she randomly grabbed passers-by to keep herself upright and maintain forward momentum.

Eliza: "I do beg your pardon... Sorry... Excuse me..."

She accidently tugged out a girl's hair extension and they both looked at it in horror.

Eliza nearly dropped it with surprise.

Eliza: "Urgh! Oh, my goodness, I thought that was attached! Isn't hair normally kept on by some means? Like your scalp or something?"

The girl whose extension had been unceremoniously yanked out by a heavy-handed Eliza, spat at her with distain: "Give it here, you clumsy cow."

Eliza lobbed it at her and carried on her way to the toilets.

When she got there, she joined the queue and watched in amazement as girls fought for the mirror to daub more make-up on their faces.

It's not a wise move. These lights aren't favourable for blusher application.

When it was her turn, she gratefully threw herself into a cubicle, locked the door and rested her head against it.

I do believe I am a bit drunk.

I can hear swishing in my ears but my brain is still.

Eliza looked down and started to fumble around.

Hang on where's me buttons?

Do I have buttons on this dress?

How did I get it on?

Ooh, I'm feeling a bit scared.

I can't recall how to get out of this dress and I'm desperate for a wee.

I must not drink any more.

I've lost the ability to work clothing.

She looked around helplessly at her dress and in the end just hauled it up and went to aim at the toilet.

She looked round to lift the seat and was greeted by a massive poo the previous occupier had left.

Oh, that's just charming.

Eliza turned round, had a grateful wee and flushed the chain.

As she shimmied down her dress, she looked down the pan.

The poo was still in there.

Oh brilliant.

I've got to sort that out now.

I can't leave here with that still in there in case the next person thinks it's mine.

She tapped her foot and looked around the cubicle whilst she waited for the cistern to fill up. On the back of the door there was an advert which she read.

"Do you suffer with erectile dysfunction? We can help…"

Hang on. Am I in the wrong loos?

Eliza opened the cubicle door and poked her head out and a girl ran forward to take her place.

Eliza: "No! I'm not coming out! I'm just checking I'm not in the gents. Go back!"

Eliza waved her back and shut the cubicle door in her face and heard the girl muttering "stupid bitch" under her breath as she walked back to wait her turn.

So, it is the ladies.

I think they need to have a word with their marketing department with regard to their targeted promotion campaign. At no point in my life will I ever have a requirement to have my penis looked at.

Hang on.

I'm still in the toilet.

Why is that?

Oh yes, I'm on poo patrol.

She listened to the cistern and decided that it had filled up enough to give it another go.

She flushed again and crossed her fingers.

It wasn't shifting,

Go down, you bastard!

What did the maker of that eat for heaven's sake?

Lead based cake?

The flush ended and it was still sitting in the bowl.

One more bash and then I'll have to think of something else.

She lowered the lid and sat on it, waiting for the cistern to fill up again.

Well, isn't this the most wonderful evening?

I've got shoes I can't walk in

Three-hundred-odd-degree mid-air whiplash.

A dress on that I don't know how to work.

And Barney the milkman bashing, bare-chested building bear from Bolton is in the house.

I think this may be the point in my life I decide to rethink my path.

When I'm old and batty, I'll tell my carer in the home that it was when I was sat on Vertigo's toilet looking at an advert for erectile dysfunction waiting for a stranger's poo to go down the U bend that I decided to take stock of my life. I'll tell them that it was at that point I decided I would no longer leave the house unless it was for emergencies.

The cistern stopped and Eliza stood. She lifted the lid and flushed it again.

Go down!

Aargh! I hate the person who generated this!

How can you blithely go about the rest of your evening and leave me to deal with it?!

At what point did that become socially appropriate?

I am rapidly finding out I'm living in a world I don't understand.

Full of people who speak in a language I don't understand, who find people like Barney wonderful and leave poos for passers-by.

I've been in here ages.

I need to give up.

I can't stay in here all night.

Eliza admitted defeat and pulled off a load of toilet paper and threw it into the bowl.

She let herself out. The next woman in the queue was a tall brunette with long brown hair down to her bottom. Eliza went up to her.

Eliza: "Just for the record, that poo isn't mine."

The girl looked at her with distaste and went into the freshly vacated cubicle.

Eliza fought her way to the taps and washed her hands. She caught sight of her face in amongst the sea of youth and sighed.

I don't belong here.

I want to go home.

She pushed her way out of the toilet and when she got out, looked for Lydia.

She saw her with her back to the toilets a few feet away and rushed as fast as her shoes would allow and tapped her on the shoulder.

Eliza: "I'm so sorry I was in there so long. I took ownership of a massive poo and have spent the past ten minutes trying to flush it down the pan!"

Lydia turned round, smiling.

As she turned Eliza's face switched to horror as the person in front of her was revealed.

Her mouth fell open and one of her knees gave way.

Lydia caught her and steadied her.

Lydia: "Are you alright, darling? I was wondering where you were. Look who I've just found!"

Eliza nodded and stared at who she'd found.

Jude.

He looked at her and smiled, cautiously.

Lydia: "I need a wee now. Hold these will you. I'm off to venture into the depths of the ladies' bogs."

Lydia slung the drinks at her and left Eliza and Jude staring at each other.

Eliza: "He... hello! Oh my god. You heard me say about the poo! Forget you heard that. It wasn't mine so you don't need to remember anything about that..."

Jude raised his eyebrows and continued to smile at her.

Shut up Eli.

No more drivel must exit your mouth.

He's here. In person. His body. His face.

Aww, his crinkly eyes.

He's just a lovely as you remember.

Jude: "Hello Eli. Fancy seeing you here. Are you a Barney lover?"

He's talking to me.

I think I might be sick.

Breathe.

Eliza: "I thought he was a dinosaur. Why are you here? Are you a BLOB watcher?"

What a truly scintillating conversationalist you are, Eli.

"Are you a BLOB watcher?"

Really??

Jude: "Er no, I can't say I am. I'm here tonight in more of a professional capacity."

Just then Gaz rolled up to them.

Gaz: "Hey, twice in one day?! Are you stalking me, bomb lady?!"

Go away paper boy.

Can't you see I'm talking to the man of my dreams?

Eliza: "Ha ha, aren't we funny? Don't you have friends you need to be with?"

Gaz: "No, I'm here working. I's on a journalistic mission, innit."

Eliza: "Off you go then."

Gaz remained where he was and looked at her then at Jude.

Piss off!

Gaz: "Barney won't talk about that model or the milkman incident but says he'll cover all other questions."

Stop talking and go away!

Eliza: "Why are you telling me this?"

Jude replied.

Jude: "Ok, we'll cut those questions, though to be honest they're the only thing that would make the article interesting. How about you get a couple of pictures of him on stage and we can pad it out with that. Let me know when you've finished with the photos and I'll come over for the interview."

Huh?

Gaz: "Sure thing, boss."

Huh?

Gaz melted back into the crowd and left Jude and Eliza stood together.

Eliza: "You're his boss?"

Jude turned his attention back to her.

Jude: "Indeed."

Eliza: "You work at the Billington Gazette?"

Jude: "Indeed."

Eliza: "I Googled you. You didn't come up."

Aarrgh.

Cease wordage.

Jude cocked his head and looked at Eliza, enquiringly.

Jude: "Did you now?"

Retrieve the situation before he calls the police.

Eliza: "Can I just say at this moment in time I'm not fully aware of my verbal functions. Please don't judge me on what comes out. My brain and mouth are polar opposites at present due to my inability to cope with alcoholic beverages. I've had a peculiar evening so far. I met a man earlier who only had to say the word "sandwich" and I'd take my pants off. That's quite a disconcerting position to find yourself in."

My mouth is a liability. It's official.

Jude raised his eyebrows again.

Jude: "I can imagine it would be."

They were interrupted by the tall brunette with poker straight hair down to her bottom. She smiled at Jude as she approached.

Jude straightened up.

Jude: "Ah, brilliant you're back."

Huh?

You again!

It is absolutely not brilliant you're back.

Who are you?

Activate 'rival woman' radar.

Ping... Radar is assimilating visual information.

Height: Perfect.

Weight: Perfect.

Hair: Perfect.

Dress sense: Tut. Perfect.

Result of 'rival woman' audit?

I hate her.

You complete and utter fool, Eli.

He's found someone else. Of course, he has.

He's perfect. She's perfect. They are both perfect.

I could cry.

I'm so far from perfect it's laughable. I can't even work my clothing.

Poker hair brunette: "It's chaos in those toilets and they're disgusting. Can you believe some filthy tart was in there for ages and left a ruddy great poo down one of the loos?"

Eliza looked down at her feet.

Jude: "If you'll excuse us, please Eli, I was only waiting here for Charlotte. I've got to go."

Eliza looked up to see Jude smiling at her, kindly.

Eliza: "Oh, oh of course. Sorry."

Those eyes.

Sigh.

I'm screaming inside.

I want Charlotte-long-hair to disappear.

I want to talk to you.

I want to see you again.

I want you.

Jude: "Bye Eli."

Well, that's that.

Again.

I think I am definitely going to cry.

Eliza gave him a sad smile.

Eliza: "Bye Jude."

As Jude and Charlotte turned away from her, she heard Jude speaking to Charlotte as they merged into the crowd.

Jude: "Thank goodness you returned when you did. I got caught by someone I really didn't want to see again."

Charlotte: "That woman you were talking to. She was the one who left the poo."

Eliza's heart stopped; she suddenly felt sick.

He hates me.

I had my chance and I blew it.

He doesn't know his note went in the bin.

And now he's got a perfect girlfriend.

This is horrible.

Lydia blustered up to her and reached out for her drink.

Lydia: "Jeezus, I'm high on hairspray fumes. I feel quite dizzy."

I know the feeling.

Eliza: "Hit me, please, Lydia. Hard enough so I pass out."

Lydia: "Don't rely on me for anything at the moment, darling; my aim would be diabolical. I just got chatted up by a woman in there and gave her my number. She had a wonderful pair of knockers. I'm turning into a lesbian when I'm drunk. I'd not give bosoms a second look in the cold light of day but I was positively drooling in there."

Eliza's eyes hadn't moved and they bored into where she'd seen Jude merge into the crowd.

I need to go home.

Eliza: "Can we go home please, Lydia? I feel a bit wobbly."

Lydia looked at her.

Lydia: "You do look rather pale, darling. Ok. Let's call it a night and go and find a taxi."

They finished their drinks and Eliza looked around frantically as they left. Torn between desperately wanting to see him again and feeling completely rejected.

Eliza: "Hold me up please, Lydia. I'm unstable in every respect."

Lydia: "Of course, darling. In drink as in life, we'll be a mutual support for each other."

Lydia hooked her arm through Eliza's and led her past the stage on the way to the exit. Barney, who had now left the stage, was signing Becca's bra and could be heard as they tottered past.

Barney: "What you on about, laydee? Barney ain't no Michael Flattery. Barney don't do no Irish jigging."

I could step in at this point and correct matters but I have decided my life is in ruins so meh, as you were.

Barney looked across at Eliza and Lydia and shouted out to them.

Barney: "Hey laydees! Do you wanna make your friends jealous by sayin' you had a hug with Barney?"

Huh? Oh you?! You stupid idiot of a man.

Do I look like someone whose friends would be jealous that I met a non-famous, famous man like you?

Eliza looked him square in the eyes and hollered back to him.

Eliza: "Sorry, Mr Egotistical-BLOB-man, but I rather like milkmen. They are bastions of British life and should be treated with respect. They also get up very early in the morning and should be excused for accidently picking up the wrong bottle from the van; not threatened by a baby-oiled ball of muscle who wears inclement clothing. Plus, skimmed milk is rubbish in your tea so he was doing you a favour."

Barney looked at her with utter astonishment, unaccustomed to any form of refusal.

He brusquely waved Becca off and stood as he faced Eliza.

Barney: "That milkman, he were asking for it laydee. He'd been goading me for weeks with his... "Do you want bread?" ... "Do you want pastries?" ... I kept saying to him "Nah man, all I want is the skimmed." He weren't stopping with the selling of his wares. It wore me down, laydee. I don't need peddlers upsetting my mind; I have a body to maintain. I'm wheat intolerant; I can't be crumbling to the lure of the bread. It's like offering an addict a needle, innit? It's just cruel. When he gave me the wrong lactose I just flipped. I saw red."

You complete and utter cock.

Eliza: "You poor lamb. On a good note, you have, however, made me reconsider my feelings towards Barney the Dinosaur as I'd find a hug from him more preferable to you even with the paunch. Plus, he's educational. There's nothing educational about signing women's tits. Good evening to you."

Barney turned to Becca who still had her bosoms thrust in his signing direction.

Barney: "She must be frigid. Move along, you've had enough time with the Barney. I got other fans I need to gratify with my presence."

All he's got is a chest and an ego.

A bouncer came up to Eliza and Lydia and put a guiding hand under each of their elbows.

Bouncer: "Come on ladies. I think it's about time you both called it a night."

Lydia: "Don't bundle me in with old motor mouth here. I was just standing there!"

Bouncer: "You might wanna keep a bit of an eye on her in future. We can't be having disruption with our guests."

The bouncer continued to guide them towards the exit.

Eliza: "Yes, well he probably wants to keep his offers to himself."

As they were being chaperoned out, Eliza saw Gaz, Jude and Charlotte stood round the back, behind Barney. Gaz was writing feverishly onto his ringed note pad. Jude smiled broadly at her, winked and gave her a thumbs up.

What?

What have I missed?

Eliza: "Please, Mr Bouncer can I just go back and see that man? I need to speak to him."

Bouncer: "I think you've said quite enough. Come on. Out you go."

Eliza: "Are you Ramone?"

Perhaps Ramone: "Yer, why?"

Eliza: "Neville said you were lovely and not remotely petty minded. Please let me just go and speak to him. I'll be one minute."

Ramone: "That geeky twat?! Out!"

Meh. Neville was right.

Give him a lanyard and he thinks he's god.

He unceremoniously shoved them out of Vertigo's front doors and stood in the doorway, exerting his presence to ensure they didn't try and go back in.

Lydia grabbed Eliza by the arm and started walking off towards the taxi rank.

Lydia: "For the record, I would have quite liked a hug from him. That's never going to happen now thanks to you and your runaway gob. We might have to consider sticking duct tape over your mouth next time you drink. What do you reckon?"

Eliza: "I consider it to be a shrewd idea."

Why was Jude so happy when I left?

Oh. It's because I was leaving.

Forcibly leaving.

He was happy I was being thrown out of Vertigo.

Oh. That's not good.

Number of times the benefits of becoming tee total considered in the past half an hour: *Eight hundred and fifty.*

Number of times sworn under breath about agonising footwear: *Eight hundred and fifty.*

Chapter Thirty-two

Sub sub sub quote for the day: *You know you're getting old when you stoop to tie your shoelaces and wonder what else you could do while you're down there. George Burns*

The fresh air made Eliza and Lydia even more aware of their inebriated state and they doddered along to the taxi rank. As they passed the Merrythought Café they were surprised to see lights on and people sat at tables.

Lydia: "Dave's open late."

They pressed their faces up against the glass and watched through the window as Dave came out of the kitchens. He had an apron on over a white shirt and chef's trousers. He did a double take at the two figures pressed up against the window and a broad grin spread across his face as he spotted Eliza. He signalled for her to come in.

Lydia groaned.

Lydia: "Really? Do we have to?"

Eliza: "Come on, only to say hello. After the evening I've had, I feel quite buoyed at the patent joy seeing my face brings someone."

I feel wretched. If I go home now, I'll have to confront my own mind.

I'll delay that as long as possible, I think.

Lydia, tutting: "Ok. Two minutes."

Eliza nodded, pushed open the door and started to walk in. As soon as she stepped on the new highly polished, ceramic tiles she started to skid.

Eliza: "Oh!! Buggering bollocks!"

Dave watched in horror as Eliza grabbed the nearest man who was just about to suck up a forkful of spaghetti and skidded to almost full splits.

Eliza: "Flip-flopping balls!! I think I've done myself a permanent!"

Dave came hurrying over.

Dave: "Oh my goodness Eliza! Here, let me help you."

Lydia had remained in the doorway and was bent double, laughing.

He thrust a chair under Eliza's bottom and went to check on the spaghetti sucking man who was now coughing, wildly.

Eliza sat splay legged on the chair and started to rub her inner thighs. Unaware of her unladylike stance courtesy of the amount of alcohol she'd consumed.

Eliza, inelegantly: "Oi, Cowbell! Get yourself in here but take it steady. It's like a bleedin' ice rink!"

Lydia knelt and crawled across the tiles on all fours until she reached Eliza.

Eliza: "I think I've pulled something."

Lydia: "Well it's certainly not a man."

This, I am painfully aware of.

Eliza: "Welcome to my life. The only thing I can pull on a night out is a muscle."

Dave came over to a still crouched on all fours Lydia.

Dave: "Sit on a chair for Christ's sake, Lydia. You're drawing attention to my floor choice."

He thrust one at her and she plonked herself down.

Lydia: "I don't think covering your floor with Teflon was the wisest move."

Dave: "It's quick with the mop."

Lydia: "How many injury claims have you had?"

Dave: "Only two so far. I think I might have to get mats. I'll have dialogue with Health and Safety when they do their next check-up."

Eliza was still rubbing her thighs and Dave loosened his collar as he tried but failed miserably to divert his gaze.

Dave: "You look ravishing tonight, Eliza, if I may be so bold."

Eliza: "Thank you. A compliment at this particular juncture is gratefully appreciated."

Eliza looked around at the people eating.

Eliza: "You're open late."

Dave: "I know. I need the income due to the refurb so I'm trying out having it as a bistro in the evening."

Eliza: "Oh, that's a clever idea."

Dave: "It's proving somewhat hair-raising if I'm honest as the level of clientele alters after dusk. They expect a different level of cuisine."

Lydia: "You mean they want it edible and without a layer of lard on it?"

Dave: "Yes and with garnishes... Apparently."

He wiped his brow.

Dave: "Can I interest you in our evening menu?"

Eliza: "I'm not sure my innards can face food at the moment. I've had a bit of an eventful evening. However, at least I can rest assured that if you offer me a sandwich, I'll keep my clothes on."

Dave pulled his attention away from her lower half and flapped his shirt.

Dave: "Would you mind terribly stopping what you're doing with your thighs? I'm meant to be serving crème brûlée in a minute and I fear I may be hazardous with the blow torch. I need my mind fully on the job when dealing with such puddings."

Eliza: "Eh?"

She looked down to see her dress up round by her bottom with her hands resting on a thigh each, an inch from her crotch. She whipped her hands away quickly, yanked down her dress and clamped her thighs closed.

Eliza: "Oh good lord! I am sorry, Dave. I appear to be slightly puddled and neglectful of social graces. Forget you saw that."

Dave: "It'll be a struggle. I might choose to recall it after the crème brûlée. Pot of tea?"

Eliza: "Yes please. I think it prudent otherwise I might end up mooning out of the taxi without my knowledge."

Dave turned his attention to Lydia.

Dave: "And you? What do you want?"

Lydia: "I see the day hospitality continues through to the evening. I'll have a black coffee... You've pushed the boat out with the table decoration."

She pointed at a dribbling candle in an old wine bottle.

Dave: "It's ambient. Apparently, fifty-watt halogen is deemed inappropriate for eventide gourmet."

Lydia: "What's this?"

She picked up a minute jam-jar of tomato ketchup nestled amongst the condiments.

Dave: "Belinda decants our catering size sauce into them for the evening service. It's been a learning curve for her but there's been less wastage since she started using a teaspoon. I'll fetch your drinks."

He wandered off towards the kitchens and returned a couple of minutes later, balancing two mugs on a floor tile. Perched on the corner was a bedraggled strawberry with a dusting of icing sugar on it.

He plonked it down in the centre of the table. Eliza and Lydia looked down at it and then up at him.

Eliza: "Why?"

Dave: "Why what?"

Eliza: "Why a floor tile and not a tray?"

Dave: "It's all part of the dining experience. I was going to go for slate but I had a load of these left over. I'm thinking outside the box."

Lydia: "You'd be best off in one."

Eliza: "Your thinking might be a bit too far away from the box, Dave."

Dave: "Really? Fair enough. I've got a friend who lives near Delabole. I'll give him a call in the morning; see if he can help. I can use these in the gents; waste not, want not."

A diner at a nearby table raised his hand to get Dave's attention and he excused himself.

Eliza let out a big yawn which she didn't bother covering her mouth for.

I feel very sleepy all of a sudden.

I'm not used to being out in the evening.

Lydia: "Are you alright, Eli?"

Eliza: "I'm whacked!"

She leant her head heavily on one arm as she swigged her tea.

I could just drop off right here and now.

Ooh my whiplash neck has gone all weak.

Oh...

Eliza's head lolled off her arm and she smacked her brow on the floor tile tray.

Eliza: "OW!!"

Lydia: "Blimey! You silly mare! Are you alright?"

Eliza looked at her a bit dazed and rubbed her forehead.

Lydia: "It's that alcohol induced necrophilia thing you get. You need to get to bed."

Errr.

The tables around them stopped mid-chew and stared at them.

Lydia: "What? What are you looking at? Go back to your Beef Bourguignon on a tile. She's fine, she's just bit tired that's all."

Eliza: "Narcolepsy."

Lydia: "Eh?"

Eliza looked at the admonished beef eater.

Eliza: "I don't get the sudden urge to sleep with dead people when I'm drunk, she means I drop off not cop off."

Lydia: "Whatever, same thing. Come on, let's go."

Eliza nodded in agreement.

They threw their drinks money on the tile and crawled on all fours to the door.

I've had enough injuries for one evening.

Well, wasn't that a roaring success?

I've made a mental note never to venture out after dark again.

I have conceded that the going out part of my life is over.

Relief at removal of all clothing and falling into bed: *Absolute.*

Chapter Thirty-three

Quote for the day: When you have no winds, take to the oars. Anonymous

Early the next morning, Tom and Eliza were sat at the breakfast table. Eliza rubbed her forehead ruefully and Tom looked up, mid-munch, from his cereal.

Tom: "You've got a right bump there, me old finger and thumb."

Eliza: "Indeed. I hit it on a floor tile."

Tom looked concerned.

Tom: "You fell over?! What happened? Did someone put their foot out? Charlie did that to Lily at school. We all laughed but Miss Gardner told us off cos Lily hurt her face. Charlie a bit of a naughty boy. He got bad feet."

Eliza: "It was on the table. I didn't fall far just with a bit of velocity."

Tom looked confused.

Tom: "What a silly place to put the floor."

Eliza: "Lydia and I quite agree but Dave seems to think it is cutting edge evening tableware."

Tom ignored her and carried on eating his breakfast.

Eliza's fuzzy head tried to make some sense of the previous day's events.

I've got a headache.

I'm never drinking again.

I'm never going out again.

I saw Jude.

I saw Jude but rambled on like an imbecile.

I saw Jude and his girlfriend.

I feel a bit sick.

I am angry at the air for ruining my chance.

He doesn't know Henry threw him in the bin.

I told him I'd Googled him.

Oh Eli, you complete mental case.

No wonder he said to Miss Perfect he got caught by someone he didn't want to see again.

Eliza rested her head on the table.

Our shop has been the subject of village tittle tattle.

The villagers buy our cabinets in the hope they'll get a cream horn.

There's another shop near Billington which sells the same stuff... cheaper.

Eliza lifted her head slightly and took a glug from her tea before putting it back down on the table.

I need to know if we've been getting our stuff from there.

Surely not. It must be a co-incidence.

Lydia would have said.

It's Sunday. I shouldn't really contact Margaret - she'll probably be at some caravan conference.

I could text her. She's got a phone from the ark, though. Margaret's still coming to terms with the wonderment of fax machines.

Still, it's worth a go.

Eliza pulled her mobile towards her still resting head and texted her.

Tom: "Mummy, you in a bad way. You gone all floppy and I didn't get me fried brekkie. Ewwington and me not happy about that."

Tom looked down at a begging Ellington who was waiting for an interesting titbit to be lobbed his way.

You need to get a grip.

You can't change things. Jude is with her.

You've texted Margaret. There's nothing more that can be done about that at the moment.

Get on with your day with your doolally child and forget about everything else.

Eliza gingerly lifted her head from the table and nodded, carefully.

Eliza: "How about we go down the park and I shall make up for the lack of fried lard with a home-made roast later."

Tom beamed at her.

Tom: "Now you're talking. You're not a bad old stick, really."

Eliza: "Oh well, isn't that heartening to hear?"

Eliza picked up her phone and texted Lydia.

Eliza: "We'll see if Lydia and Freya want to come, shall we?"

A few moments later, Eliza's mobile sprung into life with The Girl from Ipanema blaring out.

I might have to swap this for something slightly more this century.

Eliza picked it up hastily to stop the racket from rattling her, already, delicate brain.

Eliza: "Hi Lydia. Did you get my text?"

Lydia's phone: "Yes, hence the phone call. I'd love to go to the park but unfortunately your cheating ex-husband is due in two hours at your house with old mardy bum and their newly delivered offspring, if you hadn't forgotten."

Aaaaargh!!

Eliza looked around the state of her kitchen, frantically.

Eliza: "Oh. My. God! I had totally forgotten!! Help me, Lydia! I have nothing in and the house is like a bomb site!"

Lydia: "Fear not, I spoke to Brian yesterday and he's bringing the food. Freya's going to stay at Roy's which I'm not very happy about but she's with me for Christmas so that makes me feel a bit better. Didn't your mum mention it last night?"

Eliza: "She said, see you anon. I don't know when anon is. I presumed that was next month. It always sounds a long way away."

Lydia: "I'll be over in an hour. I've got to meet someone first."

Eliza: "Who?"

Lydia: "Oh, er... an old friend. No-one important. You make a start on the house and I'll be over before you know it. I'll also pick up some bits as I'll be in town"

Eliza put down her phone to find Tom looking at her expectantly.

Eliza: "Your dad is coming over today. I forgot. Grandma is too."

Tom: "Oh yes. She said last night she was going off to get some shut eye and then we were going shopping before they all turn up. I forget; my memory is not as it was. My head is full of too much stuff now. I forgot where I put Bob the Builder, the other day. I found him in me PE kit when I got to school. I losing my mind; I blame the alphabet."

Tom clambered down from the table and looked himself up and down.

Tom: "I'd best put me glad rags on then."

He looked at Eliza.

Tom: "I think you have quite a lot to do. Cheddar Chicken and me will be in me room if you need us."

Eliza: "Cheddar Chicken and I, you mean."

Not Cheddar Chicken and me.

Tom: "You need to look at the state of yourself; you don't have time to sit about with him, mummy."

Just go, child.

I need to drag my bones and house into some semblance of order.

Eliza just pointed upstairs and Tom dutifully toddled up to his bedroom.

Times ran around house with arms in the air going "Aaargh": *Four.*

Times told to get a grip by child: *Four.*

Chapter Thirty-four

Sub quote for the *day: It is easier for a father to have children than for children to have a real father. Pope John XXIII*

Lydia looked out of Eliza's window to see Lewis and Geraldine faffing about outside the house, collecting all manner of baby paraphernalia from the boot of their boxy people carrier.

Lydia hollered towards the kitchen

Lydia: "Warning! Brothers Grimm approaching!"

She took in Lewis's appearance.

Lydia: "What's happened to Lewis? He looks like a tramp. Has Gerry made him live in the shed?"

Eliza joined her at the window.

Eliza: "He's gone for the surfer look."

Lydia: "Does he realise we're seventy miles inland? That's one very big wave to run him aground that far. He may have been a boring fucker when he was with you, but at least he looked like he washed."

Yes, thank you.

Eliza: "He does have an air of vagrant about him, I do agree. Perhaps it's the late nights."

Lydia: "Maybe she's like one those "feeders" you read about."

Eliza: "Eh?"

Lydia: "You know. Some men are like it; they get a perfectly normal salad eating woman who feels comfy in a bikini, they fall in love with her and then they make her eat pork pie and pizza for the next five years so she has to wear something akin to a burkha on the beach so no one else wants her."

Eliza: "Ah, yes. I know what you mean. Controlling types."

Lydia: "Yes, she is probably one of them. She made him leave you, didn't she? She probably thinks by making him look homeless it'll keep him with her. No one wants to date a hobo, do they? What's the prospects there? Though, how any man can take style advice from a woman who thinks it's socially acceptable to wear a ninety-eight percent polyester maxi dress, is beyond me."

A couple of minutes later, Lewis and Geraldine wandered down Eliza's path carrying a car seat with a blanket thrown over the top and she opened the front door to greet them.

Eliza, towards the approaching guests: "Hello, congratulations. Let's have a look at the little fella."

She ushered them in and Geraldine theatrically whipped the blanket off the baby carrier.

Eliza and Lydia, in unison: "Ohhhh!"

Christ on a bike, I wasn't expecting that.

That really is a face only a mother could love.

Lydia peered in at him and shook her head in dismay.

Lydia: "I've seen enough. You can put the cover back over him now."

Geraldine: "Oh, we only do that so the sun doesn't go in his eyes."

Lydia: "What are you going to do? Put sunglasses on him for the rest of his life? Probably best though if you put it back over him. We've got more people coming and some are of a sensitive disposition."

Geraldine: "It's indoors. He's fine now."

Lydia: "Nah, put it back over."

Geraldine looked around her.

Geraldine: "Where's the dog and cat? I don't want them near us."

Eliza: "Why, is he allergic to animals?"

Geraldine: "No. I just don't want him breathing in their germs. Those things are riddled with disease."

I bet you're riddled with disease.

I'm quite put out.

Eliza: "They are living creatures and for the record they have had their jabs and are wormed regularly. Tom's grown up around them."

Geraldine: "That's your choice if you want to expose your child to such dangers. Lewy and I, however, wish to be cautious."

Oh yes, Lewis is very cautious. So cautious, in fact, he didn't have anything to do with his child for years.

Eliza stared at Lewis to step in.

Sort your ignorant girlfriend out. She's not even two feet over the threshold and she's insulted three of its inhabitants.

Geraldine: "I don't want Tom touching him, either. Children never wash their hands properly."

Make that the whole household.

Lewis, sensing imminent uproar: "Gerry, he'll have to get used to all those things in his life. He won't live in a bubble. Hello, by the way."

Geraldine: "I've told you, Lewy. Precaution. Eliminate the dangers as far as possible."

Lydia: "Yeah, Lewy. Life's all about taking precautions. I bet you think about that quite a lot now."

Lydia raised one eyebrow at him and catching her look, he looked at his feet.

Poor child. The odds are stacked against him from the outset.

Eliza: "Right well, allow me to bleach the house and remove all animal dwellers and you can come through."

Geraldine: "Bleach isn't required. Just give me a packet of anti-bac wipes and I'll just go over where we're sitting."

Cheeky cow.

Eliza made her way out of the room and left Lewis, Geraldine and Lydia standing by the front door.

Lydia, eagerly: "Hang on, I'll come with you."

Eliza and Lydia got into the kitchen and gasped, audibly.

Lydia, whispering to Eliza: "Some genes just shouldn't unite. It looks like The Grinch."

Eliza: "I don't think you're meant to say babies are ugly. Isn't there some sort of law against that? Don't you have to say they're all beautiful?"

Lydia: "Darling, the poor child was doomed from the minute he was deposited out of that woman's womb; but on the bright side, the NHS looks favourably on plastic surgery in these sorts of cases so he'll only have to endure a miserable childhood before he can get himself a new face."

They went in search of the animals.

Eliza located Norris who was peacefully snoozing on a dining room chair and picked him up. She carefully carried a still prone cat, with a lolling head, across the kitchen and with an elbow, opened the back door. She went outside and placed him carefully on top of the patio table. Norris, picked his head up, looked around at his new surroundings and mewed in dismay.

Lydia, meanwhile, prodded a foot twitching Ellington who had drifted off into a dream. Making a Scooby-Doo noise he sat bolt upright in shock with one ear up and the other, flopping. He looked around bemused as to why he'd woken with such a start.

Lydia: "Come on dog, you've been given your marching orders by old pernickety pants. You've got to play outside for a bit."

She ushered him outside to join Norris and he looked back at her with confusion.

Eliza came back in and called towards the front door.

Eliza: "Coast clear, you can come in."

Geraldine and Lewis wandered in and she gestured at Eliza:

Geraldine: "Wipes."

You truly are quite objectionable.

To think I felt inferior to you when you wore a black bra and straightened your hair.

Eliza threw the wipes at Geraldine and, due to the fact she was holding the baby, they whizzed past her left ear, missing by a millimetre.

Eliza: "Oops, sorry."

I think we both know that I'm not remotely.

Geraldine tutted loudly, put the baby on the kitchen table and went to pick up the wipes. Upon retrieving them she stuffed the whole pack into a pocket in her voluminous, misshapen cardigan.

Geraldine: "I'm off for a wee. Watch him will you, Lewy."

Geraldine then dashed off upstairs.

Lewis, Lydia and Eliza stood awkwardly in the kitchen.

Lydia, pointing at the baby carrier: "What have you called it?"

Eliza, quickly: "Him, what have you called him?"

Lewis, slightly uncomfortably: "Orson."

There was a moment's silence whilst this name choice was digested.

Lydia: "Eh? Why would you do that? As if he hasn't got enough against him already."

Eliza: "You what? As in Mork and Mindy; Orson?"

Lewis: "Er no, as in Welles. Citizen Kane is Gerry's favourite film."

There was a knock at the back door, Eliza looked out to find Philip standing there.

Eliza went and opened it.

Eliza: "Hello Philip. Would you like to come in?"

Philip: "Seasons of goodwill and other such niceties, my dear girl. No, it's just a fleeting visit to inform you that your dog is digging up my daffodil bulbs. Would you be so kind to call him in?"

Due to the ridiculous fence, Ellington occasionally wandered into Philip's garden, generally without causing any problem. However, he must have been annoyed at being roused from his slumbers.

Eliza: "Oh gawd, sorry Philip. I can't let him in, Geraldine is here and she's trying to protect her new baby from all living creatures."

Philip: "Is that the big old barge, your myopic ex-husband ran off with?"

Lydia burst out laughing.

Aargh, awkward!

Eliza, panicky: "He's here. In earshot!"

Philip, towards the kitchen beyond: "Oh, I do beg your pardon. No offence intended!"

Philip pulled a "whoops" face.

Eliza: "I'd put Ellington in the car but he chews the seatbelts. Can I put him in your house for a while please, Philip? We're having a bit of a Christmas get together, if you'd like to join us."

Philip: "Well, why didn't you say?! I'd be delighted to partake, my dear Eliza. I'll go and pop him in the kitchen and will return, forthwith."

He added pointedly towards the kitchen.

Philip: "Why anyone would leave you is beyond me, my dear. You epitomise all that would satisfy a man."

Dear me.

Lydia pulled a face and Lewis looked dispiritedly towards the back door.

Eliza: "Yes, thank you. See you when you've contained the dog."

Philip: "Righty ho. Back in a jiffy."

Geraldine came back into the kitchen.

Geraldine: "Your toilet won't flush properly. We need to move him, he's in a draught. We'll sit in the lounge. Can you turn the heating up, please? Babies need to be kept warm."

Ohhh right I see, you've instantly become an expert on babies within five minutes of shucking one out.

If it had escaped your attention, I have managed to keep my own son alive for four years without him catching frostbite.

Geraldine picked Orson up in his baby carrier and swept off back into the lounge and shouted over her shoulder.

Geraldine: "Lewy, warm some milk up for him. It's nearly his feed time."

Anything else you'd like done? Shall I peel you a grape?

Geraldine looked around the lounge with disapproval and called back towards the kitchen.

Geraldine: "It very cluttered in here."

Your face is very cluttered.

Lewis, was I really that bad for you to run off with such a despicable woman?

Eliza looked at him. He looked henpecked and miserable.

Oh, that's cheered me up a bit.

Eliza: "Right, I'd best attend to the toilet."

Eliza scooted off upstairs.

Lydia to Lewis, sarcastically: "You must simply adore your life."

Lewis sighed.

Lewis: "Gerry wasn't like this before. She was fun and carefree."

Lydia: "When was that? When you were married to Eliza?"

Lewis, sadly: "You'll never forgive me, will you?"

Lydia: "No, though you did her a favour. She's better off without you."

Eliza came back into the kitchen and was pushed out of the way by Geraldine, whisking back in.

Geraldine, annoyed: "LEWIS! Why do I have to repeat myself, hmmm? It's not a particularly difficult request for you to warm up some milk, now is it? Why is your son still waiting? You're effectively starving him whilst making small talk. Now chop, chop."

She swept back into the lounge.

Lydia to Lewis: "She's just perfect for you. I couldn't be happier."

Lewis, sighing: "I'd better warm the milk or she'll really kick off. Eli, can you help me, please? I don't know what to do."

This, I am painfully aware of.

Eliza: "Give me his bottle, I'll sort it out."

Lewis gratefully handed Eliza a bag of paraphernalia he had over his shoulder.

Lewis: "Where's Tom?"

Ah, you finally realised your first born isn't here.

Eliza: "He's gone Christmas shopping with mum. They'll be back in a bit."

There was a knock at the back door and Philip had returned. Lydia swung the door open.

Philip: "Hello, dear Lydia, you look particularly bewitching today."

Lydia: "Cheers. Want a vol-au-vent?"

Philip: "You know what they say; the way to a man's heart is through his stomach. This certainly holds true for me."

He winked at her.

Lydia: "That's good to know; at least I know where to aim the bullet."

Philip paled, slightly.

Philip: "Ohhh."

He threw the vol-au-vent into his mouth whole.

Eliza handed the warmed milk to Lewis which he took gratefully.

Eliza: "Let's go through to the lounge, shall we?"

Philip picked up a mini-Cornish pasty from the kitchen work surface and led the way.

Philip strode over to where Orson was and caught sight of him.

Philip: "Whoaaaaah!"

With the surprise, he dropped the remainder of his pasty on him. He leant over and started roughly brushing crumbs away.

Geraldine, shrieking: "Get out of the way, you inept little man!"

Geraldine batted him out of the way and bent down and gently started removing bits of pastry from her baby's face.

Geraldine, cooing: "Poor wittle Orson, did nasty man dwop a pasty on you? We should smack him right in the face, shouldn't we? Yes, we should."

Philip whispering to Eliza: "Is that hers?"

Eliza: "Indeed."

Philip guffawed.

Philip: "Good Lord! I say, it must buoy you to know that the best years of your ex-husband's life are already past him. Look at what he's lumbered with now, my dear girl; a gargantuan woman who lacks any ounce of femininity and an alien offspring. It must truly warm your heart... Now where's the booze?"

I hadn't thought of it like that but now you mention it...

Just then the door rang. Eliza went over and opened it. It was Brian.

Eliza looked over his shoulder for Clive.

Eliza: "Hello. Where's Clive?"

Brian: "Hello poppet. He's had to visit his aunt who's got gout."

Eliza: "Which one?"

Brian: "Phyllis."

She led him through to the lounge.

Eliza: "I didn't know he had an Aunt Phyllis."

Brian: "Me neith..."

Just then a gurgling Orson caught Brian's eye.

Brian: "Fuck me! Those forceps did a bit of damage, didn't they?"

Philip laughed, heartily.

Gerry: "What do you mean? He slid out like an angel."

Lydia scrunched her face up.

Lydia: "I don't think angels slide out of there."

Brian looked around helplessly.

Brian: "Oh, only his head is erm... "

Eliza came to his rescue.

Eliza: "His head is on his shoulders. Just where angels have them."

Geraldine picked up Orson, cradled him and shoved the bottle of milk in his face.

Geraldine, cooing: "My bweautful Orson. You're so handsome, aren't you? Yes, you are."

Brian: "Pardon? Orson?"

Eliza and Lydia raised their eyebrows and nodded.

Brian: "Oh, that's very unusual. Hmmm, you don't get many of them outside of Ork."

There was an awkward silence, broken only by the gulping of a thirsty Orson.

Eliza looked around the room. Philip, Lydia and Brian were all staring at Orson whilst Lewis had slumped into a chair and was picking bobbles off his jumper.

That baby is certainly a show stopper.

Eliza: "Indeed you don't. Who wants cake?"

Grateful for a diversion, Lydia, Philip, Lewis and Brian all hollered with relief: "Me!"

On the way out, the doorbell went and Eliza was greeted by her mother and an exuberant Tom.

Tom: "We buy presents. I wanted lots but Gwandma not happy at price, she told me to stroll on."

Eliza's mother: "Hello Sparrow, it's madness out there. I need a cup of tea to calm my kundalini."

Eliza: "Your kundalini will need more than that in a minute. Come through."

Tom and Eliza's mother went through to the lounge.

Tom: "Oooh a baby!"

Eliza's mother: "Hello everyone. Ah, Lewis good afternoon and you too."

She sniffed in the direction of Geraldine.

Philip, Lydia and Brian all waved hello and Lewis scrabbled to his feet.

Lewis: "Mrs Turner, hello. Please meet my other son."

He motioned towards Orson who had just finished his bottle. Geraldine yanked it out and pulled him up hastily to wind him.

Eliza's mother's jaw momentarily went slack but she gathered herself quickly.

Eliza's mother: "Ooh, he's an interesting little soul, isn't he?"

Geraldine: "Yes, Christine. Isn't he the most beautiful boy ever born? May I call you, Christine?"

Eliza's mother straightened up.

Eliza's mother, tightly: "I'd rather you didn't. Mrs Turner is fine, thank you. My grandson, Tommy, is the most beautiful boy ever born but as his mother, I can understand your bias. What's his name?"

Everyone shifted, awkwardly.

Geraldine, proudly: "Orson."

Eliza's mother tilted her head.

Eliza's mother: "Come again?"

Lewis, sighing: "As in Citizen Kane, not Mork and Mindy."

I have a feeling you'll be tripping out that phrase for the next eighteen years.

Eliza's mother looked with uncertainty at Eliza who nodded.

I know mum. What can I say?

Eliza's mother, shrugging: "Oh, fair enough. These funny names are all the rage these days; I read about it in the Daily Mail. Of course, it's for people with affectations who insist on imparting their whimsical attitude on to their children without any consideration of school playground bullying and the limitations within the workforce. You'd never take a Managing Director seriously if her name was Elderflower, would you?"

Oooh, mum's on a roll.

Divert! Divert!

Brian got there first.

Brian: "Mrs Turner! I've got some tremendous Christmas nibbles in the car which Carlos has made. Would you mind terribly helping me put them on plates? You're marvellous at such activities."

Eliza's mother: "Eh? Oh, naturally Brian; I'd be delighted."

Brian cocked his elbow at Eliza's mother which she hooked her arm into and they went into the kitchen.

She could be heard whispering loudly into his ear.

Eliza's mother: "Fancy calling your child Citizen Kane. That's her, that is. Her and her over familiarity. Not even the woman in the post office calls me Christine and I've been buying commemorative stamps from her since 1986."

Geraldine's face turned to thunder and she looked sternly at Lewis who just shrugged.

Tom: "Can I hold little person?"

Geraldine: "Absolutely not."

Lewis: "Come on Gerry, he is his half-brother."

Oh. My. God. They're related!

This thought had never even entered my head before!

Tom, bewildered: "He's my brother? I not see mummy with fat tummy."

He looked at Eliza.

Eliza: "Well, sort of but we won't think of it like that. Let's just think of it as dad's other child."

Geraldine, pointedly: "Him not "it"."

I meant the situation but whatever.

Consider yourself lucky you're even in my house, you miserable old tart.

Lydia: "Oh god yeah, she'll not saddle you with that as a brother Tom, you're ok."

Tom: "Oh."

Philip had been watching from by the sideboard.

Philip: "It's confusing these modern relationship set ups, my boy. Just be safe in the knowledge you have an exceptional mother who is raising you marvellously and is gracious in the extreme. Not many women would let the tramp who stole her husband and who subsequently expelled a very disconcerting looking child into her home but your mother has and for that she has exceeded my already high opinion of her. The woman is to be worshipped."

Ohhh... and wait for the fall out...

Three... Two... On...

Geraldine, spluttering: "Expelled!! Tramp!! Lewis, I insist you do something, this instant! Not only did that man drop a pasty on Orson's head, he has insulted me. What are you going to do?"

Lewis clicked his neck as if limbering up.

Lewis, rather limply: "Steady on now, Philip. Geraldine has a lot on her plate at the moment. She's got post-natal things going on."

Geraldine gasped apoplectic with rage and thrust Orson at Lydia.

Geraldine: "Hold him."

Lydia pulled a very displeased face.

Lydia: "Oh. Must I?"

Lydia held Orson at arm's length and jiggled him, awkwardly.

Geraldine put her hands on her hips and squared up to Lewis.

Geraldine: "Oh I see. Everything's my fault, is it?"

Her lip curled and she spat in his face.

Geraldine: "You got us into this state. You and your... Cock!"

Ohhh!

Eliza covered an agog Tom's ears.

Lewis, stunned: "Now, come on Gerry. Don't use that word in front of Tom."

Geraldine: "Cock! Cock! Cock! What are you going to do, Lewis? I tell you what, shall I? Fuck all! Because that's what you always do. You're a useless, pathetic person who can't even stand up for me when I'm being insulted."

Brian came running back in with Eliza's mother trailing behind holding a cocktail sausage.

Brian: "Did I hear a lot of cocks?"

Lydia was still holding Orson at a distance.

Lydia: "You did. Gerry's lost it. She said the word fuck an' all."

Brian called over his shoulder to Eliza's mother.

Brian: "Brace yourself, Mrs Turner. The new mother is having a freak out."

Eliza's mother: "Oooh, lovely. Let me through."

Eliza's mother pushed past Brian and popped the remainder of the sausage in her mouth.

Lewis stood facing a thunderous Geraldine as her eyes bore into him, full of hatred.

Lewis, stammering: "I... I think you ought to apologise Gerry. You used filthy language in front of my son and wife."

Ahem. Ex-wife.

Lewis, continuing: "Eliza's been kind enough to let us be a part of Christmas proceedings and I don't think foul language is very lady like."

Geraldine breathed deeply with contempt.

Geraldine: "Don't you now? Well, you're a poor excuse of a man so we're a perfect fucking match, aren't we?"

Eliza quickly put her hands back over Tom's ears.

Eliza's mother stepped forward.

Eliza's mother: "Now, then young lady, I think it's time you took a hold of yourself. Young ears are present, as well as old, and none of us want to be privy to your domestic strife. If you can't be civil and eat this rather delicious finger food then I think you should go home and settle your differences on your own."

Geraldine snatched Orson back off Lydia.

Geraldine: "We're going. I trust you're coming with us Lewis or are you going to stay with your *wife*?"

Ah, that slip up didn't miss her then.

Lewis sighed heavily.

Lewis, flatly: "I'm coming."

Geraldine: "Good. Are you capable of picking the stuff up?"

Lewis ignored her and put Orson's empty bottle in the changing bag.

Geraldine looked on with Orson.

When he'd gathered everything, they headed silently to the front door.

Eliza, Tom, Lydia, Philip, Brian and Eliza's mother followed behind them and Eliza opened the door to let them out.

Lewis, sadly: "Sorry."

Eliza shrugged.

Lewis: "I hope you all have a Happy Christmas. See you soon, Tom."

Tom: "Yeah, ok. Don't bring shouty Gewwy though. She moody."

Philip: "Indeed she is."

Geraldine harrumphed and strode off towards the car with Orson without looking back.

Lydia shouted towards Geraldine.

Lydia: "Merry Christmas to you too!"

Brian, calling after them: "Na-nu na-nu, Orson!"

Geraldine put two fingers in the air and carried on walking.

Brian: "I think she meant this V sign."

He put his hands into an Ork hand gesture and Lydia shook his hand using a mirrored action.

Eliza's mother pushed her way to the front of the group, pulled a piece of paper out from her pocket, quickly scribbled on it and handed it to Lewis.

Eliza's mother: "Geraldine might want to have a go at this course. It's called 'Hormone levelling through the medium of dance - A guide to new mothers.' They run it down the old snooker hall in Billington."

Lewis looked at it.

Lewis: "Right, thank you Mrs Turner. It's got to be worth a bash. Happy Christmas."

Everyone else: "Happy Christmas!"

Lewis turned and followed Geraldine.

Eliza shut the door and leant against it.

Philip: "How he dipped his wick into that is beyond me. I'd never even get a flicker with that sprawled out in front of me."

Ohhh. An image I don't wish to have. Clear my mind... clear my mind.

He clapped his hands

Philip: "Right now then, fingering food you say? Lead me to it."

Glee at state of Geraldine now: *Unrestricted.*

Chapter Thirty-five

Sub sub quote for the day: *An obstacle is often a stepping stone. William Prescott*

Eliza was flumped on the settee having waved a reluctant Philip out of the door.

Tom was fast asleep in the shape of a starfish on the lounge rug with his head using a snoozing Ellington tummy as a pillow. Ellington's floppy jowls reverberated to his gentle snores and his legs were held straight out forming the arms of Tom's makeshift lounger. On Tom's chest perched a curled-up Norris who was purring in his slumbers.

All of a sudden, The Girl from Ipanema blasted out, shattering the silence and everyone leapt up with shock.

Oh, flipping flip-flops!

Eliza scrabbled around and picked it up, hastily.

She fanned her hands down and the other three settled back down to their dozing.

Eliza: "Oh! Hello Margaret! I didn't know you picked up messages on a Sunday."

Margaret's phone: "Hello dear. Geoffrey bought me a clever phone from the internet as I accidently dropped the other one down the chemical toilet in the caravan. I've been playing a game where you slice fruit with a swipe of your finger. It's frightfully clever, if a bit of a fruitless activity, if you excuse the pun. However, I've been married to Geoffrey for twenty-five years so I'm quite accustomed to undertaking activities which are a waste of time. I was going to call you tomorrow, anyway, but when I received your message, I decided to ring you straight away. I can't text; my forefingers are not dextrous enough for intricate screen movement. Swiping a watermelon has taught me that."

Eliza: "Oh, thank you. I had a lady in the shop, yesterday, and she said there was another place near ours which has opened and it was selling similar stock. She seemed to think we were getting our stuff from them."

Margaret: "Ah indeed, my dear. This was to be the purpose of my call to you tomorrow. When I was going through last month's accounts, I noticed that a number of items had been purchased from FunkyFurn. However, due to the lack of stock records I cannot tell what specific items are selling for but you're not making enough to cover outgoings, dear. I don't see any records for you opening a wholesale account, though. If you insist on buying retail and not wholesale from there you're going to be in hot water. It's not looked very good for the past few months and I can't stress enough the seriousness of the situation. How did your competition go?"

Eliza: "Alright. It would appear people only entered so they would be in with a chance of winning Mr Hicks's cake though."

Margaret: "Oh, I'm not remotely surprised. His baking abilities were the talk of Pilkington before the demise of his wellbeing."

There was a pause and Eliza heard muffled conversation before Margaret continued.

Margaret: "My dear, I need to go; Geoffrey says the volume needs to be turned up on the television. With regard to the matter to which our conversation originated. If you insist on purchasing further stock from FunkyFurn I would suggest you try and obtain a wholesale account. It's all looking a bit bleak my dear... Yes, Geoffrey, I'm coming... Pass me the remote for goodness' sake... There... On the side by the goldfish... No, not the lamp... Sorry Eliza, I must attend to domestic matters. I'll speak to you later in the week once I've finished last month's accounts."

Eliza sighed, heavily.

Eliza: "Ok Margaret, leave it with me. Speak to you soon."

Time wasting task of the day: *Downloaded fruit swiping app and spent half an hour playing it.*

Guilt at carrying out such a pointless activity: *Eighty percent.*

Chapter Thirty-six

Quote for the day: *The nicest thing is to open the newspapers and not to find yourself in them. George Harrison*

The next morning, Eliza stopped off at the newsagents on the way to the shop to buy a copy of the current week's Billington Gazette.

I wonder if the competition coverage will be good.

I wonder if I can see Jude's name in it.

She looked at the second page.

Editor: Julian Hardy

Marketing: Charlotte Anderton.

Nope...

Oh, hang on, what was that?

Eliza flicked back to the front page and emblazoned across the top was "Exclusive" and a picture of a bare-chested Barney on stage at Vertigo.

She scanned down and read the accompanying paragraph.

"It was the exclusive they all wanted but thanks to a female reveller's snub of Barney's advancements in Billington's top nightclub, Vertigo, last Saturday night; the Billington Gazette can reveal the real reason why Barney the star from Triffic Channel's hit show Bright Lights of Bolton, won't be appearing for the rest of the series. Turn to page 3 for more on this article."

Ooh something must have happened after we left.

Gossip. I like gossip.

Eliza paid for the newspaper quickly and ran into the shop. She slung the door open, ran behind the counter and turned to page three to continue reading the article.

The headline read "Wheat Intolerance drove Barney to the Brink of Despair" by Gavin Wild.

After an outburst at a female reveller who indicated she would rather be hugged by Barney the Dinosaur than him; Barney, 21, who often refers to himself in the third person, has booked himself into rehab to deal with his demons.

BLOB producers have issued the Billington Gazette the following statement:

"Since Barney opened up this weekend about the struggle he faces on a daily basis with regard to yeast foods, he has decided to admit himself into rehab in order to come to terms with his intolerance issues. He has found mornings particularly tough. Toast used to be the mainstay of his morning diet, however, since the diagnosis he has had to turn to porridge. This has severely impacted on his emotional wellbeing. As a result, he has relapsed on a few occasions and the bloating he received as a result made his life unbearable.

He acknowledges his behaviour towards the local deliverer of dairy products was unforgiveable but wishes to stress that this was as a result of consuming a bacon sandwich.

He requests privacy at this difficult time, but wishes to express his gratitude to his fans for the messages of comfort he has received since it has been disclosed that he won't be featuring in forthcoming episodes of Bright Lights of Bolton.

BLOB producers support him in his decision and look forward to welcoming him back into our bricklaying arms soon. Bolton's foundations depend on him!"

The Billington Gazette approached the milkman for his views on recent events and he expressed the following:

"Barney should have said. I stock a nice range of wheat and gluten free products. It really would have saved us all a lot of bother and dental bills. I'm on first name terms with my dentist now thanks to him and I've still got a dodgy molar. Here's hoping he sorts his head out. I must go, it's a warm day and my milk might curdle."

Erm.

Re-read the female reveller paragraph.

Eliza re-read the article.

Oh no, that is most definitely me.

Hmmm.

I might stick to non-alcoholic beverages in future.

Saying that, it doesn't matter because I'm never going out again.

I went out in a blaze of exclusive article glory.

That'll be something to tell my carer in the old people's home. I'll tell her the tale of Barney the bread intolerant bear and they'll go home at the end of a day's shift and tell their family about the batty old woman they look after. They'll think I made it up but everyone in Vertigo knows it was me.

Oh god. Jude knows it was me.

Hang on. Who wrote this article?

Eliza looked at the top of the article.

Gavin Wild?

Oh, Gaz.

Just then in blustered Lydia.

Eliza: "Have you read the paper?"

Lydia: "Eh? Oh no. I've been busy. I need a cup of tea; I'll go and put the kettle on then come and read it."

A few minutes later Lydia looked up from the paper.

Lydia: "Buggering balls, darling. You've sent him to rehab!"

Eliza: "It rather appears I was the catalyst for his stint, indeed."

Eliza looked around the shop and took in the stock.

Do it now. Broach it.

Eliza: "Have you been buying stuff from that new place in Billington?"

Lydia shifted uncomfortably.

Lydia: "Ah well, you see, I was going to talk to you about that."

I bet you were.

Eliza: "Crack on then, I'm all ears."

Lydia: "Well, you know I'm bezzies with Dorothy now?"

Eliza: "Indeed."

Lydia: "I was over there the other week and she was showing me her garden. Old Kenneth the Killjoy turned up. Well, you know, he leaves me a bit agitated. He's the reason why I started thinking about things and left the cellar."

Eliza: "Indeed."

Lydia: "I was expecting to be thrown out, as per usual and was already on my way to the door when he starting chatting to me about our shop and told me about FunkyFurn. He said it had just recently started up and I should take a look. He said it would open my eyes to the world of upcycling and preloved furniture."

Eliza: "Did he really?"

Lydia: "So I pootled along and god, Eli, it's amazing. It knocks our little shop into a cocked tin hat. I simply had to get some of the stuff."

Eliza: "That's nice. It also saves you from having to do anything."

Bit harsh, Eli.

Tone it down.

Lydia: "Well, there was that added bonus, yes. I have been very busy, darling. The talking to men was taking up a lot of time and I can't use the sander in case I miss a client."

Eliza: "I spoke to Margaret; we're paying over the odds for it. Why didn't you get a wholesale account?"

Lydia: "Well, that's the odd thing and why I've had to hike the price up in our shop. For some reason they won't give us one. I would have got away with it if old blabber woman hadn't noticed the other day. I had no idea people in this village would also go to Billington to get their furniture."

Eliza: "We do live in a society where we have cars, Lydia. It may be a bit backwards but they don't use a flippin' horse and cart."

Lydia: "Maybe you'll have more success. You're good at that sort of thing."

Am I? I don't feel I'm particularly adept at anything these days.

Eliza: "I might nip along today. I want to see it for myself."

Lydia: "Go now, darling. I'll man the pumps. You'll be blown away by the vastness of the place. It's truly marvellous."

Eliza: "I rather wish it wasn't marvellous, quite frankly. We're in the poop and fabulous shops opening up in the vicinity are not helpful to our coffers."

Lydia: "Oh, I didn't think of it like that. When you put it like that, it is a bit of a bummer."

Times shouted at Queen voiced sat nav for being too slow offering directions to FunkyFurn: *Six.*

Times threatened to throw her out of the window to see if she can work out how to find her way home: *Five.*

Chapter Thirty-seven

Sub quote for the day: *Defeat is not bitter unless you swallow it. Joe Clark*

Eliza parked up in the large car park behind FunkyFurn which was housed in a converted lace factory. Two brand new delivery vans with logos were reverse parked up to large open double doors to the rear. She sat in her car and watched two men with a trolley jack wheel a beautifully restored tallboy down a ramp and lift it into the back of one of the vans.

Blimey, this is all a bit efficient.

Right well, let's have a look at the competition.

Eliza locked her car and went to find the main entrance.

When she found it, she was greeted by a lobby area with a well-dressed woman sitting behind a leather topped writing desk.

Stretching out behind her were a series of individual room sets all decked out in various home furnishing styles and from differing eras. All were separated by thin walls at about seven feet high.

Well-dressed woman: "Hello, may I help you?"

Eliza: "Perhaps. Please may I have a look around?"

Well-dressed woman: "Of course. Take your time. Just call me if you require any assistance. My name is Francesca."

Eliza nodded and thanked her and wandered towards the room sets.

This is something else.

Eliza walked into the first room. There was a little plaque to the side which identified it as "Fifties Fever." The walls had retro wallpaper and an old radiogram in the corner. To the right was a reupholstered geometric patterned settee with tapered legs. Above it was a Sputnik mirror. To the left was a low teak sideboard and in front of the settee was a leaf shaped mid-century coffee table. The whole look was cohesive, co-ordinated and very well thought out. She looked at a sign on the wall which provided a cost for each item and also a complete room cost.

Francesca joined Eliza.

Eliza: "Wow, you can literally buy everything in the room!"

Francesca: "Indeed. People purchase the look, lock stock and barrel. It's proving very popular. We also have a team of experts who can lay the carpet, hang the wallpaper; everything really. We provide the buyer with a complete cost from the outset based on their room measurements. It's a complete design service. We specialise in renovated furniture and pre-loved items, restored to the highest standards by our dedicated team. If you wish to see them at work, they are based on the second floor."

As Lydia would say, this has knocked our little shop into a cocked hat alright.

Francesca: "Would you like a cup of tea, madam?"

Eliza: "Yes please."

I need one.

I need a face fanning service whilst you're at it.

Our shop is well and truly buggered.

There's absolutely no way we can ever compete.

We'll end up flogging Marjorie's bicycle pump wind chimes at this rate.

Francesca wandered into an adjoining room and Eliza followed her.

She found herself in a country style kitchen, complete with flagstone floor and a scrubbed pine kitchen table. There was a half-sliced loaf with an old knife positioned in the middle and a series of mismatched oak chairs placed around it.

The assistant was stood at a range and popped a brightly polished copper kettle on the hob.

Eliza: "Don't tell me you've got gas?"

Francesca: "Ha, no. This is electric. It's the look and lifestyle we exhibit in the design warehouse."

Eliza: "It is amazing."

Francesca: "I am lucky to work here for sure. I love it. When I've made tea would you like me to show you the other rooms?"

Eliza: "Yes, ok."

Francesca and Eliza wandered around the ground floor and Francesca pointed out objects of particular interest. In the Art Deco room, she highlighted the Lalique vase and Bauhaus chair they'd just got in.

Francesca: "Have you seen anything you'd like?"

Eliza: "Well, to be honest I came here on a fact-finding mission. I own a similar shop but it's nothing on the scale of this."

Francesca: "Oh really? Which one is that?"

Eliza: "Illusions of Grandeur Crafts in Pilkington."

Francesca: "Oh yes, I know you. I usually see another lady. You buy some of our shabby chic range."

Eliza: "Yes, that'll be Lydia. I was wondering if we could set up a wholesale account with you."

Francesca's amiable stance changed and she straightened up.

Francesca: "I'm afraid, madam, that won't be possible."

Eliza: "Oh, don't you have that facility then?"

Francesca: "Oh yes, of course. Just not for you."

Eliza: "Pardon?! Why not?!"

Francesca: "Oh sorry, I didn't mean to offend. I enquired previously when your colleague came by but the owner informed me to decline. You are, of course, more than welcome to purchase at retail prices. Follow me, I'll show you our range."

Francesca made off towards a corner of the warehouse.

Hang on, hang on.

Eliza: "Hold up. Why did the owner decline?"

Francesca turned back.

Francesca: "He didn't go into details, I'm sorry."

Eliza: "I'd like to talk to the owner, please."

Francesca: "Of course, madam. He doesn't spend his time here but I shall fetch you his details."

Francesca put down her cup of tea on a passing console table and went back to her counter.

She came back a minute later with a lacquered business card.

Francesca: "Here you are, madam."

Eliza looked at the heavy cream card and read the script. On one side was the name and title and the other the contact details.

Kenneth Cuthbert
Director
FunkyFurn Ltd

Eliza put her hand up to her mouth in horror.

Eliza, stammering: "How long have you been open?"

Francesca: "A few months, madam."

Eliza: "But he owns Cuthbert Promotions, doesn't he?"

Francesca: "That is correct. This is his little venture on the side, if you wish. Apparently upcycled furniture is a new found love of his."

I bloody bet.

Francesca smiled and looked wistful.

Francesca: "He has many enterprises. He is a true visionary."

Eliza: "Is he now? Thank you, Francesca, for your time. It's been a real eye opener."

Francesca looked slightly wrong footed.

Francesca: "Oh, erm... Wouldn't you like to see the shabby chic range for your little shop?"

Eliza straightened her shoulders.

Eliza: "No thank you, I've seen enough."

Eliza put down her cup of tea and wandered out of the shop.

Song playing on Francesca's Bakelite radio perched on top of the writing desk: *Don't look back in Anger. Oasis.*

Chapter Thirty-eight

Quote for the day: *Man is free at the instant he wants to be. Voltaire*

Dorothy stood in the lounge and looked around, taking in her surroundings. She looked out of the French windows at the garden and caught sight of the bird table.

She walked into the kitchen and went to the bread bin, pulled out a complete loaf of bread and began crumbling it into a bowl. She then went to the pantry and pulled out a bag of bird seed which was three quarters full.

She picked up the bowl and seed and went out into the garden, sprinkling them as she walked around the patio. She emptied the remainder of the seed and breadcrumbs onto the bird table and checked on the bird bath. She fetched the hosepipe, turned on the outside tap and filled it to the brim. With these tasks done she surveyed her garden and nodded to herself.

Dorothy muttered under her breath.

Dorothy: "Be free little birds and fly to where your hearts settle."

She went back indoors and locked the door. She walked into the hallway and looked around. A moment later she picked up two cases which stood beside the bureau and purposefully strode out. She slammed the front door behind her with finality.

As she stood on the driveway, she took a deep breath and exhaled long and hard.

Dorothy: "Be strong. Don't look back."

She walked briskly away to the waiting car.

She pulled the passenger door open and threw her cases into the back seat and collapsed into the passenger seat.

Dorothy: "It is done. Let's go."

Poem: *Beckoning*

A light so pure and loving
No room for doubt allowed
Believe my friend
As the time is coming
For you to be found
A life's purpose is calling
But what? You seem to ask
Be aware of your helpers
In whatever guise they take
They are here to help your journey
And the decisions you will make
Act with the best intentions
Love and healing in your mind
This love will manifest itself
My friend, you have been found.

Eliza Wakeley

Chapter Thirty-nine

Quote for the day: *To expect the unexpected shows a thoroughly modern intellect. Oscar Wilde*

Mr Hicks flicked up the valance and tucked it under a corner of the mattress in order to get a better view under the bed.

He crouched down and shuffled as close as he could beside the bed and reached his hands out underneath. He flailed about until his right hand finally found the box he'd been searching for.

He scuffled his knees backwards and pulled the box towards him but it caught on the bottom of the bed frame. As he leant down to free it, he caught sight of something and gasped.

He dropped his grip on the box and pulled the remaining sheets off the corner of his bed.

Mr Hicks: "Oh my goodness. It's Charles Dickens!!"

There under the corner of Mr Hicks's bed post was indeed Charles Dickens. Hard Times was being used as a prop to level the bed on a decidedly wonky floorboard.

Mr Hicks threw his hands to his mouth and muttered out loud.

Mr Hicks: "Please don't let there be any damage."

He bent over and gingerly lifted the corner of the bed with one shoulder under the frame and delicately pulled out the book from under the leg.

He inspected the top cover and sighed with relief that there was no obvious damage. He groaned as he straightened up and leafed through the old book.

The first page bore an inscription and a swirly signature with several pen underscores.

Mr Hicks started to shake and sat down on the edge of the bed.

Mr Hicks: "Oh my heavens. I am in the presence of antiquity."

He delicately put the book on his bedside and ran downstairs to find Eliza, who was quietly wandering around the shop picking up items and replacing them, deep in thought.

Mr Hicks emerged from the kitchens, breathless.

Mr Hicks: "Eliza. I have news!"

Eliza: "Do you? Me too. I hope yours is better than mine."

Mr Hicks: "I've unknowingly been on Hard Times!"

Eliza: "We all are. It catches up on you, doesn't it? The business is looking very bleak, Mr Hicks."

Mr Hicks: "No, no! I've been asleep on it. It's been propping my bed up! I wondered why it didn't rock anymore when I had... cough...erm...activity."

Eliza looked wide-eyed at Mr Hicks as the information filtered through.

Eliza: "You've found Dickens?!"

Mr Hicks: "I have!! Bunty must have put him under there to stop the noise. She was rather vigorous in that department. My sciatic nerve took quite a pummelling."

Too much information.

Eliza: "Go and get him. Let's have a look!"

Mr Hicks dashed off upstairs and brought down the book on one of his pillows and presented it to Eliza.

Mr Hicks, grandly: "I present to you a leather bound, first edition signed copy of Hard Times by Charles Dickens."

Eliza flapped her face.

Eliza: "Oh my flip-flopping heavens. I think I'm going to faint. I need to call Henry."

Eliza picked up the phone and scrabbled around trying to find the number on her mobile.

She unsuccessfully tried dialling his number five times before shaking her hands in frustration.

Eliza: "I'm a bag of nerves. Please dial it for me, Mr Hicks."

Mr Hicks nodded, took the phone and dialled Henry's number.

He handed the receiver to Eliza.

Eliza: "Hello Henry... yes, I'm fine thank you. Mr Hicks has found the book! ... Yes, really... Yes of course, I'll wait around... Ok, see you about five."

Eliza replaced the receiver.

Eliza: "It's safe to say he's quite excited."

Mr Hicks: "This could be the good news you were waiting for."

Lydia came running into the shop with a beam from ear to ear.

Lydia: "I have news!"

Eliza: "I do too!"

Lydia: "Me first."

Eliza: "Ok."

Mr Hicks: "If I may excuse myself. I was doing something before I found the book. I'll go back to it."

Lydia: "Book? You found the book?!"

Eliza: "That was my news! He's found Hard Times!"

Lydia looked across at the pillow with the book grandly placed.

Lydia: "Oh yeah! That's it alright. Dusty old thing. Have you called Henry?"

Eliza: "Yes, he's coming over later. What's your news?"

Lydia grabbed Eliza's arm, excitedly.

Lydia: "I'm happy to report that Clarabelle has left the field. I'm seeing someone now and I want to make a go of it. I can't be talking about hammer drills and ball bags now, it's inappropriate."

Hammer drills? Ball bags?

Eliza: "Oh I see. That was a bit quick. When did that happen?"

Lydia: "We went out before but, of course, it didn't work out. I've regretted my actions ever since I lost him. After seeing each other at the weekend we realised we had to be together. He contacted me yesterday and we met up. No one else comes close; we're like magnets to each other. I can't muck it up. I'm in my new white room and I am going to be pure."

Jude.

Eliza: "I thought he was with someone else."

Lydia: "Not anymore. He wants me. He couldn't sleep, apparently, after bumping into me on Saturday night."

I can't hear any more.

It's too upsetting.

Change the subject.

Eliza: "Oh well that's marvellous. When I went to FunkyFurn yesterday, I found out a bit more about it."

Lydia: "It's amazing, isn't it? Did you manage to get a wholesale account?"

Eliza: "Nope."

Lydia looked disappointed.

Lydia: "Oh. Why not?"

Eliza: "Kenneth has blocked us."

Mr Hicks had put his coat on and was walking through from the kitchens holding the box he'd found under the bed and stopped mid step.

Lydia: "Who?! Killjoy Kenneth? Dorothy's husband who said he wants to help us?! What's he got to do with it?"

Eliza: "He owns it."

Lydia's face fell, as did the box Mr Hicks was holding. The contents spilled to the ground and he muttered under his breath as he scrambled around picking them up.

Lydia: "Oh, are you alright Mr Hicks?"

Lydia and Eliza bent down to help Mr Hicks pick up the box contents and Lydia continued.

Lydia: "I don't understand. How can he own it? Why would he set up a business like ours but better? He said he was going to help us."

Mr Hicks straightened up, placed the box on the shop counter and sighed heavily.

Mr Hicks: "Ladies, I feel I may be responsible."

Song playing on Billington FM: *Is There Something I Should Know. Duran Duran.*

***

Kenneth flung his case on the mahogany bureau and stopped in the silent hallway.

Kenneth: "Dorothy?"

Something was different. It was too quiet.

Kenneth: "DOROTHY?! Where are you?"

He strode into the kitchen to find everything laid out as usual. He opened the fridge and all the food was neatly placed in the correct positions.

He nodded with satisfaction then looked around at the empty kitchen.

Kenneth: "Where the bloody hell are you woman? I'm sick and tired of this. Why aren't you here with my dinner on the table?"

He flexed his hands with annoyance and went into the lounge.

All the cushions were neatly stacked and surfaces dusted. His attention was diverted by movement in the garden and he looked out of the French windows. Jostling at the bird table were an abundance of starlings pecking at a mountain of seed which was overflowing onto the ground below. He looked closer and saw haphazard lumps of bread strewn around the patio.

He stood straighter and his muscles tensed.

Kenneth paced into the kitchen again and opened the bin lid.

Laying on the top was the empty seed packet.

He let out an almighty roar as his fury rose and ran upstairs.

He raced into the master bedroom and flung open Dorothy's side of the wardrobe.

The sight that greeted him physically winded him and he stumbled back and sat heavily on the end of the bed.

All of her clothes had gone.

She had gone.

She had finally done the unthinkable.

She had left him.

Poem: *Strength*

The pull it has gone
The eagerness to please
The irrational allegiance
That brought me to my knees.

The time has finally come
For me to stand up tall
And to look back at you
No longer an insurmountable wall.

The pain you inflicted

Will never be erased
But whilst there is life
I am determined to live it
To find joy and share
With those of a like-minded spirit.

As I go forward on my path
I thank you for the lesson
That time with you has brought
I know one thing for sure
I'll never tolerate what I did before.

Eliza Wakeley

Chapter Forty

Quote for the day: *Every moment is a fresh beginning. T. S. Eliot*

Dorothy sat on the edge of the unfamiliar bed and lightly stroked the creases on the cover. She looked to the ceiling.

Dorothy: "I did it, granny. I finally did it."

There was a gentle tap on the bedroom door and a head poked round.

Poking round head: "Would you like a cup of tea? I've also got some biscuits if you'd like?"

Dorothy: "I would love one, thank you, and do you know what? I am going to have a biscuit; I might even have two!"

The poking head smiled and retreated from the room and Dorothy was back with her thoughts.

She straightened up and inhaled deeply.

She smiled up at the ceiling again.

Dorothy: "Thank you, granny. You sent me darling Lydia. If you hadn't, I would never have seen the depths of Kenneth's contemptuous behaviour. How could he stoop so low?"

She shook her head in dismay.

Dorothy: "If only we could make it better for them, granny. They're such wonderful ladies. They don't deserve to be ruined because of him. Please help granny. Please."

She put her hands in silent prayer and kissed the top of her fingertips.

There was another tap at her door and the head poked back round, announcing tea was ready.

She smiled and went to join her host.

They sat in amiable silence as Dorothy delicately nibbled on her biscuit and sipped her tea.

There was a knock at the door and Dorothy sat bolt upright, startled. She involuntarily pulled her cardigan up around her neck.

Her host's brow furrowed and patted her gently on the hand.

Host: "Don't worry, I'll not let him in."

Dorothy nodded uncertainly and fiddled nervously with the buttons on her cardigan.

The host stood and went to answer the door.

Dorothy looked to the ceiling and pleaded to the air.

Dorothy: "Please don't let it be him. Make him stay away."

A couple of moments later her host strode back into the room, smiling.

Host: "It's ok, it wasn't him. I have something for you."

Her host reached into their pocket and pulled out a photograph and handed it to Dorothy.

Dorothy looked down and gasped with shock.

Dorothy: "Granny!!"

She looked up with astonishment. In her hand was the photograph of her beloved grandmother with her looking up, taken at the restaurant where they ate Dauphinoise potatoes all those years ago. The familiar image was no longer faded by years of tears but fresh and bright as if it had been taken yesterday."

Dorothy: "How? This was torn up!"

Host: "He said he'd found the negative in a box under his bed. He just dropped it round as he knew it would mean a lot to you."

Dorothy: "Oh but of course, he took the photograph. We'd had the most wonderful day. How did he know I was here?"

Host: "I hope you don't mind but I told him; he's been worried. We all have. He didn't want to intrude so just dropped it off but did ask one question."

Dorothy looked up from the photograph, expectantly.

Host: "He asked if you'd meet at the café in Billington. The one Eliza and Lydia go to, at eleven tomorrow."

Dorothy looked back down at her photograph and inhaled deeply. She put it to her mouth and kissed the image of her grandmother.

Dorothy: "I see. I am ever so tired. Would it be alright if I went up to my room?"

Host: "Of course! Treat this as your own. You are welcome to stay as long as you wish."

Dorothy: "You are a kind soul. I am truly touched by your humanity."

Host: "Dorothy, I have always been here for you and always will. I wouldn't have it any other way. After all, what is family for?"

Dorothy stood and hugged her host.

Dorothy: "Thank you."

Song drifting in from the kitchen: *Run for your Life.*
The Beatles

Chapter Forty-one

Quote for the day: *Holding on to anger is like grasping a hot coal with the intent of throwing it at someone else; you are the one who gets burned. Anonymous*

Eliza picked up the phone and dialled the number.

Eliza: "Hello Margaret. How are you?"

Margaret: "Hello Eliza dear, I was going to call you."

Eliza: "Mr Hicks has found the book! He's found Hard Times! Henry came over and valued it. He went a bit of a funny colour and is speaking to a few experts. This could be the lucky break we need. I went to that FunkyFurn and found out why we can't get a wholesale account. It's owned by Kenneth Cuthbert."

Margaret almost spat with contempt down the line.

Margaret: "Oh my goodness. That Kenneth Cuthbert has a lot to answer for."

Margaret huffed and continued.

Margaret: "He was a trouble maker from the outset, my dear. Far be it from me to cast aspersions but that man is conniving. What he did to Mr Hicks is unforgiveable."

Eliza: "Eh?"

Margaret: "Of course, you don't know the background, do you? Kenneth Cuthbert and Mr Hicks used to be best friends. They grew up together. Kenneth was always the leader and was invariably found up to no good whilst Mr Hicks trailed along behind. I'll never forget the time Kenneth stole all the vicar's wife's undergarments off the washing line and because Mr Hicks was a slower runner, he got the blame. Mr Hicks comes from good stock, you know? His family were very highly regarded. The same can't be said for Kenneth Cuthbert. Less said about his family the better."

Margaret paused, lost in reminiscence.

Margaret: "Anyway, Mr Hicks and Dorothy used to go out. They were a delightful couple. They were first loves. Everyone thought they'd end up together. Then Kenneth put his oar in."

Margaret sighed heavily.

Margaret: "Mr Hicks was about to propose, he'd arranged a special dinner and had made a beautiful cake. He'd placed the engagement ring on an iced cushion with filigree roses around the side. Dorothy always liked flower arranging you see. There were red ones, pink..."

Yes, yes, get to the interesting bit.

Eliza cut across her cake recollections.

Eliza: "What happened?"

Margaret's voice was full of disdain.

Margaret: "Mr Hicks had told Kenneth about his plans to propose. He was so excited. From what I have since gleaned, Kenneth then did the most hateful thing... He contacted Dorothy and told her Mr Hicks had been having... cough... relations with another woman, if you take my meaning."

Eliza: "Yes, Margaret, I get your drift."

Margaret: "Good, because whilst I'm becoming accustomed to speaking on a modern phone, I do still feel uncomfortable with modern parlance and Geoffrey's within earshot... Anyway, Kenneth told Dorothy that Mr Hicks had said he was only with her as he wanted to secure the bakery, and was seeing someone else whom he truly had feelings for. Dorothy knew they were best friends so had no reason to doubt the truth of his revelations."

She paused and huffed with anger before continuing.

Margaret: "Dorothy's family own quite a lot of property around Pilkington. Her parent's used to own the bakery which Mr Hicks bought. It transpires Kenneth had apparently had his eye on it for his new business. Because he lost out, Kenneth had to move his business into the new industrial estate on the outskirts of Pilkington. It has a terrible view. No one wants to look at a septic tank while they're at work, do they? He harboured a grudge and it would appear that Dorothy was the pawn in his sick game of one upmanship. He was used to getting his own way in that friendship and he wasn't prepared to let Mr Hicks win."

It's too much information for a weekday. My brain aches.

Margaret: "Kenneth made it up to hurt Mr Hicks. Dorothy was heartbroken; Mr Hicks was heartbroken. It was a dismal state of affairs. He had no idea what had happened. He sat for hours by that cake waiting for Dorothy but, of course, she never showed. He tried calling her and went round to her house but she refused to speak to him. It was at this time Kenneth seized his opportunity with Dorothy. I despise that man... Oh now, I'm getting upset. I can feel my rash coming on, dear."

Eliza sat in a state of shock.

Eliza: "I'm trying to take all this in. How did Kenneth get with Dorothy then?"

Margaret: "He lured her with his ways. He's so Machiavellian it gives me heartburn just thinking of the man. She was in a terrible state after hearing the news about Mr Hicks. She wouldn't eat. I've since found out that Kenneth would turn up, all innocent and coy with Shepherd's pie and would spoon feed her it. He's despicable. He did that to her; got the woman so low she couldn't feed herself. Then he pretended to be her saviour."

There was a pause whilst Margaret gathered herself, before continuing.

Margaret: "Then her beloved grandmother died. Shortly after that, I heard that she'd married Kenneth... The truth came out though, it always does."

I can't assimilate all this. It's all too much.

Eliza shook her head, trying to make sense of it all.

Eliza: "How do you know all this, Margaret?"

Margaret: "I used to do the accounts for the bakery; Mr Hicks and I became very close. In a strictly professional capacity, you understand. Geoffrey has his faults but we share a love of cribbage which is truly binding."

Eliza: "How did Dorothy find out?"

Margaret: "It was after Patricia left Mr Hicks. I do believe he loved her dearly but it wasn't the same. He was a broken man after Dorothy and Patricia was his support. She was a strident woman and he needed that. They were good companions and ran the business well together. That is until she ran off with that foreign waiter. I can't say I blame her, though. Mr Hicks was in the bakery all day, every day; it wasn't much of a life for her. Between you and I, dear, she did eat a lot of the stock. Her thighs truly suffered. I only hope she eats more salad now she's out in the sun every day."

Oh Margaret, you don't half go on.

Keep to the interesting bits, please.

Some of us are losing a business here.

Eliza: "Carry on."

Margaret: "Oh yes, sorry. Anyway, after the loss of Patricia to foreign climes, Mr Hicks's emotional wellbeing became quite fragile again. He and I were in the shop one day and we'd been going through the accounts as he'd decided to step down from running the bakery. Mr Hicks was very messy with regard to such matters; his cost of sales were all over the place and he started to struggle with pest control due to lack of management of his wholemeal flour. Had it been anyone else, I would have charged more for the extra time it took me to attend to his book-keeping. Geoffrey wasn't best pleased."

Stop rambling!!

Eliza: "Carry on, but with just the important bits, please. I'm running out of free minutes."

Margaret: "Sorry dear. I'll be more succinct. This day, when I was in the bakery; Dorothy's brother came in and asked if it was true that Mr Hicks was going to sell the freehold to Kenneth. Kenneth had asked Dorothy to put up the money as he wanted to put an offer in on the place. Of course, that wasn't the case. Mr Hicks told him that selling to Kenneth would be akin to selling to the devil after what he did to get Dorothy all those years ago. Kenneth Cuthbert only wanted Dorothy for her money; he's built his entire empire using the purse strings of the Hardy family."

Hardy? I recognise that name from somewhere.

Come on brain, think...

Oh, she's still talking.

Margaret: "Her brother is a lovely man. He's become fully aware of the depths of Kenneth. He's tried to protect her but you can only rescue someone if they allow themselves to be. Kenneth made her a virtual recluse. She's such a sweet woman but she's afraid of her own shadow these days because of him. She barely has any friends. He sees to that."

Eliza: "How awful for Dorothy. Oh, poor Mr Hicks. Why didn't Dorothy leave Kenneth as soon as she found out?"

Margaret: "Only she can answer that question."

Eliza: "This is awful. What a despicable man."

Margaret: "The book is your only hope I'm afraid, dear. You won't be able to compete with such a force. He now has the finances and business acumen to make anything he touches a success. I fear this may be the end for your delightful little shop. If you wish to undertake my advice, you should sell the book, clear the debts and try and get out an element of capital you put in."

Eliza shook her head in dismay. The writing was on the wall.

Our shop has become a statistic.

Eliza, sadly: "Ok Margaret, thank you. Pay yourself any outstanding invoices whilst you can and hopefully the revenue from the book will sort any other suppliers out."

She said goodbye and looked around the shop, sadly.

Just then Kenneth Cuthbert came striding into the shop.

I am not in the mood for you.

Or rather, I am just in the right frame of mind for you.

Block your ears good natured fairy – I'm gonna blow.

Eliza: "Well looky here. If it isn't just the person I was talking about. What do you want?"

Kenneth: "You insolent woman. Show some respect. No wonder your pathetic little venture is on its knees."

Eliza: "It is thanks to you it's on its knees, as we both well know. If you've come here to gloat you can just flip-flop off. You're not welcome."

Kenneth: "I've come for my wife. Where is she?"

He started to march behind the counter to the back of the shop.

Eliza blocked his path and started to shake with rage.

Eliza: "How dare you! You can't come in here throwing your weight around. You don't own this shop."

Kenneth: "Get out of my way, you stupid woman. You and your little tart of a friend should never have got involved with my wife and you certainly shouldn't have got involved with Mr Hicks."

He started to push past Eliza when the door of the shop swung open.

Eliza looked past Kenneth to find Jude stood in the doorway.

His voice was full of anger.

Jude: "Kenneth! Stop harassing Eliza this instant!"

Kenneth swung round and saw Jude who was approaching him.

Kenneth: "Eh? Oh, it's you. What's it got to do with you?"

Jude: "It has everything to do with me. It stops now. Do you understand? You've done enough damage to our family. She's gone and won't be coming back."

Kenneth: "Well we'll see about that, won't we? She'd never be able to live without me. She is my wife and she will do as I say."

Jude: "She's a human being with a mind of her own, not a possession. How many people's lives are you going to ruin on your warped power trip? I warn you now, Kenneth, if you so much as approach Dorothy again I will expose your dubious business practices in the Gazette."

Kenneth stood stock still; rooted to the spot.

Kenneth spoke with a voice like ice.

Kenneth: "Are you threatening me, Julian?"

Julian?

Jude shrugged.

Jude: "You can call it what you like. I call it honest journalism. I have contacts with the nationals and I would quite happily pass on all the information. It would make a lovely front page."

Jude and Kenneth stood in the middle of Eliza's shop, staring at each other; neither breaking the deadlock.

Kenneth relented first.

Kenneth: "Fine. I'd had enough of that ridiculous old hag anyway. Her obsession with her grandmother was most unappealing."

Kenneth tossed a look of distain in Eliza's direction and pushed past Jude as he left the shop.

Eliza and Jude stood facing each other in silence, both in a slight state of shock

They started speaking together.

Eliza and Jude: "I'm sorr…"

They both stopped.

Jude: "Can I sit down, please? Confrontation with that man can be quite wearing."

Eliza: "Of course."

She waved him in the direction of the Lloyd Loom chair which he gratefully flumped into.

Your beautiful little face is all sad and dishevelled.

I want to stroke it and give it butterfly kisses all over.

Eliza: "Why did he call you Julian?"

Jude: "It's my name. My parents are keen Beatles fans and I was born at the time Paul McCartney wrote "Hey Jude." I've always been called Jude."

He smiled and continued.

Jude: "Only Kenneth and the police call me Julian."

That's why I couldn't find him when I Googled him.

Eliza: "How do you know each other?"

Jude: "He, regrettably, is my brother-in-law. Dorothy's my sister. I had a feeling he'd come over here. Looks like I got here just in time. I'm very sorry you got involved."

Eliza: "He's set up a rival business. We've had our chips."

Jude shook his head, sadly.

Jude: "I know, Dorothy told me. It was the final straw. She thinks an awful lot of both you and Lydia."

He looked up at Eliza and paused.

Jude: "I've not mentioned to her about Lydia and that day I called you. She doesn't need to know about that aspect of her."

Eliza: "The chained to the bed aspect?"

Jude smiled.

Jude: "Yes, Eli, that aspect. Let's keep that from her, shall we? She's a delicate flower and need not know the more salacious facets of her new best friend."

Eliza smiled.

Eliza: "You're back together then."

Jude: "She's staying with me at the moment. She can stay as long as she wants."

Eliza: "Blimey that moved fast."

Jude looked at her with a confused look.

Jude: "It's what you do for loved ones, isn't it?"

Eliza nodded, sadly.

He loves her.

I feel a stab in my heart.

Eliza: "Love... I see."

Jude: "I want to thank you."

Eliza: "Do you? What for?"

Jude: "Without you, we wouldn't have got the exclusive with Barney."

Eliza: "Oh, it was nothing. Anyone who'd consumed three quarters of a bottle of vodka would have done the same."

Jude laughed and shifted awkwardly in the Lloyd Loom chair.

Jude: "Eli, erm... That day, at the auction, with the box... I waited you know."

I had my chance and he's telling me I blew it.

Eliza: "I wanted the box but I lost the note. A man poured his tea on it."

Jude looked up and looked her straight in the eyes.

Eliza felt a flood of blood rush to her ears.

Jude: "Ah, did you? I presumed you'd changed your mind."

As if!

Eliza: "God no! It's the best box I've ever clapped eyes on."

Jude's eyes widened.

Jude: "Oh really. Oh, I see."

He scratched his head.

Jude: "Do you still want the box?"

Eliza: "Yes."

Do I want the box?! I could jump on the box right here and now.

She looked earnestly at him.

Eliza: "Very much so."

Jude flushed slightly and looked awkward.

Jude: "Oh, oh I see."

He pulled at the neck of his jumper and stood.

Jude: "I need to go. I need to sort some stuff out. I also need to make sure Dorothy's alright. I don't want to leave her for long; there's nothing to say he won't turn up at my house and try and bang the door down."

He patted his pockets.

Jude: "Have you got a pen and paper, please?"

Eliza ripped a page from the stock/doodle pad and passed it to him with a pen.

Their fingers touched as he took the pen and they both jumped.

They looked at each other and grinned, broad teethy grins.

Jude: "I've got a couple of days off work due to domestic issues. I'll be in town tomorrow, meet me for a cup of tea there if you want."

Eliza took the piece of paper and looked at it.

Jude went towards the door to leave and she called after him.

Eliza: "Jude! What about Lydia?"

Jude looked surprised.

Jude: "Lydia? What's it got to do with her? This is about us."

Oh my god, he used the word "us" in relation to him and I.

I feel quite faint.

Number of times folded and unfolded piece of paper with place and time to meet: *Twenty-six.*

Chapter Forty-two

Quote for the day: *Everything comes in time to him who knows how to wait. Leo Tolstoy*

After a restless night, Eliza had made her decision.

She couldn't betray Lydia.

She seemed so happy and had stopped the cow calling to make a go of it with Jude. Eliza mustn't stand in her way.

Their friendship would be ruined if she took Jude off her.

There was an undeniable attraction. They both felt it but she must remain strong and not give in.

It was a test from the resolve fairy.

Still, at least they'd found the book. It would get them out of the pickle with the shop and they'd walk away without any debts, maybe even with a bit left over.

She wandered into the shop and called out to Mr Hicks but he was nowhere to be seen.

Ah great, another day on my own in an empty shop.

She started putting "SALE" stickers on items and set about slashing the prices on the stock.

She looked at the clock.

Jude would be getting ready now.

Perhaps he'd be putting on his coat.

She studiously looked down and carried on with her stickers.

Half an hour later she looked up again.

He'd definitely be on his way now.

Oh god, I feel awful.

She started to cry and continued reducing the prices on the stock and labelling them.

She heard the door go and she wiped her eyes quickly on her sleeve.

It was Lydia. She was beaming from ear to ear.

Lydia: "Morning darling! Oh, are you alright?"

Eliza: "Hi, I'm ok. Just a bit sad, that's all. You look happy."

Lydia: "I am darling, I am. I finally feel complete. He's the black-out blind in my white room of life. When he's there, the rest of the world is blocked out and doesn't matter. He's simply divine. I've not had a night like last night in living memory. He made me feel like the only woman on earth."

Eliza: "That's nice."

Eliza sniffed, inelegantly.

Lydia: "What are you doing?"

Eliza: "Clearing stock ahead of the shop closure."

Lydia looked shocked.

Lydia: "Closure?!"

Eliza: "Yes, we can't compete. We need to quit whilst we can still clear the debts. I'm waiting to hear from Henry with the outcome of the book. You can have everything that is left over, seeing as it's your book but can we settle everything we owe first?"

Lydia: "Darling, of course! I don't think I'm really cut out for work. As it transpires, I don't think I'll have to in future."

Eliza: "Really? How come?"

Lydia: "He wants me to do whatever makes me happy and as we both know, work doesn't, so I'm not going to bother."

Eliza looked at her aghast.

Eliza: "Blimey. Ok. Lucky old you; newspapers must pay well."

Lydia: "What are you talking about?"

Eliza: "Jude. He works at the Gazette."

Lydia looked at her utterly dumbfounded.

Lydia: "What the bollocking balls has Jude got to do with it?"

Eliza: "He's who you're going out with, nay, shacking up with."

Lydia: "No he isn't! Where did you get that from?!"

What??!

Eliza started to gabble.

Eliza: "You said about seeing each other the other Saturday and that you'd been out before and were powerless to contain your ardour."

Lydia: "You stupid mare. I was talking about Tony. He's got an undeniable hold over me. I'm powerless to resist. It's his voice... and well, a few other attributes. No one else has ever come close, not even Roy. I'm going to be mahoganous from now on. I'm a one-man woman."

Monogamous.

Shit! I've got it all wrong!

I am such a stupid cow.

What time is it?!

Eliza looked at the clock.

Buggering flip-flops, he'll be there!

Eliza: "I need to go out. Can I just check something? Would you mind if I went out with someone you went out with?"

Lydia: "Darling, it would ease my conscience."

Eliza: "What do you mean?"

Lydia: "Don't be cross but the cellar me had a quick fling with Henry. It's weighed quite heavy with me and I've felt really rather guilty in case you told me off. It wasn't very good as I think I engender an element of fear in him. He was a bit quivery and it put me off. There's nothing attractive about a man who shakes as he undoes his flies."

Eliza burst out laughing with relief.

Eliza: "Oh thank god. It's Jude. I would like to see Jude, if you're happy with that? Nothing might come of it but are you ok with it, just in case?"

Lydia: "Oh my god darling, I'd be delighted! I think he's got a huge willy; you'll have a field day!! How absolutely fabulous! He's definitely worth breaking the celibacy for. He was very displeased to see me at Vertigo. I definitely blew my chance with him. It doesn't matter though as I've got Tony and would have had to dump him anyway. Tony's my soul mate."

Eliza: "I have to go. He's waiting for me and I'm late."

Lydia: "Go, go go! Put some make-up on in the car though or he might change his mind."

Eliza picked up her bag and hurtled as fast as she could to meet him.

Number of times hollered at the car in front to get out of the way: *Ninety-six.*

Number of times pleaded with the ether that Jude was waiting for her: *Over a hundred.*

Number of bargain pleas made with the karma fairy: *Twelve. (A lot of charities are going to be very joyous for the foreseeable future if Jude is there).*

Chapter Forty-three

Quote for the book: *Love is a fruit in season at all times, and within reach of every hand. Mother Teresa*

A new year and a new beginning; that's what they say and it certainly rang true for a number of the residents of Pilkington on the Moors that year.

Hard Times created quite the stir in the bibliophile world and Henry asked if his auction house could sell it, to which Eliza and Lydia agreed. They sold off their stock and even with their prices slashed realised the bottom had indeed dropped out of shabby chic chairs. They used the remaining Hard Times funds to clear debts and put a bit aside to cover expenditure for the coming weeks. It also had to be noted that Kenneth's FunkyFurn had well and truly cornered the home furnishings market in that locality for the future. His promotional power alone rendered them dead in the water.

However, an offer to take over the shop was put on the upcycled table to which they agreed.

Who made the offer for the premises? It was Dorothy and Mr Hicks. They decided to join forces (in more ways than one) and once Illusions of Grandeur Crafts closed, they opened a new shop of their own. It was called 'Blooms and Bloomers' and it combined their shared passion for bread and floristry in this rather unique shop.

Kenneth had slunk back to his stacked cushion lair and had raised little fuss since. It's amazing what the threat of national exposure of your rather dubious business practices can do to silence a person. Sometimes it takes someone else's cowardice to make you realise your own strength and this was certainly true for Dorothy. With the support of her family, friends and the quiet love of Mr Hicks she regained her identity and joy of life.

Dorothy and Mr Hicks shared long conversations reminiscing about Dorothy's grandmother and the times they spent together all those years ago. Being allowed to speak freely about her beloved granny helped Dorothy deal with the loss. It was as if she was still a part of her life and through their shared memories, her grandmother's spirit lived on, once again. Mr Hicks's patience and quiet guidance gently supported Dorothy whilst she overcame the trauma of life with Kenneth. The emotional scars, whilst always remaining visible, were no longer raw to the touch. She had emerged stronger and more determined to enjoy life as a result.

Poem: *Wholeness*

The future is yours to hold
Happiness unabound
A Blessed celebration
In every sight, smell and sound

Keep love your intent
For peace so true and pure
Like you knew once before.
A memory of your life
Before you opened the door

Take the step again
To enjoy your life and heal
The pain you hold inside
Bow your head and kneel.

Eliza Wakeley

Epilogue

Quote for the future: *I dream of a better tomorrow; where chickens can cross the road and not be questioned about their motives. Anonymous*

It was a bright February morning just before Valentine's Day when Eliza and Lydia pushed their way through the familiar shop door into the heavily scented aroma of flowers mixed with baked bread.

Dorothy was stood behind the counter delicately placing stems into a cut glass jug. There were a collection of photos hung on the wall behind her; in pride of place, in an ornate frame was the photograph of her looking up at her grandmother. Around that were other photographs of her and Mr Hicks when they were in their twenties; some by the seaside, others with her grandmother. It was as if the last decades of Dorothy and Mr Hicks's lives had been put in a box and stored away. Erased and forgotten.

Dorothy looked up and smiled, broadly.

Dorothy: "Hello dears. How absolutely tremendous to see you; it's a very busy time for us. Love is everywhere!"

Mr Hicks came out from the kitchen with a tray in his hands.

Mr Hicks: "Ah, would you like to test these? We thought we'd put a few in a box with the Valentine bouquets."

Placed on the tray were delicately iced pink and yellow petit fours. Some had little iced roses and others had a small red heart.

Eliza and Lydia picked one up and spent the rest of the afternoon sampling cakes and drinking tea.

Later that evening Eliza sat down at the computer and opened her blog.

Hello, you're no doubt wondering why I've been posting up random poems for the past few months. These were ones I wrote when I was at my lowest ebb but at the time I didn't feel ready to share them. As my life moved on, however, I felt able to post them up for you. I hope they've struck a chord and, in some way, helped. Even if it's just to know other people share your thoughts and worries. You're not on your own when you feel there isn't any way out.

But I've learnt something. Life is a wonderful gift and no matter how low I once felt, just knowing I can still feel the undiluted joy again at living makes me happy. (It all sounds very hippy and unnecessary of me, I know). It sometimes takes the love and patience of others to change your path and with that your whole way of being.

That's what it's all about though, isn't it? Optimism. If you haven't got that you're pretty buggered... Oh and cake. It obviously takes cake too.

I've written you a poem that epitomises my frame of mind now, though.

Is too much excitement good for you?

I am so excited
I am fit to bust
I am so excited
To be with him, I must
I am so excited
Of that there is no doubt
I am so excited
I could scream and shout
I am so excited
Our life will be just great
I am so excited
I have got a mate

I am so excited
Life suddenly looks so good
I am so excited
I am in a brilliant mood
I am so excited
I've taken to writing prose
I am so excited
I've rid myself of clothes
I am so excited
Even though I've been arrested
I am so excited
I'm being lunatic tested
I am so excited
I even like the cell
I am so excited
The padded walls and pink go well
I am so excited
I like being confined for my own protection
I am so excited
I'm going to stand at the next election
I am so excited
Though the medication's kicking in
I am so excited
What's your name again?

I thank you ☺

A cup of tea and some biscuits were placed on the coaster beside her and she looked up and smiled.

Jude: "What are you doing?"

Eliza: "Oh nothing, really. I used to write a blog. It's called Adventures of a Failure."

Jude: "That sounds cheery."

Eliza: "You can read it if you want but promise me you won't think I'm dolally."

Jude: "I already know you're dolally. It's part of your charm. Shuffle up and let me have a read."

Eliza sat with one buttock on the chair and Jude perched with one of his on the other side.

He read through the many blog entries and poems. He stopped every now and again to lean over and kiss Eliza on the forehead, cheek or lips.

When he'd finished he looked at her.

Jude: "I've been thinking. What are you going to do now the shop's gone?"

Eliza: "I'll have to get a job."

Jude: "We've got a part time position at the Gazette which might suit you."

Eliza's eyes lit up.

Eliza: "Part time would be brilliant! Would it fit round Tom's school hours?"

Jude: "I don't see why not. It's only minimum wage, though."

Eliza: "What is it?"

Jude: "It's typing in the classifieds but also, I was wondering about having an agony aunt column. It could cover everything from relationships to the pothole issue people have. You could answer in a whimsical way. I reckon it could prove to be a popular column. You'd be able to do most of it from home."

Eliza: "Oh, Jude! I'd love that! Hang on, though; you'd be my boss. Am I allowed to sleep with the boss?"

Jude: "I believe it constitutes part of your contract of employment."

Eliza: "Oh. When do I start?"

Jude: "Now?"

Eliza: "I'd better put down my custard cream, then."

Soundtrack as the last page turns: *"At Last" Etta James.*

Oh, I expect you're wondering about the prologue and who the couple meeting at the Merrythought Café were.

Was it Eliza and Jude meeting up when she realised he wasn't back with Lydia?

Was it Mr Hicks and Dorothy meeting up after she left Kenneth?

Was it Lydia and Tony meeting up after all those years?

It could be all of them or none of them. It doesn't matter really who it is; it's about love and second chances. It's about opportunities. It's about life.

If Dorothy's tale strikes a chord with you, as it did with Lydia, I sincerely hope you are able to find your light.

See you in Fortitude Amongst The Flip-Flops x

Printed in Great Britain
by Amazon